PRAISE FOR

Caged in Winter

"The slow build of Winter and Cade's relationship is satisfying and real. Walsh's debut raises the bar for NA books and will leave readers hungry for more." —Booklist (starred review)

"This is why I love New Adult! Everything about *Caged in Winter* felt real. And Cade? Perfect book boyfriend."
—Jennifer L. Armentrout, #1 *New York Times* and *USA Today* bestselling author

"With characters so real I feel like I've known them my whole life, *Caged in Winter* is pure, sweet, hot romance. It's a must-read!"
—M. Leighton, *New York Times* bestselling author

PRAISE FOR

Tessa Ever After

"*Tessa Ever After* is a delight: womanizing college party guy falls for single mom and her daughter — it's an awesome premise and Brighton Walsh has written a winner." —*USA Today Happy Ever After*

"The swoonworthy hero belongs on the 2015 best fictional boyfriends list." —RT Book Reviews

"In true Brighton Walsh fashion, *Tessa Ever After* was hilarious, sexy, & emotionally vulnerable." —Prisoners of Print

"There are a lot of New Adult books on the market...but few that combine incredible characters, sexy times and great story that has you turning the pages quickly." —Stuck in Books

Other titles by Brighton Walsh:

Paige IN PROGRESS

BRIGHTON WALSH

bright PUBLISHING

Bright Publishing, LLC
P.O. Box 580238
Pleasant Prairie, WI 53158

Edited by Tamara Mataya
Proofread by Sarah Henning
Cover Art by Brighton Walsh

Paige in Progress is a work of fiction. Names, characters, places, and incidents are either products of the author's imagination or are used fictitiously, and any resemblance to actual persons, living or dead, business establishments, events, or locales is coincidental.

To every girl who's ever been underestimated, looked down on, or pushed aside just because you don't have the "right" parts. This one's for you.

ACKNOWLEDGEMENTS

It's a damn miracle I got to this place, another published novel under my belt, and I have a horde of people to thank for it.

As always, to Christina, my Plot Whisperer Extraordinaire, for everything you say, everything you don't say, every answer to my frantic babbling, every encouragement to my freak-outs, and every time you are there, pom-poms in your hands and smile on your face, to help me however I need it. Thank you could never be enough.

To Jeanette Grey for reading an early copy of this, even when you didn't have time, even when you were on deadline, and giving your always valuable, always honest, always helpful feedback. I love you like whoa.

To Jamie J, who jumped at the chance to read early and give me a reader's perspective of the book, even if your feedback was, "I love everything! I'm sorry!" Love you.

To Ellis Leigh, because this book *literally* would not have been possible without your help and guidance. I hate myself a little bit for using that word, but it's true. I can never thank you enough for holding my hand through this whole process and answering my endless (and probably stupid) questions. But I shall try to pay my debt to you through drinks and desserts. As we do.

To my agent, Mandy, who stood by my decision when I made the choice to self-publish this book, who still offered insight and opinions, even when you didn't have to. I'm so thankful I've found an agent who supports me, not only when it benefits them, but when it benefits my career.

To my editor, Tamara, and my proofreader, Sarah, thank you

both for your knowledge and expertise and polishing this book to be the shiny, pretty thing it is.

To everyone who helped with all different parts of the book— some small and some large: To my sister Amy for helping with the criminal analyst details. To Jim O'Donnell for helping with the cop info. To Michael Mammay for helping with the career Army details. To Nikki G., Katherine Locke, Funmbi, Shireen, Season, Mistress M, and anyone else I'm forgetting for helping me come up with pet names for Paige. You guys rock.

To the readers who, immediately after finishing *Tessa Ever After,* asked whether they'd get to read Paige and Adam's book. This book exists because you wanted it. As always, thank you for your support.

Last but never least, to my guys. We've survived nine drafted novels, despite ups and downs, and you've learned what the frantic pounding of my keyboard means and have accepted when I have to go to Starbucks *again.* You never roll your eyes when I'm on deadline and a frazzled mess who maybe doesn't smell very good. Instead, you say, "How about we order pizza?" For that and a million other reasons, thank you. I love you.

ONE

paige

Being a blonde with a nice body and a rockin' set of Cs isn't all it's cracked up to be. People tend to take in the packaging and not concern themselves with what's underneath, underestimating me and comparing me to Barbie before I even open my mouth. Before they know anything about me other than how I appear on the outside. They think because I'm beautiful I don't also have brains in this head of mine…that I'm just another girl with lofty goals and nothing with which to back it up.

Which is why it's always so goddamn satisfying to watch the faces of those fuckers who underestimate me as I blow their assumptions and preconceived notions out of the water.

Sitting across a worn, oak desk from one such fucker right now—a fucker who will, hopefully, become my boss in the near future—I have to work to maintain my calm. Outside, I am the picture of serenity. My face is impassive…bland, almost. My posture is relaxed but confident. But inside…oh, inside, I'm dancing the fucking Cha Cha Slide, because I just wowed my potential-probable-boss with my knowledge of the criminal investigative field. A field I've never worked in, but one I've immersed myself in for as long as I can remember.

As I spoke, his body language changed from someone appeasing me—allowing me in here for an interview as a favor to my older brother, no doubt—to someone interested. And not just *interested*, but nearly salivating at the thought of what I could offer to the team, not only during the internship, but in the future as a bonafide new hire.

"Well, Paige, I have to say I'm impressed," Captain Peters says.

My lips lift in an amused smile. "You sound surprised by that."

He becomes visibly flustered, broken words escaping his lips before he shakes his head, waving a dismissive hand. "No, no. Tanner assured me you were the real deal. I'm just glad he wasn't bullshitting me."

I nod. "You can't always believe my brother, I understand that. But I'm happy I proved him right this time."

The Captain relaxes back in his chair, his beer belly protruding over the belt of his pants, his full mustache twitching almost like he wants to smile but he refuses to do so. "In all honesty, I think you'd be a real asset to the team dynamic we have here. It's obvious you wouldn't be coming into this starry-eyed and unaware of the pressures and responsibilities of the field. You know your stuff, and I think that would only help you be able to really jump in with both feet during this internship."

"Thank you, I appreciate that."

He pushes up from his chair, and I follow his lead, shaking his hand when he offers it. "I hope to get this wrapped up by the end of the week. I'll let you know one way or another by Friday."

He'll let me know I've got the internship is what he means.

Instead of saying that, I nod. "Sounds great. I look forward to your call." I grab my messenger bag and purse and walk out of his office and through the station. My brother said he wasn't planning on stopping by headquarters today, otherwise I'd hunt him down before leaving. Thank him for giving me this in, because even though I'm certain I'll get this job based on my own merit, I'm also not an idiot. I know exactly how much pull he has after being a cop in this city for so many years. I also know the reason I even got the interview in the first place was as a favor to him.

My heels click against the floor as I make my way toward the elevator, and I'd have to be blind, deaf, or both not to notice the people noticing *me*. And I'd be willing to bet each and every one of them are underestimating me. Scoffing at the thought of me working here with them. Probably assuming I'll get the job thanks to my rack—that, admittedly, looks amazing today—or the sum of my parts. When I push the down button, I let the smile I worked hard to keep hidden finally emerge, overtaking my face, because I know the truth.

I'm going to get this internship. I can feel it in my fucking *bones*. I'm going to get it, and I deserve it. I'd work harder than anyone else they could get, and I have no doubt I want it more than anyone. This is the last step before I get my master's. The last step before I get my dream job as a criminal analyst.

Despite all the crap piled on me, despite having a wrench the size of a semi-truck thrown into my life plan, I busted my ass and got shit done. And here I am. Twenty-three and *happy*. I'm living in a city I love near people I love, and I'm so close to getting everything I've wanted, I can taste it.

A brief flash from the corner of my eye causes my heart to flip-flop, my pulse speeding as I whip my head to look at the silhouette I glimpsed. As I do so, flashes come to me unbidden. Brown hair. Blue eyes. Height and muscles to feast on for days. Except the person I was hoping—no, not hoping, *never* hoping—I'd see isn't there. It's just some nameless guy walking down the hall, his back to me. He doesn't have the right stance. The right walk. The right build. He's all wrong.

And the fact that he's all wrong should be right.

Except it feels anything but.

I should be thinking about anyone—*anyone*—other than the guy who's haunted my thoughts for the past five months. The guy I've tried diligently to get out of my mind, but the same one who keeps creeping in, popping up unexpectedly when I'm just going about, minding my own business. I'll be on a date with a nice and interesting guy, a *hot* guy, and suddenly an image of a head covered in dark hair and piercing blue eyes looking up at me from between my thighs comes to me. Or I'll hear the exact cadence and tone of dirty words he whispered in my ear as he took me from behind. Or I'll feel the rough wood of my door pressed into my shoulder blades as I wrapped my legs around his pumping hips. And when all of that happens, I can't dive into a new guy fast enough. Just to avoid. Just to forget.

Because the last person I need taking up every waking—and non-waking—thought I have is the one guy I shouldn't have been with in the first place.

The one guy who's all wrong for me.

The one guy I can't get out of my head.

Adam Reid.

A COUPLE DAYS later, I let myself into my best friend's house, throwing open the door and bursting into the living room, bellowing, "It's celebration time!"

Except the living room is empty. As is the dining room—no trace of Tessa or her boyfriend, Jason. I toss my purse on the couch and peek around the corner into the kitchen—empty, too. There's a thud down the hall, and I turn around, narrowing my eyes at the darkened hallway. Their house is small enough that noises carry easily, but it's eerily silent for a place that houses a walking, talking, five-year-old pixie stick. I'm not sure where Tessa's daughter, Haley, is, but it's clear she's not here or a screeching tiny person would've already assaulted me. As I listen harder, a rhythmic thumping reaches my ears, and I spin on my heels and head back to the living room. I plop down on the couch and turn on the TV, cranking up the volume to overpower the sounds coming from the master bedroom that no best friend should ever have to listen to.

One-and-a-half episodes of *Forensic Files* later, Jason comes strolling down the hallway, his lips quirked up on one side in a cocky-ass grin, his brown hair sticking up in all directions. At least he's fully clothed, his jeans and rumpled T-shirt fitting his frame better than should be allowed. He tips his head toward me in acknowledgement and continues into the kitchen.

Propping my arm over the back of the couch, I call after his retreating form. "You can't spare me a hello? What, did you fuck all the sound out of your vocal chords?"

He laughs, that low, satisfied male sound that both grates on my nerves and makes me wish I had a date tonight. "Not me. Can't say as much for your best friend, though."

"What can't you say for me?" Tessa walks into the living room and sits next to me on the couch. Her clothes aren't rumpled like Jason's are, but her short hair is definitely of the freshly fucked variety. And even the blue stripe running through said hair can't distract from eyes so bright, they might as well be flashlights.

"Apparently he fucked the voice right out of you. But since you're speaking fine, looks like Little Jason's performance wasn't quite up to snuff. There are pills for that, you know," I call over my shoulder.

Jason walks—struts, really—into the living room, one hundred percent cocky male. "First of all, there's nothing little about my cock." I scoff and roll my eyes, but he talks right over my interruption. "Second, if I wanted her to be hoarse, she would be. I was being considerate because I knew you were out here."

Tessa's eyes bug out. "You were here the whole time?"

"Nearly."

She drops her head into her hands and groans, then glares at Jason, her face flaming. "And you knew? God, why didn't you tell me?" Bringing her attention back to me, she says, "I'm sorry. If I'd known, I wouldn't have let him go for the second round."

"And *that* is exactly why I didn't tell you." And then he ignores us as he drops to the couch and grabs the remote, switching off the show I had on and changing it to something mind-numbingly boring.

Tessa turns toward me on the couch, tucking one of her legs under the other. "But seriously, I'm sorry."

"But seriously, it's okay. Not like it's the first time I've heard you two going at it. I do expect that diagram of his cock now, though." I glance over Tessa's shoulder and see Jason shrug.

"Don't look at him," she says. "He doesn't care who sees his junk. He'd put it in the Hall of Fame if he could."

I snort. "Like it could be in there."

"Just wait for the diagram, Paige." He shoots me a wink. "Just wait."

Reaching into my purse, I pull out a small notebook and a pen and shove it at Tessa. "You heard the man. If this isn't better than those GIFs I absolutely do *not* have saved on my computer, I'm going to be very disappointed."

Instead of gracing me with the illustration of Jason's junk, she rolls her eyes and tucks the pen and paper back into my purse. "So why are you here? We didn't have a girls' night planned, did we?"

"Not officially, but we're sure as shit going out. We have to celebrate."

"Yeah?" she asks with a smile. "What are we celebrating?"

"I got the internship!"

"You—wait." Tessa's bright smile drops as she furrows her brow. "You told me on *Tuesday* you got the internship."

I wave my hand at her. "Semantics. I got the *official* call this afternoon, and that means *we* are going out dancing and drinking and whatever other shenanigans we can get into."

She glances at Jason. "We don't have anything going since Haley's staying with my brother, do we?"

"Nah. If you guys go out, I think I'll head over to Adam's.

He's been bitching about his mom doing his laundry and shoving food in his face at every turn. And I'll be honest…I could really go for some pizza rolls and apple pie. I don't know why he doesn't appreciate that more. Ungrateful little bastard."

They continue talking, discussing details, but all I can focus on is hearing it confirmed that Adam is home. *Home.* As in, here in my town. Close enough that I could run into him at the grocery store or the movie theater. Close enough that I could call him up for a booty call and have him at my place in fifteen minutes, tops.

Fuck.

Fuck.

Tessa mentioned back around Christmastime that Adam's parents' business wasn't doing well. In the months since then, there's been talk about him coming back to help, but that's all it was. Talk. It had never been confirmed—not to me. Though why would it be? As far as Tessa knows, Adam is just the best friend to her boyfriend and her brother. He's just the guy she practically grew up with.

Definitely not the guy who was her best friend's one-night stand.

I also might have, *maybe,* made Tessa think I hate Adam, so she never talks about him when I'm around. I thought that was self-preservation, but it turns out that was just me burying my head in the sand, because now I'm blindsided, having had no time at all to prepare.

God. I'm going to see him.

With our small circles connecting so intricately, there's absolutely no hope that I can avoid him indefinitely. I tune into Tessa and Jason's conversation just when she mentions the six of us going out to celebrate my internship and Adam's homecoming.

"I know you don't like him," she says, "but maybe you just got off on the wrong foot. I really think you'd get along if you'd give him a chance."

And that's exactly what has my hackles up, what has my

defenses set to a Code Red status. Because giving a chance to a guy I had a one-night stand with? That's a big, fat *nope*.

TWO

adam

Being here should fill me with ease, or at the very least a sense of bittersweet nostalgia. And I guess it does. I love my childhood home. No matter what ups and downs my parents' shop faced as I was growing up, home was always perfect—Mom made sure of that, never letting the downs of the business bleed into our home life while we were kids.

I've loved coming back over breaks from college and during brief stays since I started my job a couple years ago. There was always an expiration date on those visits, though. And knowing my time here was only a blip in the grand scheme of things, it was easier to take my mom's pampering—hell, I *enjoyed* it. But now? Knowing I'm here for the foreseeable future, stuck in a bedroom forever preserved to my junior year of high school—the last time my mom redecorated it because the store was having a great year—is un-fucking-bearable. It's made that pampering suddenly feel a lot like smothering.

And even thinking that makes me feel like an ungrateful

douchebag, because what twenty-five-year-old guy doesn't want home-cooked meals every night and his laundry done for him?

This one, apparently.

"Adam, honey?" my mom calls from down the hall. "Jason is here to see you!"

It's like high school all over again.

"I'm too old for this shit," I grumble as I open my bedroom door and head down the hall to the living room. Jase is sitting on the arm of the floral couch my parents have had forever, bullshitting with my dad who's stretched out in his recliner.

"Haley needs a bigger bike, so we'll probably swing in to the shop sometime this week so she can pick something out. You have anything with unicorns and shit on it?"

"I'm not sure about the shit part, but probably some unicorns or princesses or something."

Jason laughs. "She'll probably like your version better."

"Oh! We have some glitter tassels I bet she'd love," mom offers from her corner of the couch.

"If it sparkles, that girl is all over it." Jason turns around and lifts his chin in acknowledgment. "Hey, man. Tessa's out with Paige, so I thought I'd swing by and see what you were up to."

I try not to show any kind of reaction at the mention of Paige's name, and since Jase's eyes don't narrow, apparently I'm successful. I just pray no one glances south, because the mere sound of her name has my dick twitching in my jeans, memories of what happened all those months ago at the forefront of my mind. Clearing my throat, I say, "Not much. Just got home a while ago."

Mom cuts in, "He's been working so hard at the shop. There before we get in and stays well after we leave. The boy never even takes a lunch break, just eating what I packed him in the office." Her admonishment is tinged with pride, and I can't help the warmth that spreads through my chest when I hear it. Even though my parents never forced me to come back and help, it still feels a little like I didn't have much choice. If I didn't come, who was going to?

"Well, you boys don't want to hang out here all night with us old people," she says. "Why don't you head back to Adam's room, and I'll bring in some snacks for you."

Jase grins, and I should, too. On any other day, it would be a nice, normal offer. Today, however, after Mom flew into my bedroom this morning to set out my newly ironed clothes for me, and after I ate a bagged lunch consisting of a ham and cheese sandwich—sans crust because I didn't like them when I was a kid—and apple slices, and after I found my supply of boxer briefs freshly washed and folded on my bed when I got home, it grates on my goddamn nerves. I have to take a few deep breaths to stop myself from snapping, because I don't snap. I don't lose my temper in general. It takes a lot to piss me off, to irritate me even a little, but I'm there, and I have been since day-fucking-two in the Reid house.

Jase doesn't say anything until we're behind the closed door of my bedroom. He goes to the gaming rocker set up in front of the TV, sprawling in it as he grabs a baseball and tosses it in the air. "What's on the menu tonight for snacks? Is it pizza rolls? Please, sweet sparkling Jesus, tell me it's pizza rolls."

I grab the other chair and move it over next to him, then pull out a game controller for myself and toss the other to him, not looking to see where it flies as I sit down.

"The fuck, man?" He fumbles the baseball trying to catch the controller.

I flip through my games, finding one where I can get out the most aggression. "Since you're so excited about the food, maybe you should come live here, and I'll move in with Tess. If you made a list, I bet Mom would make you whatever you wanted."

"Aw, is the honeymoon over? I sense a little hostility in your tone. It hasn't even been a week yet."

Before I can answer him, a knock sounds at the door. "Honey? I've got some snacks for you boys."

Jase looks at me, then a shit-eating grin spreads across his face. "Come on in, Mom! I'm freakin' famished."

She smiles as she opens the door and carries in a tray, setting it down between us.

Just like in high school.

"Pizza rolls are in the oven. I'll bring them in as soon as they're done, but I thought you could use a little something to tide you over until then."

"Have I told you I love you today, Judy?" Jase grabs a chip from the bowl and scoops up some of my mom's homemade salsa with it.

Mom beams, her cheeks turning pink at the same time my dad yells down the hall, "Quit hitting on my wife, Jason!"

"Can't blame a guy for trying." He winks at my mom—the same mom *he's* called Mom since we became friends more than fifteen years ago—and takes another bite. "Outstanding as always, Mom," he says around a mouthful of food.

She waves off his compliment and heads out of my room. "I'll bring in the pizza rolls when they're done. You boys have fun."

As soon as the door snicks shut, I blow out a breath and sink back into my chair, queuing up the game. Maybe it'll do my mood some good to blow shit up since Jase isn't doing it—not with that shit-eating grin on his face as he shovels chips in his mouth.

"What do you have to be so happy about?" I ask. "You're here with me which means you're not getting laid tonight."

His grin gets larger, if possible. "Already got laid, man. Twice."

"Bragger."

He shrugs. "You're the one who brought it up, not me. And why the hell *wouldn't* I be smiling? I have homemade salsa, homemade guac, pizza rolls on their way, and if my nose is not mistaken, I do believe there are some cookies out there with my name on them."

"You should definitely just move in. Trade places with me. You're a lot happier about this than I am."

"As much as I love your mom's cooking, I love Tess more. Can't do it. I'll just come here and intrude weekly...okay, daily." He scoops some guacamole on a chip. "But, seriously, I don't get why you're not thrilled with this situation."

"You wanna know why?" I blow out a deep breath and lean back on the rocker. "This morning, she barged in here to drop off the clothes she picked out for me to wear to the shop today. After she'd ironed them."

"Still not seeing the problem. So she picked out your clothes." He shrugs. "At least she ironed them. I'd kill for Tessa to iron my shit for me. She tells me to fuck off."

"Yeah, well, it wouldn't be bad if your girlfriend caught you rubbing one out. My mom walking in on me doing it?" I shudder all over again, reliving the mortification I felt and the same mortification I saw spread across her face when she realized what I was doing.

He stares at me for a minute, slack-jawed, then he barks out a laugh and continues until he starts choking on a chip. Serves him right.

"It's not funny, assbag." I punch his shoulder. Hard. "I can't even jack off, for fuck's sake. What kind of life is that for a twenty-five-year-old guy? I don't care how many apple pies she bakes. A man needs his space."

Jase gets himself under control and shakes his head at me. "You only have yourself to blame. You should've done that shit in the shower like any self-respecting man. Jesus."

I don't say anything because he's right. And normally I would have, especially being back home. What I don't tell him, though, is that I woke up with wood to rival an oak tree, dreams so fresh in my mind, I couldn't do anything but grip my cock and stroke. And the worst part was that the dreams were so vivid because they weren't dreams at all, but a replaying of events that already happened. Waking up did nothing to dispel the image that was playing on a loop in my mind—Paige spread out on her dining room table, legs parted for me and back arched as I licked her to orgasm. And even though it wasn't happening right then, hadn't happened for months, I could practically taste her pussy, just like I did that night in December.

"Seriously, though, it sounds like you just need to get out more. Maybe you're working too much," Jase says, interrupting my thoughts. Thank fuck, because the last thing I need to be doing is getting wood while sitting next to my best friend. "Have you found anything at the shop yet?"

I've been back for a few days, each one spent at my parents' shop, Reid Sporting Goods, trying to find where it all went wrong for them, and thus the reason I took a hiatus from my life and showed up in Michigan, more than a thousand miles from home. Though *all went wrong* isn't quite right, considering the ups and downs the shop has faced every year since I could remember. It's worse now than it's ever been, though. So much so, bankruptcy is knocking on my parents' door. No way for me to ignore that and stay in the stable bubble I created for myself in Denver.

Each day at the store has been about as productive as shoveling during a blizzard. The books are a mess, receipts in boxes and stacks and piles here and there, and it's going to take me a hell of a lot longer than a few days to get it sorted out. But if the plethora of IOUs I found are anything to go by, I have a pretty damn good idea of why the shop is nearly in the red for the first time since their first three years in business. My parents are too goddamn nice.

I shake my head. "Nothing concrete, but I have a few ideas of why they aren't pulling in as much money." Or any money, really. But having spent every day and night worrying about it, I don't want to talk about it now. "But, yeah, I could use a night out. Cade up for something?"

"Actually, Tess mentioned the six of us getting together. Paige just got this internship she's been salivating over. Last step before she gets her master's." He scoops up some more salsa. "Speaking of Paige, what'd you do to her that night I asked you to drive her home after

Christmas?"

I'm pretty sure the answer he's looking for isn't *fuck her in every room of her apartment*, so instead I just shrug. "Nothing, why?"

"Because Tessa's under the impression that Paige can't stand you." To anyone else, it might seem like he's just looking at me while having a conversation, but we've been friends nearly all our lives, and I know he's being anything but indifferent right now. His eyes aren't narrowed, but he's studying me just the same.

I work hard to school my features into disinterest, making sure the shock doesn't show on my face. Shock at the fact that Paige would think of me in any way but happily. I should be her favorite person in the world, considering I got her off five times that night— not that I was counting.

Granted, she was adamant that what we had that night was a one-time deal. Or a three-times-in-one-night deal, anyway. Maybe she's pissed that I'm back here, even if temporarily. Maybe she's pissed that I never called or texted her, even though she specifically told me not to and never gave me her number. Maybe she's pissed that I never said anything about it to the guys, even though that was one of her stipulations, too.

At the time, that was fine with me. I was stressed from dealing with all the shit with my parents, the burden of helping them falling to my shoulders since my older sister has her own family to worry about several states away, and I needed an outlet. One-night stands aren't my usual M.O. In fact, Paige was my first and only. But, Jesus. If all of them are as amazing as that night was with Paige, I need to rethink my stance.

I have a feeling, though, it isn't one-night stands that are so great.

It's her.

And I'm damn well going to figure out why she's got a problem with me and get that shit settled, because I'm not going to be satisfied until I get another taste of her.

"You know anything about that?" Jase asks after my too-long silence.

I shrug. "Your guess is as good as mine for why she's got a problem with me. But we can find out when we all go out. Set it up and let me know."

THREE

paige

Why does he have to look so *good?* I know five months isn't a long time, but it's long enough that I hoped maybe he'd have developed a bit of a gut, started getting a receding hairline or going prematurely gray, perhaps. But no. His hair is dark—not a strand of silver in it— and just as thick and full as it was when I gripped it while he was stationed between my legs. And a gut? Hah. He's all solid muscle, the breadth of his shoulders and the planes of his chest filling out that red Henley like no one's business. And I'm only a little ashamed to admit I glimpsed his ass in those dark, low-slung jeans when he went up to the bar in the far corner of the pub when we first got here. Bitable, just like I remember. And I can't, for the life of me, remember why I *didn't* bite it when we slept together. Because an ass like that deserves to have teeth marks on it.

Since the only time I've ever spent with him was while he was between my thighs, our communication restricted to grunts and dirty talk, I thought—prayed, really—that maybe I'd find him obnoxious or annoying. Irritating or frustrating. And while I'm both irritated and frustrated, it has nothing to do with his personality and everything to do with his *presence*.

Because all I can think about is shoving these plates and beer bottles and martini glasses out of the way, crawling to the other end of the table, and sitting in his lap so I can grind on him until we both come. Never mind the four other people here with us.

And the way he keeps looking at me. *God.* His face gives nothing away, his expression impassive. But his eyes. Those crystal blue eyes several shades lighter than my own, noticeable even in the dim light of the pub, stay focused on me throughout the night. Even when I'm not looking at him, I can *feel* his gaze on me. It's like he's trying to undress me with that alone.

The worst part is, I'm pretty sure I'd let him.

Okay, there's no *pretty sure* about it.

Someone says something, and it isn't until Tessa elbows me in the ribs that I realize it was apparently directed at me. I snap my gaze up from my food—the food I've been staring at to avoid looking at Mr. Hot Pants. "Huh? What?"

Tessa's brother, Cade, laughs across from me, his arm slung around the back of his girlfriend Winter's chair. "I asked when you start the internship."

If there's one thing that can get my mind off Adam and his delicious abs and rock-hard chest and delectable cock, it's my coveted internship. I smile my first authentic one all night. "Monday. It'll probably be a lot of filling out paperwork and shit like that, but I'm hoping they'll let me get into the thick of things before too long. Tanner says they don't usually, but I'm crossing my fingers that with his pull and my knowledge, they'll let me get a little more involved than they've done in the past."

"That's awesome." Cade nods, smiling at me before taking a drink from his beer.

He and Winter have only been back from their relocation to

Chicago for a few weeks, and I'm about to ask him how the restaurant is doing, how he likes being head chef, when I'm interrupted before I can get a word out.

"Who's Tanner?" Adam asks. By some miracle, we're seated on opposite ends and across the table from each other. Probably Tessa wanting to keep everything mellow tonight, thinking I hate his guts.

I look at him, and, oh boy, that's a mistake. Especially when I replay how he sounded when he asked who Tanner was. It's not the first time I've heard his voice tonight, but there's a note to it now I haven't heard before. No, that's a lie. I've heard it before. Just never in mixed company. It's one that speaks of possession—like even the mere mention of another guy's name in the same airspace as mine is unacceptable—and if there's one thing I don't stand for, it's guys treating me as a possession.

So then why are my panties so fucking wet?

I try to swallow and impart some moisture into my too-dry mouth, but nothing helps. I don't dare even attempt to croak out an answer, too afraid it'll sound a lot less like, "He's my brother," and a lot more like, "Fuck me now."

Finally, Tessa takes pity on me and steps in. "Tanner's one of her older brothers. He's a cop."

That's all she says, but she glances at me, her eyebrows lifted in a silent question. A, "What the hell is going on?" kind of question. A question I am definitely not answering tonight. Or ever.

Conversation starts up again around the table, Jase, Cade, Tessa, and Winter all diving into talk of the restaurant, while Adam and I have a stare-off. To everyone else, I'm sure he looks the same, but I notice his shoulders relax the tiniest bit and the tension around his mouth dissipates after those brief words from Tessa. And as much as I shouldn't be happy about this, I can't help the satisfaction that sweeps through me. He wants me just as much as I want him.

Except him not wanting me would be a lot easier on both of us, because then I wouldn't have any problem keeping my distance.

And I need to. Because Adam has Relationship Material written all over him, and the only relationship I'm interested in is the one I have with my vibrator.

I knew the night we slept together he wasn't a one-night-stand kind of guy. And even if he didn't give off that vibe, Cade, Jase, and Tessa have all said enough over the years that I've assumed as much. The guys had all graduated from high school by the time my family moved here when I was a junior, so I never spent much time with Adam since he went to college in Colorado. He came home on breaks, I assumed, but we never saw each other in more than passing. Never long enough for me to learn I wanted to ride him like a pony. Oh, no. That was reserved for the one night months ago I was off my game, having had too many appletinis in an effort to help Tessa forget Jason's douche-like behavior—best friend that I am.

That night, Adam drove me home at Jason's request, walked me to my door, and then instead of thanking him and telling him good night, I was just tipsy enough to ask him if he wanted to come inside. Even knowing his relationship stance. Even knowing how close he was to *my* closest friends. Even knowing how it could potentially blow up in my face.

But it doesn't have to blow up in my face. I can totally handle this. He isn't going to be here forever—only as long as it takes him to get his parents' business back on track. I can wait it out.

I'll just stock up on batteries.

"—walked in on him choking the chicken the other morning," Jason says through a guffaw.

As laughs erupt around the table, Adam scowls. "Thanks, man."

My head snaps up again, zeroing in on the conversation that managed to go on around me once more. I look between Jason and Adam, a grin spread over the former's face. Adam lifts his eyes to me and notices me staring and stares right back. Then he quirks a brow as if to say, "Picturing it?"

And yes, yes, I am.

My entire body ignites, and if my panties were wet before, there's a fucking tsunami going on in there now, because all I can see is Adam with his thick fingers wrapped around his even thicker cock, slowly stroking it up and down while he stares at me just like he is now.

Breathing shallowly, I shift in my seat and take a deep pull from my vodka cranberry, avoiding his gaze. Thank God for the low lighting in this place, because my face is absolutely on fire.

"I told him to do it in the shower like every other guy," Jason says over the laughter still rolling through everyone at the table, and I choke on my drink, because now I'm picturing him in the shower, and that's not any better. Thinking of the water sluicing down his chest and the ridges of his abdomen as he grips his length...

We never made it to my shower, but now I sure as hell wish we had so I could draw from memories rather than my imagination.

Tessa laughs along with the others and distractedly slaps my back as I attempt to catch my breath. To Adam, she says, "I know you're trying to save as much as you can to help your parents, but have you thought about getting a place while you're here? Something cheap? I'd offer you to stay with us, but we only have the two bedrooms."

"No offense to your boyfriend, but I would kill him if we ever lived together," Adam says.

"Hey, I'm not that bad." Jason grabs a fry and throws it toward Adam, who flicks it away before it can hit him.

"Oh, babe, you kind of are." Tessa pats Jason on the head and smiles. "I put up with it because of the sex."

"Jesus Christ," Cade groans. "How many times have I told you I don't need to hear that shit?"

Winter laughs and shakes her head. "Like you can talk. How many times has poor Tessa walked in on us?"

"God, don't remind me. I could've gone my whole life without seeing that." Tessa shudders, then she gasps and turns to me, her smile bright. "Hey, what about that studio apartment that's always for rent in your building? You said people are moving in there every other month. Is it available now?"

I open my mouth to tell her there's no way Adam is moving in across from me, and then snap it shut. This is not the time or the place to bitch her out for suggesting that. But seriously, why the hell would she offer this to him, especially since she thinks I can't stand him? Except I don't even have to think about it. Tessa likes for everyone to get along. And knowing two of her closest friends don't is probably killing her. I totally fucked myself over by acting like I hated him.

Goddammit.

"I'm not sure if it is or not," I hedge. It's open. The last douchebags who lived there got evicted a couple weeks ago, and there hasn't been a moving truck around since. Can't tell her that, though. Instead, I try a different tactic and turn my attention to Adam, ignoring that flutter in my belly when I find his gaze already on me. "And, actually, you probably wouldn't want to live there. It's in kind of a shitty part of town."

Tessa opens her mouth, no doubt to argue, at the same time Adam leans back in his chair and crosses his arms. "You live there."

I shrug. "I like to live on the edge."

He continues scrutinizing me, his stare unwavering, and I will not shift in my seat. Will. Not. After a million years, he says, "Your brother's a cop."

"Yeah…?" I draw out the word, having no idea where he's going with this.

"Your brother's a cop, and I'm pretty sure if you lived in a shitty neighborhood, he wouldn't allow you to live there."

"First of all, my brothers don't *allow* me to do anything. I do whatever the hell I want, because I'm a grown-ass woman." And as a grown-ass woman, I obviously need to step up my game if I have any hope of deterring him from looking at the apartment across the hall from me. So I tell a teeny, tiny white lie. "Second, I'm pretty sure the last people who lived there were cooking meth. And then there were all the cats. Like, at least six. In a tiny studio apartment. I can, you know"—I wave my hand in the air—"smell it through the door. It's that bad."

He does that staring thing again, and this time he does it long enough that I do shift in my seat. Goddamn him. Then he turns to Tessa and shoots my entire survival plan to hell with a handful of words. "Thanks for the tip, Tess. I think I'll check it out on Monday."

He looks at me, one corner of his mouth tipping up in a sly grin, and holy shit I am so fucked.

FOUR

paige

I've never come just from a guy staring at me, but if I have to sit here for another minute under the intense gaze of one Adam Reid, I'm not so sure I'll be able to say that when I walk out of the pub tonight.

Everyone's finished eating, plates cleared from the table and replaced with second or third drinks. Talk of Cade's restaurant and Winter and Jase bullshitting about website-something-or-other and Tessa recalling Haley's latest mishap goes on around me, but I can't pay attention. I can barely listen or offer any sort of input, because my words don't work. Adam has no problem, though. His velvety smooth voice, rich and deep, has filtered through all the other noise in the pub and planted itself inside me when everything else has gotten lost amidst the cacophony of sound around me.

But it's not just his voice that has me squirming in my seat like a whore in church. Oh, no. That wouldn't be cruel enough for the devil himself. Nope, he's continued his torment of looking at me, too. And not just looking, all casual like, taking peeks here and there. No, he's *looking*. His gaze is as hot as the sun, sweeping over me like he wants to devour me right here on the table, and he doesn't give a shit if our friends watch as he does it. I know that gaze. I *remember* that gaze. It's the same one he used on me that night in December. When I stripped for him. When he took me against my front door.

My nipples have been saluting the entire table for the past twenty minutes, and my panties are a lost cause. All from his voice and those looks. It's like he's done some kind of crazy voodoo magic on me. He's dickmatized me.

And that's really goddamn sad, considering I haven't seen his dick in nearly half a year.

When his eyes lock on mine again, I can't take it anymore and stand abruptly, my chair scraping loudly across the floor. Conversation halts as five pairs of eyes snap to me.

"Uh, just gotta tinkle." I jerk my thumb over my shoulder and spin away from the table, pretending I don't see Tessa's questioning look, and head to the back of the restaurant, finally escaping into the dark hallway housing the restrooms. It's still pretty early—the lights have dimmed around the pub, but it hasn't yet filled up with the late-night crowd—so I don't have to wade through throngs of people to get to my refuge. And, thankfully, I don't have to wait in a long-ass line for the single-stall bathroom.

I shut and lock the door behind me, then lean against it, taking several deep breaths to get myself under control. This pull I feel toward Adam is unacceptable and so atypical I barely recognize myself. If I want a guy, I have him. Sometimes more than once, but never for more than a week. And once I've had my fill, I'm done. I move on. They get on my nerves, all their little flaws building up until it's all I can see, and I'm over it. Over them.

Why can't it be like that with Adam? I've already had him—more than once—so why do I want him again? Why do I want him *still?*

Regardless of the *why*, I have to figure out a way to get past it, to deal with this unending attraction somehow, because until he finishes up what he needs to with his parents' business and heads back to Colorado, these nights where the six of us are together are going to happen more than I'm comfortable with.

Pushing off the door, I head to the sink and run a paper towel under the cold water, then press it against my flushed face. I look like I've just run a marathon. Or had marathon sex.

God, why does he get to me so much?

I've had my fair share of guys, and some of them even knew what they were doing. But I've never—*never*—felt this insatiable need before, like fire burning under my skin. I've never been so thirsty I didn't think there was the possibility of that thirst ever being quenched. I've never *wanted* like this. Not even when I was seventeen and in love. Not even with the guy I thought I'd spend the rest of my life with before he crushed those plans right in front of my eyes.

"That's enough of that," I mutter and toss out the paper towel. My open-weaved, lightweight sweater hangs off one shoulder as I adjust my skirt. I wish I'd worn something else. Jeans and a T-shirt, maybe. Something I'd wear while running to the store instead of what I wear when I'm looking to hook up.

Because I'm not.

I roll my eyes at myself, because even I don't buy my lie, and reach for the doorknob to head back out to my doom. The darkness of the hallway looms as I pull open the door, but I don't even cross the threshold before there's a big, male body in front of me. I don't have time to react before hands are around my waist, pushing me back into the bathroom. My heart jumps into my throat for half a second before the familiar scent fills my nose—citrus and sandalwood—and a whole different kind of fear grips me.

Lashing out the way I do best—with my mouth—I pull out of his grasp and turn around, my back to the door, as I snap, "This is the *ladies'* room, Adam. Did you lose some parts since I last saw you?" And I don't want to, try to stop myself, because I *know* what a bad idea it is, but my gaze still drops to the front of his jeans. And, nope, he's definitely not missing any parts. I can make out the outline of his obviously hard cock straining against soft denim, and my mouth waters. My mouth actually fucking waters.

When I lift my eyes to meet his, he doesn't even dignify my accusation with a response, just raises a single eyebrow. "You've been avoiding me."

There may have been a few times this past week when I ducked out of Tessa and Jason's place once I heard Adam was on his way over. Or maybe I just had shit to do. I scoff and cross my arms. "I can't be avoiding someone when I don't care one way or another if I see them."

He takes a step closer to me, and I flatten my back against the door. "Oh, you care, Paige."

"I do not." Apparently being in his vicinity turns me into a mouthy teenager.

His eyes lighten in amusement, the side of his mouth quirking up, and he's so fucking smug, I want to smack the look right off his face.

"If you don't care, why are you hiding in the bathroom?"

"I'm not *hiding*. Did you miss the part where I said I had to pee?"

"Uh huh." His voice is taunting, and it makes me want to kick him in the shin. And then maybe bite him. On the ass.

He takes another step toward me, and *God*, how did I forget how big he is? Even with my heels adding three inches to my already tall five-foot-ten I have to look up to see him. I'm used to looking most guys in the eye, and I like it that way. Puts me on a level playing field.

But not with him.

My eyes don't listen to my brain when I tell them to focus and instead decide to take a leisurely path up his body, feasting on his defined arms and wide shoulders encased in that red Henley, a couple of the buttons at the top open and hinting at the skin underneath it. Skin I know the exact texture and taste of. That night we were together, his face was smooth, freshly shaven, but not now. Now, there's a shadow of stubble gracing his jaw, and I want to know what it'd feel like against my neck. Between my thighs.

His lips are full, the bottom pouty and too lush on his angular, masculine face, but I love it. I love how it adds some softness to all his hard edges. Separately, his features are nearly perfect—square jaw, straight nose, full lips, and high cheekbones. By all accounts, he should be a pretty boy, but he's not. Somehow, when you put everything together, he has this…hardness to him. This mystery about him that makes me want him all the more.

God, he is tasty.

He takes another step, and I can feel the warmth emanating off him. I want to rub myself all over him like a cat in heat. If I don't get out of this bathroom right the fuck now, I might actually do it.

"Is this because you were too drunk that night? Did I take advantage of you?" His voice is low and gruff, his eyes surprisingly sincere.

That isn't at all what I was expecting. Does he really think that? I meet his stare, take in his penetrating gaze, and uncertainty looks back at me. This is the first time I've ever see him be anything but confident. And it would be so easy to say yes, to let myself off the hook of having had sex with him because I actually wanted it. But he looks so torn up about that being the case that I can't bring myself to, especially when I was completely cognizant of everything that happened that night. Especially when I wanted it as much as he did.

"No." My voice is hoarse, the single syllable coming out in a throaty near-moan. "I wasn't and you didn't."

Another step, and now he's crowding me against the wall next to the door, one of his feet between my parted legs, his hard thigh pressed against my pussy and his hard cock pressed against my hip. I have to force myself to stay upright. To not let my head tip back to the wall, to not open my mouth and ask him to push harder against me—or worse, ask him to replace his leg with his cock or his fingers.

He leans into me, his nose skimming my jaw until his lips brush my ear, and I force myself to hold my breath so I don't moan. "And now? Are you too drunk now?"

Needing something to steady myself, I reach up and grip his biceps, the muscles hard and unforgiving under my fingers, and that was possibly the worst idea I've had all night. Because now all I want to do is pull him closer. Before my brain can signal to my hands what a bad idea it would be, I tighten my fingers around him, and then his hand is on the inside of my thigh. His fingers make a slow path up, moving under my skirt, and God. *God.* In about two-point-five seconds, he's going to know exactly how wet he's made me, exactly how much I want him. Exactly how full of shit I am. And I'll die of mortification.

If I don't first die from whatever the girl form of blue balls is.

But he doesn't trace the leg of my panties, doesn't feel the soaked lace cupping me. He stops just short of exactly where I want him, and I realize he's waiting for an answer. I should tell him yes. I should play the drunk girl card, because I know he'd step back. He'd walk out of here without a second thought, because Adam isn't the kind of guy who takes unless you're explicitly offering.

I should tell him yes, but somehow I shake my head and that's enough for him. Finally he closes that last inch of space, his fingers slipping under the material of my panties until he's running them along my slit. A low, satisfied sound leaves his throat when he finds how wet I am, and I was wrong. Mortification is the last thing I feel as he traces circles around my clit. The only thing I feel is overwhelming desire and the need for more.

We're in the bathroom of a public place, and our friends are twenty feet outside this door. I shouldn't be with him at all, because I've already been there, done that. And I don't do repeat performances. Not like this.

But instead of pushing him away, I tilt my hips up, a moan ripping from my throat when he takes my unasked plea and fills me with two fingers, pumping them in and out in a slow, agonizing pace.

"I need to ask you something." How is his voice so perfectly controlled when I feel like I'm about to come undone?

"Now?" I pant, eyes closed, as I grind myself on his hand trying to get friction on my clit, not at all ashamed of how greedy I am. I'm past that point, and now all I care about is the finish, the release.

"Yes, now. Why don't you want me to move into your building?"

It takes me a couple tries to get out the words because his fingers are *so good*, but I finally do. "Because I don't like you."

"I don't believe that."

"I don't—" I gasp out a moan when he dips his head, his teeth scraping against the juncture where my neck meets my shoulder, and I clench around his fingers. I swallow and try again. "I don't care what you believe. I'm telling you that I don't like you."

He places an open mouthed kiss below my ear, sucking the flesh there, and I arch into him. How does he remember all my weaknesses? Against my skin, he says, "Your pussy seems to like me just fine."

"She's a very bad judge of character."

He hums deep in his throat, and I feel the vibrations of his chest against my own, my nipples hardening even further. "I think she's just attracted to men she knows can get her off like she's never gotten off before."

I dig my fingernails into his cloth-covered skin. "God, you're a cocky—" He finally presses his palm to my clit, and I nearly see stars.

"I am cocky. Know why?" He puts his lips right next to my ear, so the smoothness of them brushes against the shell with every word. "Because even though we only spent one night together, I still remember exactly what it takes to get you off. I know exactly what it takes to make you writhe, to make you moan, to make you scream.

I know if I tug your top down and pull your nipple into my mouth, you'll arch your back, trying to get closer. I know if I curl my fingers and hit that spot deep inside you, you'll moan low in your throat." As if to prove his point, he does just that. I try to hold it in, clamp my lips shut as if I can stop the sound from sheer force of will alone, but it comes out anyway. His lips curve against the skin below my ear. "And I know if I press my thumb hard on your clit right now, you'll come. So, yeah, I'm a little cocky. Now, do you want to finish or should I keep playing with you?"

"I hate you."

He pulls back, his eyebrows raised and his fingers frozen inside me. "Finish or play, Paige?"

I groan and latch my fingers in his hair to tug him closer to me. "You are such an asshole. Now make me come."

"You didn't say please."

Fuck this. And fuck him. I don't need an orgasm that bad. I can get one just as easily with my fingers or B.O.B. at home. I don't get the chance to push him away, though, before he's doing exactly what he said he would to get me off.

And he's right.

One hard press of his thumb on my clit and I'm flying, my mouth open in a silent moan as my head falls forward, my forehead pressed against his chest while I ride out the best orgasm I've had since forever.

Since him.

The quick thud thud thud of his heart beats against my forehead, and it's a small consolation that he's as worked up as I am. When the sound returns to my ears and breath fills my lungs, I pull back, pushing against his chest to get some space. His fingers slip from inside me, and he gives me some room to breathe, but not much. Not enough.

And then I make the mistake of looking at him. His eyes are dark and hungry, the baby blue eaten up by black pupils, and a flush blooms on his cheeks. It smells like sex in here, and with his fingers still wet from me and him looking at me like he wants to devour me, I can't take this. I need to get out of here. Regroup. Maybe give myself a lobotomy.

I spin for the door, and my hand closes on the knob, ready to turn.

"This isn't finished, Paige." His voice is low and rough and halts my movement.

My shoulders tighten, my posture going rigid, because I'm afraid he's right. And worse, I'm worried that getting any more involved with Adam Reid will completely demolish all my defenses. Defenses I've worked years to perfect.

Looking at him over my shoulder, I say, "I finished just fine. You'll have to work yourself out on your own." I pull open the door and march out into the pub, faking a confidence I certainly don't feel.

Because I know he's right. This definitely isn't finished.

And I'm afraid I don't want it to be.

FIVE

adam

My fingers are still wet from Paige when she rushes out of the bathroom. And all I can do is stare at her back as she flees. It smells like sex in here, like *Paige*, and my cock is hard enough to pound nails. I want nothing more than to bring my fingers to my mouth and suck, get a little refresher of her taste, because my memories don't do it justice. But I don't. I refuse to.

The next time I taste her pussy, it's going to be straight from the source while her legs are over my shoulders and I can listen to her out-of-control moans while I do it.

By the time I get out to the table, there's no Paige in sight. Though that's not exactly a surprise. I knew she was going to bail, but she *bailed*. I wasn't that far behind her, and I don't even see a flash of her blond hair by the door. The last thing I want to do is sit around with everyone a while longer. I want to go after her. Get some answers and find out why the hell she's been avoiding me, why she says she doesn't like me. Which I call total bullshit on, by the way. That girl is fighting something, and it feels a hell of a lot like she's fighting *me,* specifically.

Even though I want to leave, I still pull out my chair and take a seat. And though everyone is giving me covert glances, no one says anything about my disappearance coinciding with Paige's. Which is probably a good thing, because I'm sure none of them are interested in hearing how her orgasm felt around my fingers.

Jesus.

That girl is a damn pro at giving out mixed signals. She spouts off to me, coming at me with her defensive words at the same time she melts into my body, tilts her hips up so I can push deeper into her pussy.

I repress a groan at the thought of my fingers inside her and shift in my seat, trying to adjust the major hard-on I've had since laying eyes on her again without drawing attention to myself. When I reached into her panties and found out how wet she was—fucking drenched—I barely held my composure. I wanted to take her right there. In a goddamn *bathroom.*

I'm not that guy.

I'm not the guy who has one-night stands, who fucks on the first date, who has public sex because I can't wait to get someplace private. I'm methodical...safe in my relationships, because when it comes down to it, that's what I want. I *want* a relationship—one like my parents have. Despite all the shit they've dealt with over the years with the store—the ups and downs and plummets when they thought it couldn't get any worse—they've always maintained a solid marriage.

Because of that, it's something I've always strived for. I never went through the sowing my oats phase Cade and Jase both did. I was always content getting lucky while being in committed relationships. And if I wasn't in one? I didn't get laid. Simple as that.

And then Paige happened.

Before that night just after Christmas, I only ever saw her in passing when I'd come home for breaks, but I saw enough of her to know she was gorgeous. Like, drop-dead, is-this-girl-real gorgeous. And until that night, I didn't realize what a contradiction she is, because she isn't just a bombshell. She's a bombshell with the mouth of a sailor and an attitude to match it.

It shouldn't turn me on. *She* shouldn't turn me on. I like my women petite and a little shy. Even-keeled and mellow. Paige is none of those things. She's loud and vibrant and passionate and crass. She looks like a supermodel and acts like a trucker, and I love it, but I have no idea why.

Jase raps his knuckles on the table in front of me, getting my attention. "What happened back there, man?" He leans toward me across the table, his voice low enough to keep the conversation between the two of us.

I glance over and notice Tessa talking with Cade and Winter, her story about Haley shaking glitter all over the living room carpet holding their attention. Looking back to Jase, I say, "Took a piss."

He stares at me. "For ten minutes," he says flatly.

Instead of answering him, I shrug and take a drink from my beer, draining the bottle. He's always been one to run his mouth, sharing way more details about his sexual conquests than Cade or I ever needed to know. Until Tessa, that is. But me? I don't share shit with them—not about stuff like this. They know more about me than anyone else, but what I do with my dick is my business and no one else's. So my silence isn't unusual.

But that's the problem.

If it had been anything but sexual, I would've told him about it. Probably asked his opinion, because for having been a player, Jason has some insights that don't always occur to me. But now? He knows something's up with Paige and me. He just doesn't know what, exactly. And since Tessa can't keep a secret worth shit, especially from Jase, that means Paige never told her.

That shouldn't bother me as much as it does.

I need to get her alone…and not alone in a public bathroom

where I finger her. Someplace where I can dig deeper and find out what her deal is. I want to know what she thought of that night—if I'm the only one who's been thinking about it non-stop since it happened. If I'm the only one who dreams about it, who thinks about it when I come.

And despite her doing everything in her power to turn me away from that studio apartment in her building, you can bet I'm calling about it on Monday. Get me out of my parents' house and make it so Paige can't run away every time I get close?

Sounds like a win-win to me.

SIX

paige

It's been nearly a week since The Bathroom Incident, as I've come
to call it. Normally, Tessa and I hang out a couple times during the
week, and I *never* miss the weekly girls' night we've had every Tuesday
since forever.

I missed this week's.

I couldn't do it. Couldn't sit across from her, talk with her at
all, because I wasn't going to be able to hide this from her. She's been
harassing me all week, calling and texting, asking what the hell went
on last weekend. She doesn't mention Adam's name, but she doesn't
have to. I know that's what she's thinking.

And she's right.

I can't get him out of my head, the bastard. When I close my
eyes, I feel his warm breath on my neck, his hoarse, whispered words
in my ear. I feel his body against mine, the hard length of his cock
pressed into my hip, his fingers moving inside me.

Who *am* I? I don't do this. I don't pine or daydream over a guy unless he's Ryan Gosling. And, honestly, Ryan doesn't hold a candle to Adam and his gruff voice and naughty words. Adam looks like he was photoshopped, too, his abs and chest a work of art. A work of art I want to drown in chocolate syrup and lick up.

The only thing that's managed to occupy my mind has been my internship. It's fucking awesome, being at the station and being immersed in exactly what I want to do…

Okay, that's a lie. It sucks ass. All I've done so far is get coffee and file reports. The reports have been interesting to read, but it kills me that I'm not *doing* anything. I've been itching for the past two years to get into the field, but now it's worse than ever, being so close and still so far away. But then I remind myself it's only been four days, and I can't expect miracles overnight. I'll just have to charm them with my sparkling personality and knowledge of the field and coerce them into hopefully letting me get my hands a little dirty.

I snort into my pitiful Lean Cuisine and roll my eyes. If my sparkling personality is the only thing I have to lean on to get me where I want to go, I'm fucked.

My phone buzzes next to me on the couch cushion with a text from Tessa.

Jason's with Haley and I'm a free agent. Can I come over?

I should've known she'd corner me tonight. This isn't the first time she's asked me that this week. I purse my lips as I type back a lie I hate telling her.

Sorry, still at the station. Raincheck?

I press send and stand from the couch, bringing the paper container that held my "gourmet" meal into the kitchen when a pounding thuds at my door, sending me a foot in the air.

"You are not at the station, you little liar!"

Like she can see inside, I freeze, empty Lean Cuisine and water bottle in my hands. Maybe if I don't move or speak or breathe, she'll go away.

"I can smell whatever the hell you just cooked for dinner. I'm not going to go away!"

Fuck.

Blowing out a deep breath, I throw my fork in the sink and everything else in the garbage, then head to the door, preparing myself for a verbal beating from my best friend.

A verbal beating I can't say I don't deserve.

I don't even get out a hello before she's plowing past me, tossing her purse on my counter and spinning on me. "Time's up, Paige." She crosses her arms and taps her foot, and I repress a smile. Tessa isn't tough. She's tiny, her head perfectly in line with my boobs, and she's always been more of a lover than a fighter. Even though she's a strong woman and doesn't take shit, especially from Jason, she's just never had a rough-and-tumble personality. Seeing her all riled up like this is amusing. Probably shouldn't laugh, though.

My best course of action is to play dumb. "Time's up for what?"

"For me giving you your space. I know you're mad at me about something, so spit it out already."

This is our thing. We don't beat around the bush with each other; we just get straight to the point. Since we became friends when I moved back to Michigan as a junior in high school, it's been transparent with us. I don't do girlfriends. It might be the fact that I grew up in a military family, or that I have two older brothers who've never held back with me, or that my parents have only encouraged my tomboy inclinations, but I've always gotten along better with guys. So when Tessa and I became friends and we had our first fight, I handled it like I would with a guy. Said something to her along the lines of, "What the fuck is your problem? I wanna get lunch."

I should've known she'd do this. And I should've known she'd think it was all on her. While I *am* upset she told Adam about that apartment when she specifically thought I didn't like him, she's not the one I'm pissed off at. Nope, that award goes straight to myself.

Instead of answering her, I go to the freezer to pull out our usual indulgence—double fudge brownie ice cream—then grab two spoons and head to the couch. She follows, plopping down next to me as she tucks one leg under the other so she can face me. I pop off the top of the container and pass a spoon over to her before digging in myself.

Around a bite of creamy, sugary goodness, I say, "I'm a little pissed you offered the place across the hall to Adam."

She freezes with the spoon halfway to her mouth, her brows drawn. "Seriously?"

"Yeah, seriously. Have I done a shitty job of giving the impression that he's not my favorite person?"

"Well, no. I caught on to that when you said, 'stop talking about that asshole,' but I still don't get it. How can anyone hate Adam? He's the nicest guy in the world."

I can't help it. I snort. "Nice. He's not *nice*. He's the devil incarnate, and he's made it his mission to make my life hell."

"Okay, what the crap is going on? Because I really feel like I'm missing something here. You acted all weird at the pub on Friday and then you flew out of there like your underwear were on fire, but even before that…" She trails off, shaking her head. "I just don't get it. Something's up. What aren't you telling me?"

I avoid eye contact, digging into the ice cream and stuffing my mouth with it just to buy some time. I wonder how sick I'll get if I eat this whole container, and if that would deter her from getting answers. Might be worth puking if I can avoid this a while longer. When I reach to scoop another bite, Tessa snatches the spoon from my hand.

"Hey!" I say, trying to get it back.

"Nope." She shakes her head, holding my spoon hostage. "Not happening. Spill, or no more ice cream."

"You know I have a whole drawer of spoons, right?"

She narrows her eyes until they're nearly slits on her face. She's not budging on this.

I blow out a breath, my shoulders slumping as I lean back against a throw pillow. "Fine. You remember when you, Winter, and I went out after Christmas? When Jase came and left you that note?"

Her cheeks turn pink at the mention of those freakin' notes, and if I didn't love her so much, I'd hate her. She's actually *swooning* in front of me. Gag.

She nods. "Yeah."

"Well…Jase may have asked Adam to take me home, because I was a little too tipsy to drive. And I may have asked him to come inside. And then I *maaaaay* have fucked him. Maybe."

Tessa gasps, her eyes comically wide. She's speechless for several minutes. "*Adam?*" she finally sputters. "You fucked Adam. My sweet, caring, relationship-loving Adam had a one-night stand with you, that's what you're telling me."

I huff out a breath and roll my eyes. "He might be *your* sweet, caring, relationship-loving Adam, but to me, he's just the guy who fucked me against my front door. And over the arm of my couch. And laid me out on the dining room table and feasted on me until I was hoarse from screaming."

Her mouth hangs open as she stares at me. And it's a testament to how caught off guard she is that she's not even freaking out about sitting on the same couch I mentioned he fucked me on. Reaching over, I tap two fingers under her chin. "Close your mouth, sweetie. No cocks around."

She shakes her head as if trying to clear it and opens and closes her mouth several times, broken words spilling out. Finally, she scrunches up her face. "Holy shit, that's weird."

"Weird? Uh, no. I can guarantee that it was anything but weird. Mind-blowing? Unprecedented? Unparalleled? Yes, all of those. Weird? Not even a little."

"That isn't what I mean. It's just strange hearing about this guy I've known my whole life do all those things. Weird and a little gross."

"Wasn't that, either."

"Yeah, so now I *really* don't get it. If it was all those things, why aren't you jumping all over that? Especially now that he's here for a few months."

I just stare at her, because I shouldn't have to say it. I *don't* have to say it, because realization dawns on her face. "Paige..." She shakes her head. "Seriously, you have got to stop running scared from something that happened *years* ago."

My spine snaps straight, because I don't run scared from anything. Least of all feelings. I'd just...rather not have them. Been there, done that. Got the T-shirt that says, *Congrats, you changed your whole life for a guy and it blew up in your face.* So, yeah, forgive me for not wanting to go there again. "I'm not."

"You *are*. You haven't had a relationship—serious or otherwise—since Bryan."

I try not to cringe at the mention of his name. "That's not true. I have lots of relationships."

"It doesn't count if it lasts less than a week."

Well, shit. That pretty much makes up my entire adult dating history.

"Look, I get it," she says. "What he did was shitty. Seeing it with your own eyes was shittier. Watching me go through everything with Nick was shitty, too. And I know you were there for Dillon when he went through everything with his ex-wife, but you can't base the outlook of your entire romantic life on the bad luck of a couple people."

I snort because she's downplaying everything to a ridiculous degree. Watching her, pregnant and alone at seventeen, taking the full brunt of the judgmental stares and barely hidden gossip at school while her fucker of an ex bailed on her was hard enough. Watching my oldest brother deal with finding out his wife fucked his best friend? While he was deployed? Even worse. And all that after seeing my boyfriend—the guy I thought I *loved*...the guy I changed my life for—letting some girl bounce on his cock in the front seat of *my* car? Yeah, it affected me and every "relationship" I've had since. And I'm not sorry about that. I like my life. I *love* my life. And that includes my lack of a significant other.

"Do you know what the divorce rate is?" I snatch my spoon back and jab it in her direction. "It's not just a *couple* people. It's the whole fucking world. Plus, I like men. And I like a variety of men. There's nothing wrong with me tasting a different flavor every month."

She exhales and sags back into the arm of the couch. Probably not a great time to tell her that's the side Adam fucked me on. "Fine. You don't want to do anything with Adam—even though he was *unprecedented*—that's your call. But you better figure out a way to be around him without running like a chicken."

"Why's that? You have group get-togethers planned for the summer?"

"No. Well, yes, but that's not the main issue."

"What's the main issue?"

"You're getting a new neighbor this weekend." And then a grin splits her face, and she happily digs into the ice cream.

Well, fuck.

SEVEN

adam

"I thought you said you didn't have much shit, and that we'd just be sitting around, drinking beer and eating pizza." Jase grunts as he lifts his end of the overly heavy, pullout couch.

Yeah, I'm kind of an ass to make him and Cade carry it while I lug just a TV, but having them around to help me move is pretty much the only reason I put up with their asses over the years.

"Jesus, you're a whiny shit, aren't you?" Cade guides his end of it down the stairs and to my opened door. "Just haul the damn thing and stop bitching. *Then* we'll get beer."

I trail behind, awkwardly carrying the tube TV. I can't remember the last time I had to lift one of these monstrosities, but I can't exactly be picky considering I'm filling this place with my parents' castoffs. Nearly all of what I own is still at my place in Denver, which I'm subletting while I'm gone, and Dad certainly wasn't going to give up his 46-inch flat screen in the living room. "I knew the only way I'd get you here was to lie to you, so…"

"You're both assholes," Jase says. "And I want you to bring me a fucking Heineken as soon as we set this ugly-ass couch in your new digs."

"I'll throw the bottle at your head and hope you don't catch it," I say.

Cade snorts as he backs through the threshold into my apartment. It's small—one open room containing the living space and kitchen, plus a bathroom—but it'll work for the summer. It's a lot different than my place in Colorado, but at this point, after another week at my parents'—another week where I couldn't jack off after waking up from an inevitable dream of Paige, pick out my own damn clothes, or prepare a freakin' sandwich—it looks like heaven. We pass the kitchen—and I use that term loosely—on the right and bathroom on the left before they move the couch against the far wall opposite the battered wood TV stand that was, thankfully, left behind from the last tenants. Or meth heads, according to Paige.

"I can't believe your mom made you take the granny panty couch." Jase sets his end down and looks at the godawful floral pattern adorning my new piece of furniture.

I snort at the nickname we came up with for the couch when we were in middle school. With pink, purple, and blue flowers brushed all over the fabric, it definitely looks more like something a grandma would wear than something a dude should have in his place, but I'll take what I can get. "I'm lucky she gave me anything. She's damn upset I'm not staying there while I'm home for the summer. Pretty sure I hurt her feelings when I told her I needed to move out."

"What does she expect you to do? Your dick's gonna fall off if you don't spank it once in a while." Jason falls back on the couch and sprawls out. "Although I'm not sure you're much better off here. You gonna sleep on this thing every night? Forget falling off—your dick is gonna shrivel up and retreat inside you until you have a vagina."

"My dick's pretty big. It'll take a while."

"Not as big as mine."

"You wish, Montgomery." I set the TV down on the stand.

"You guys want me to grab you a tape measure?" Cade asks as he comes in from the kitchen, carrying three bottles in his hand. He tosses one to both of us, then twists the top off his and takes a sip as he looks around. "I think this place might even be smaller than Winter's old apartment, and that's saying something."

I sit on the opposite end of the couch from Jase and take in the room. He's probably right. It's barely big enough for the couch, the TV stand, and the pitiful excuse for a table my parents let me use. "Don't care. After only a few weeks at home, I was ready to move into one of your bathrooms and sleep in the tub, so I think I can handle a tiny-ass apartment and an ugly-ass couch. It's only temporary. I don't plan on being here a lot, anyway. I'll be spending most of my time at the shop."

Cade grabs a chair from my fancy dining set consisting of a card table and two battered folding chairs. He sits on it backward, his arms folded across the back. "How's that going, anyway? You finding anything?"

I groan and drop my head back to the couch, beer bottle resting on my knee. The past three weeks have been enlightening to say the least. "Yeah. They've been in trouble for longer than they let on, so it's gonna take a hell of a lot more work to get everything back on track. They have a stack of IOUs I plan on getting settled ASAP."

"Jesus, they were doing business with IOUs? What is this, 1952?" Jase asks.

"That's pretty much what I told them. When I put everything in black and white for them, they realized how bad it is and that they can't do that shit anymore. Besides settling those, I'm trying to come up with some events or something we can do to get in more traffic."

"What about guided classes? Hiking, fishing, rock climbing, that kind of thing," Jase suggests.

I nod. "I was thinking about that. And maybe offering rentals, too. Bikes, paddle boats, canoes... It'd take a chunk out of our inventory, but it's the perfect season to try it. And with the lake and bike trails both being close, it makes sense. I don't think it'd take much to see a return on investment and hopefully start making some money."

"You gonna suggest it to your parents?" Cade asks.

"Yeah, I just hope my mom's not too pissed at me for moving out, and she actually listens to what I'm saying."

"She will," Jase says. "Your dad will be behind you. He'll back you up."

I nod again, hoping he's right. The shop has been my parents' since...forever. As long as I can remember. They opened it when I was about three and my sister, Aubrey, was six. Despite the obligation it can be, it's as much home to me as my parents' house is, and the thought of it going under...of it getting sold to someone else—or worse, the thought of it getting run into the ground by the national chains that are overtaking every city—makes me sick.

"So...speaking of being behind people...I heard an interesting story." Jase glances at Cade, then turns his focus to me. "Once upon a time, you fucked Paige. True or false."

I freeze with the beer bottle pressed to my lips. The pause lasts less than a second before I tip my head back to take a drink, but they both see it, and I'm kicking myself for giving anything away. My poker face is better than that.

"Holy *shit*, it's true." Jase reaches out and punches me in the arm, then he looks at Cade. "Did you know about this?"

Cade shakes his head. "Nope."

Jase pulls off his backward baseball cap, runs his hand through his hair, then replaces the hat and fixes me with a hard stare. "Five months? You got with *Paige* five months ago, and you never said a damn thing? What the fuck, dude?"

"Sorry to tell you this, man, but you don't know every girl I've had my dick in."

"Uh, yes, I do." He starts counting off on his fingers. "Lost your virginity to Nikki in high school. Dated her from late sophomore year until graduation. Then it was Megan and Rachel in college—mid-freshman to junior year, and senior year, respectively. After you graduated, it was Katie until last summer. It's not a hard list to keep track of."

"Fuck off."

"I'm not saying it's a bad thing," he says, holding his hands up.

I just stare at him.

"All right," he concedes, "I'm not saying it's a bad thing for *you*. But seriously…when did you start doing one-night stands?"

"Maybe I've done them all along, and I just never told you assholes." They both snort at that. I look over to Cade, who's been uncharacteristically tight-lipped. "You don't have anything to add to this douchebag's commentary?"

He shrugs. "It's a little different than your usual M.O., but I'm not one to judge. And God knows Jase can't judge."

"Hey, I wasn't judging! I was *congratulating*. Jesus, it's like you two don't even know me."

"I don't understand what Tess sees in you," I say.

"You and me both." Cade laughs and ducks from the bottle cap Jase flicks at him.

Jason takes another drink from his beer and stretches his arm out over the back of the couch. "You gonna try and hook up with her while you're here for the summer?"

I shrug as I peel back the label from my bottle.

"Holy shit." Jase sits forward, his gaze flitting between me and Cade, his brows rising higher on his forehead with every inch he gets closer to me. "You've already done it. I *knew* something happened at the pub! I can't believe you—*you*"—he stabs a finger in my direction—"would fuck her in a bathroom."

"I didn't fuck her in the bathroom." What I don't say is that I totally would have, given the chance. I try not to remember what she felt like around my fingers. Her panting breaths on my neck and the thrust of her hips… *Jesus*. Paige isn't shy or withdrawn when it comes to sex. She takes what she wants, without embarrassment. I want to see that again. While my list of partners isn't nearly as long as Jason's, I've had my share of sex—all while within the confines of a relationship, save one, but it was still frequent. And I've always thought it was good sex. I mean, really, what did I have to compare it to? But being with Paige, I realized all the girls who came before her were…timid. Quiet, docile women who didn't ask for what they wanted. They weren't all that interested in trying new things. They were perfectly content to do it missionary every single time.

And I didn't realize I didn't want that until I had Paige bent over in front of me, begging me to fuck her harder.

Jase narrows his eyes at me. "You did *something*."

When I don't confirm or deny it, he takes that as the only answer he needs. Shaking his head, he says, "With Paige Bennett. Goddamn. You're in the big leagues now." Then in a falsetto, he says, "You're growing up so fast."

Finally cracking a smile, I grab my bottle cap and toss it at his head. Then I look over at Cade. "Nothing more to add?"

He shrugs, taking a drink before he lets his arm hang over the back of the chair again. "Unlike Jase, I don't much care what you do with your dick."

"You act like me being a supportive friend is a bad thing." Jase laughs as we both snort. "Just so you know, she pretty much hates the idea of you moving in here. I know it's been a while since you've done this whole thing, but that's not a glowing endorsement to start something with her."

I shrug, unconcerned. "I'm working on it."

"Yeah? Has she brought you some freshly baked cherry pie to welcome you to the neighborhood?"

I give him the side-eye. "Seriously, why does Tessa put up with you?"

"Because I know how to—"

"If you want to live to get home to your girlfriend, you won't finish that sentence," Cade cuts in.

I haven't been home much to see them navigate this new dynamic of their relationship, and I can't say it isn't damn fun to watch. "Please, Jase, go on…"

"You both ruin all my fun," he says.

"You're banging my sister." Cade tips his bottle toward Jason. "It's now my life-long right."

"Speaking of…" Jase gets up and tosses his bottle in the garbage. "As fun as this has been, and as much as I'd like to stick around for pizza, I need to get home, if you know what I mean." He waggles his eyebrows and dodges the fist Cade swings at him, laughing, then turns to me. "But, hey, if you wanna get a new website up for the shop, let me know. I can get something created pretty quick, depending on what you're thinking."

I walk behind him, then hold open the door as Jason walks into the main hallway. "Thanks, man, that'd be great. I'll talk to them this week and let you know."

"Beer and pool on Tuesday?"

"Works for me."

"Sounds good. Later, ladies." When he's climbed a couple steps, he turns around and says, "Oh, and Cade? Don't call your sister or me for a while. We'll be otherwise occupied."

Jase's laughter is drowned out by Cade's growl as he steps up behind me. "I hate that guy."

I clap a hand on his back. "I know."

He leans a shoulder against the doorjamb and crosses his arms. "So, Paige, huh?"

I glance around him to the door across the hall that she occupies. I've yet to run into her even once. Not when I met with the apartment manager or when I came to look at the place. Not the entire time we've been moving stuff in. "Guess so."

"Look, man," he says, his voice lowered. "Paige is an awesome girl. She's great, but she has a lot of shit from her past that fucks with her outlook a little."

"You warning me away from her or cautioning me to be careful moving forward?"

"Neither. You do what you want to do. Just giving you the info you didn't have since you were already in Colorado when she moved here. And I would give you the whole, 'don't mess with her or I'll mess with you' speech, because she's damn close to a sister to me, but considering her two scary-ass brothers, I don't think I'll have to." He grins as he pushes off the threshold to leave. "See you Tuesday."

"See ya. Thanks for the help."

He gives a wave as he climbs the steps and disappears out the front door of the building. I take another glance at her silent door before closing mine.

I can handle her brothers. It's her I'm not so sure about.

EIGHT

paige

I've managed to avoid Adam since he moved in over the weekend, but I know that can't go on forever. We live on the same floor in a tiny eight-tenant apartment building. We park in the same small parking lot. Our mailboxes are right next to each other, for fuck's sake. There's no way in hell I'm going to go the three months, or however long he's here, without bumping into him. But I'm damn well going to try. No matter how long I manage to avoid him, I can't avoid the *thought* of him, and it's messing with my head knowing he's just across the hall.

It *shouldn't* be messing with my head knowing he's there, and yet when I go to bed at night, I wonder if he's lying in his, too. When I get out of the shower, I wonder if he is, as well. And then I picture him drying off, rivulets of water running down his chest, taking a bumpy ride over the ridges of his cut abs, and trailing all the way down to the freakin' shrine Adam Reid has in his pants.

I'm not one to worship the cock, but if one were to be worshipped, it'd be his.

Shaking my head, I shove all thoughts of a naked Adam out of my mind before I have the chance to rewind my little fantasy and picture him *in* the shower, doing what we all know single guys do in there, his hand wrapped around his—

Nope.

"Get ahold of yourself, girl," I say to my reflection as I fluff my hair. Dark shadow and bold liner to bring out my eyes? Check. Pink gloss to plump up my lips? Check. Plunging neckline to show off the girls? Check. Random date with a dude I'm not even really interested in to get my mind off the one I *shouldn't* be interested in? Check, check, and check.

A knock at the door sounds, and I glance at the time on my phone, scowling when I see my date, Brent, is fifteen minutes early. Dudes should know better than to show up that early. He's lucky I started getting ready sooner than usual as a way to take my mind off Adam—which obviously did a lot of good. I take one more glance in the mirror before I head to the door just as another round of knocks sounds.

"Jesus, needy much?" I mumble under my breath, then call out, "Coming!"

I pull open the door, only it's not Brent who greets me, but my brother Tanner. And he's got one hell of a scowl on his face.

"What the fuck, Paige? You just open your door to anyone? What would you have done if I was some stalker who shoved his way into your place?" he asks…as he shoves his way into my place.

"My knee would shove its way into his balls." I shut the door behind me and follow him into the kitchen where he sets down a grease-stained paper bag, presumably filled with take-out. "Uh, not that I don't love you, but what are you doing here?"

"You. Me. Burgers. A few episodes of *CSI*. You still have that beer I like, right?" He doesn't wait for me to answer before he goes to the fridge and peers inside. He scowls at me. "You don't have any left." That scowl turns into bewilderment as he looks at me, his brows pinching together as if he's seeing me for the first time tonight. "You look like a girl. What's up with that?"

I scoff and roll my eyes. "I *am* a girl, douchenozzle."

"No, you're not. You're Paige. And she certainly doesn't wear"—he straightens to his full height and gestures to everything from my tousled hair to my skintight dress to my heels that could kill someone—"all *this*. Seriously, what's up?"

"I don't know, idiot. What does it look like? Single girl, dressed up… You seriously can't be this dumb."

"You…you have a *date*?"

"Why do you say it like it's the most preposterous thing in the world?" I grab his arm and tug him toward the front door, snatching up his bag o' grease along the way.

He studies me with narrowed eyes. "This your first date, then?"

Snorting, I work harder to pull him toward the door. "Uh huh. First one. Twenty-three and never been kissed. You got it, now for the love of Ryan Gosling, will you *leave*? Holy crap, man. We can watch *CSI* tomorrow. I'll even buy dinner, okay?"

"Fine, fine," he grumbles and snatches the bag out of my hand. "I got you extra onion rings, I'll have you know. And now I'm going to eat them. All of them."

Shaking my head, I roll my eyes when he turns his back to me and opens the door…just as Brent's fist is raised to knock. My date for the evening looks momentarily shell-shocked at seeing a dude come out of my apartment, but I paste on an overly bright smile and hope to distract him.

"Brent, hi! I'm all set, just need to grab my purse." I shove my brother in the shoulder harder than absolutely necessary while he tries to intimidate Brent with his glare, and it appears to be working. I'm just lucky Tanner's not wearing his gun, or Brent might actually pee himself. "He was just leaving."

"Uh, if this is a bad time…" Brent's gaze darts to my brother's imposing form. Seeing them stand next to each other is almost comical, and it only emphasizes Brent's wiry physique. And average height...for a guy, anyway, meaning I'm going to tower over him in these heels. Great.

"No, no! It's fine," I say as I grab my purse and head back to the door, shooing them both out and shutting it behind me.

Tanner is still glaring daggers into Brent's forehead. Brent is trying hard to look everywhere but at the cleavage I'm sporting, but he doesn't quite manage, which only makes Tanner glare harder. As if everything wasn't already horribly awkward, the front door to the building opens and Adam chooses that moment to come down the stairs. He's got a messenger bag slung over his shoulder, and his arms are full of papers. His hair is standing up all over the place, as if he's run frustrated fingers through it all day, and his eyes are bloodshot. Combine all that with way-longer-than-a-five-o'clock-shadow stubble he's rocking, and one would think he just came from a four-day bender. But that's ridiculous, because this is Adam.

Responsible, mature, sensible Adam.

Except he wasn't so responsible or mature or sensible when he fingered me against the wall in a freakin' restaurant bathroom.

A wave of heat rushes over me, and *great*. The memory of Adam doing that creeps in, and I absolutely don't need to be thinking about that now. Not when I'm standing in front of my date for the evening and my *brother*, who's taking in everything with a shrewd eye. Damn cop genes.

Adam halts in his tracks when he gets to the landing and notices us all standing there, his eyes connecting with mine almost immediately, like he can *sense* me. He takes in Tanner, then Brent, then his gaze darts back to mine again. I've spent almost a week avoiding him since the restaurant, and the first time he sees me is with two guys coming out of my apartment. I wait for him to blow up. To freak out about the guy I'm going out with and the guy Adam doesn't know is my brother. But instead of raising his voice, instead of saying *anything,* he simply lifts an eyebrow as he stares at me. "Hey, Paige."

"Uh, hi! We were just leaving! See ya!" God, who the fuck's voice is that, all high-pitched and chipper, and can someone shoot her already?

And now it's not just Adam's eyebrows that are mocking me, but those damn lips, too. How they're curved up on the side, on a one-way trip to Smirky, Smugsville, population one.

I finally get my overbearing oaf of a brother to move ahead of me, and Brent follows behind me like a puppy dog—or, more aptly, like a horny college guy who's hoping for a peek up my skirt if he lags far enough behind as I climb the steps.

My brother keeps looking over his shoulder at Adam who's standing outside his apartment, watching all this as he unlocks his front door. Tanner narrows his eyes at me, and I can practically see the wheels spinning in his mind. And then he smiles. "Can't wait for tomorrow."

Yeah, me neither.

I HONESTLY CAN'T remember ever being on a more painful date. And that's saying something, because I have been on a *lot* of dates. But this guy…this guy, man.

"Wait, wait…I can do the rest." Brent takes another huge gulp of his beer, while I try to drown my sorrows in yet another cosmo. It's not helping. No amount of vodka will help ease this insufferable evening.

Brent proceeds to burp the remainder of the alphabet. He doesn't stop when our waitress comes up to the table. Instead, he offers a smile and belches T, U, and V in her face. Understandably, she turns on her heel and leaves us, but not before shooting a commiserating look at me.

Ugh, why am I here?

Except I know exactly why I'm here. His name starts with Fuckhot and ends with Adam, and when you put them together, I'm screwed. He's been on my mind since The Bathroom Incident, and I attempted to do what I do best under those circumstances—get lost in another guy. When Brent approached me at the coffee shop on campus and asked me out, I agreed immediately. No, I don't know him that well. He's the friend of a friend, so I've seen him around before, but only ever in passing. I've never spent one-on-one time with him, otherwise I'm *certain* he would've regaled me with his burping talent before tonight.

After he gets out an excruciatingly long Z, he grins at me. "Huh? *Huh?* Pretty awesome, right? Tell me you've met someone who can do that."

"Well, you got me there, Brent." I tip back my head to swallow the rest of my cosmo, desperate for another, but I'm refraining because I want to get the hell out of here.

The waitress comes back and places the check on the table, shooting another sympathetic glance in my direction. Thank God. Now that we have the check, I can see the light at the end of the tunnel.

Brent reaches for the leather folder and cringes when he sees the total. "So, uh, how do you want to do this?"

"Do what?"

He lifts the bill folder and glances pointedly at it. "This. You just want to go halfsies, or…?"

I can only stare at him for a moment, because he can't be serious. *He* asked *me* out on this date. He selected the restaurant—one I wouldn't ever go to if I had my choice. He ordered not one but *two* appetizers for himself—he actually slapped my hand away when I reached for a bite—then proceeded to order the steak and lobster. The steak and lobster! He's a fucking college student, not Prince William. But, yeah, sure, let me get half of that for you, asshole.

"You know how this whole dating thing works, right?" I ask.

"Where the person who asks the other out on the date is generally the one who pays…"

He looks taken aback for a minute, like he didn't expect me to actually call him on it, but fuck that. I'm not known for my tact. Shifting in his seat, he says, "I…I only brought twenty bucks with me."

I snort. "What are you, twelve?" I grab the bill from his hands and check the total, grinding my teeth at how much this shitty, horrible, *awful* night is costing me, and it's a hell of a lot more than matching the twenty bucks this asshat is tossing in. Sitting on my couch and hiding from Adam would have been preferable to this bullshit, and a hell of a lot cheaper. I grab my purse, pull out some cash, and slap it in the bill folder before I stand.

"As delightful as this evening has been, I think I'm about ready to go home."

He stands from his seat and offers a frown. "Oh, I thought we could go get dessert somewhere…"

The laugh that rips free from my mouth is not even a little appropriate for the quiet dining establishment we're in, nor for the level of fun this night has been, but I can't stop it. "And how did you plan to pay for that? Gonna dig for coins on the floor of your car?"

I don't wait for an answer before I turn on my too-high heels and walk toward the door of the restaurant. This dress and these shoes and all that time getting ready were totally wasted on this douchebag of epic proportions.

I seethe the entire way home, wishing this fifteen-minute ride could be over in five. When we finally pull up in front of my apartment building, I'm so happy to see it I nearly dive out to kiss the sidewalk.

Douchebag's hand hovers over the keys in the ignition, his head turned toward me. "So, you want to fuck, or what?"

His expression is eager, and that only makes me want to punch him all the more, so I don't even attempt to sugarcoat things. "Let me get this straight. You invited me out for dinner and didn't ask where I'd like to go. You took me to a restaurant with shitty-but-expensive food, burped for a solid twenty minutes at the table, slapped my hand when I tried to eat some of the food you ordered—which, by the way, you made me pay *way* more than half for—and now you're asking if you're going to get laid. Have I got that about right?"

He doesn't say anything, his face burning with color, and I laugh as I reach for the door handle. "Uh, no. No, I absolutely do not want to fuck." After stepping out of the car, I lean into the open door. "And do me a favor: lose my number." I slam the door and watch as he speeds away, peeling out in his tricked-out Neon.

Tricked. Out. Neon.

That should've been clue fucking one.

"Freakin' wanker," I mutter, rubbing my fingers against my forehead.

I take a deep breath and reach down to slip off my heels, sighing when I remove the deathtraps from my feet. They're sexy, but holy hell do they hurt. Hooking them on my fingers, I turn and head up the walkway to the apartment building. With each step I take, I imagine different ways I could've told off Brent—like by dumping my water in his lap and telling everyone in the restaurant he has an incontinence problem.

"Bad night?" The voice I've tried my hardest to dodge, to not think about, stops me in my tracks when I'm nearly to the front stoop, making the entire night of avoidance a lost cause.

NINE

adam

It's been a long goddamn day. A long goddamn *week*, if I'm honest.
I've been at the shop from 7 a.m. to well after dinner every day. When
I was in high school, I used to love working there. I think I would
now, too, if I were doing anything but pushing paper in the back
office and trying to figure out a way to dig my parents out of this hole
they got themselves in. The funny thing is, what I'm doing now isn't
that much different from what I do back at home. My job consists
of me sitting in an office for eight hours, crunching numbers. Odd
how I feel satisfied with it in Denver, but it makes me itchy here, like
I need to be doing more.

On the plus side, my parents have never really treated me
as a child—sandwiches prepped and clothes ironed notwithstanding.
They see me as an equal in the business with valuable ideas, so they're
doing everything I suggest without complaint or argument. New
website? Yes. Guided tours? All over it. Offering rentals? They've
already taken the merchandise out of inventory to prepare it for when

the website is complete, showcasing all the new stuff we're doing and offering sign-ups for those tours and rentals.

After this week, I think I'll actually be able to dive in and help with all that stuff. I've almost reached the bottom of the never-ending paper pile my parents left for me. I've spent hours crunching numbers, figuring out what kind of income we need to have coming in to get us well into the black again. I've brought all that work home, poring over it until midnight most nights, before I crash for a few hours and start the cycle all over again.

The one interruption to my routine I didn't anticipate today was seeing Paige. I moved in almost a week ago, and I haven't gotten even a glimpse of her. And the one time I do run into her, she's coming out of her apartment with not one but *two* guys. Awesome.

I've wanted to see her, wanted to go over and knock on her door, see if she'd actually ignore me, but I've had a lot of time to think about this whole Paige situation, and I've come to the conclusion that I need to be patient. For all her bluster and bravado, Paige is a chicken—at least when it comes to relationships. And as much as I loved fucking her, I can't have *just* that. I can't. My body isn't wired that way, and neither is my mind. But no matter what we do, we'd both be bending a little. I'll only be here for a few months. Much shorter than any relationship I've ever had, but if the info Cade and Jason have slipped me is accurate, it's longer than anything Paige has done by, oh, two-point-seven-five months. I figure it's a good compromise. I just have to get *her* to actually see that before I rub my dick raw from all the wanking I've been doing.

Not able to stare at the spreadsheet I've been working on any longer, I set my laptop on the couch cushion next to me, then make my way to the fridge. I need a beer or four, and I need to get out of this tiny closet of an apartment.

I grab a bottle from the fridge, then think twice and reach for a back up before I make my way out of my apartment and up the steps to the front stoop. It's a perfect summer night, the air warm but not scorching, the light breeze making it even more tolerable. I'm just lifting the bottle to my lips when a bright blue Neon with what Cade, Jase, and I refer to as douche-wheels—the kind where the rims eat up all but a tiny circumference of tire—rolls to a stop at the curb. That car is so low to the ground, it would bottom out if it went over a pothole. And are those…florescent blue lights coming from underneath the car?

Shaking my head, I take a long drink just as the passenger door opens and a girl steps out. As I take a closer look, I realize it's not just any girl, but *the* girl. The one who's been a constant presence in my dreams for half a year. The dress she's wearing would be indecent if it wasn't so fucking hot. It's red and short and skin-tight and bunches up so it ruffles over her stomach, and I don't need her to turn around to be reminded of exactly what the front looks like. The neckline plunged so low, there's absolutely no way she could possibly be wearing a bra, and I grind my teeth again at the thought of her going out with that guy—those guy*s*? I don't even fucking know. All I know is I spent the night with my head buried in spreadsheets just to stop the images from filling my mind. Images of her out with another dude. While patience is one of my better qualities, it seems as if sharing *isn't*. I could wait for her for months. Waiting for her while watching her go out with other guys? Not so easy.

Paige stands from leaning into the car and slams the door, then flips the bird at the retreating car, muttering something too low for me to catch. She sighs so heavily, I can actually see her shoulders sag, then she reaches down and takes off her shoes before hooking them on her fingers and walking my way. Her head is down, her blond hair falling in loose waves over one of her shoulders while she focuses on the ground in front of her. This is the most unguarded I've ever seen her. Paige doesn't put up a front, I don't think. She is who she is one hundred percent of the time, but there is something there usually…an armor, maybe, that she feels she needs to have. Especially around me.

"Bad night?"

She jerks to a stop a foot from where I'm sitting, her eyes doing a slow sweep from my feet all the way to my hair that no doubt looks like I've slept on it. As her gaze travels over every inch of me, lingering on my chest, I almost wish I was wearing something other than my beat up Pumas, threadbare jeans, and T-shirt so worn it's developed tiny holes at the seams. But then her eyes snap up to mine, and there's no denying the heat there.

Patience.

She's been avoiding me for days…weeks, if I'm going to get technical. Ever since she found out I was home. But now she's here, with no way to escape without looking ridiculous, taking me in like she wants to eat me.

She tilts her head to the side as she stares at me. "I didn't know you wore glasses."

I raise an eyebrow at her blunt observation. "There's a lot of things you don't know about me."

Tilting her head down, she concedes. "I guess that's true. And to answer your question, yeah, you could say that."

"Your dates not do it for you?"

"Date, singular, and no." Her lips purse while she studies me. "The other guy, the tall one with all the muscles and the angry glower? That's my brother. One of them, anyway."

Well, that's marginally better than I thought, but that still means she went out with one of the guys. Grabbing the extra beer I brought out, I lift it toward her. "You want?"

She captures the corner of her bottom lip between her teeth, and my fingers tighten on the necks of both bottles just to stop myself from reaching up and tugging it free. Then tugging her into my lap so I can capture it between *my* teeth. But then she releases her lip, exhaling deeply, and gives me a quick nod before taking a seat next to me on the stoop. Twisting off the cap, I hand her the bottle before taking a deep pull from mine.

Resting my forearms on my knees, I glance over at her. "So what made the night so bad? You don't like Neons?"

Laughter bursts from her and bubbles around us, the sound matching her personality exactly. It's not dainty or sweet. It's carefree and loud and absolutely infectious, and I find myself smiling along.

"God, I needed that laugh tonight." She grins at me, and I think it might be the first time I've ever seen it. I've seen her face right after she comes, watched her bite her lip as she chases an orgasm, looked into her eyes when I sank deep inside her, but I've never been on the receiving end of one of her carefree smiles.

I want it again.

"You really only have yourself to blame," I say. "When you saw his car, did you not know he was going to be a douchebag?"

"I was withholding judgment." She sighs. "Of course, when we got to the restaurant and he burped the entire alphabet after finishing his lobster and steak—which, by the way, he made me pay half for—withholding judgment was thrown out the window. My judgey pants were on and securely fastened."

The off-hand comment brings my attention to her lower half, and I once again take in the tiny dress—definitely *not* pants, judgey or otherwise—that should be illegal. The hem of it comes to mid-thigh, and that's being generous, especially with her sitting down. My eyes continue past the hem and move lower without my permission, tracing the lines of her bare legs, long and sleek and muscular…like she spends time *doing* shit instead of just looking pretty. The sight of them makes my mouth go dry. I know what it feels like to have those legs wrapped around my hips. To have those thighs pressing against my ears while my tongue is buried inside her.

Christ.

I need to get my shit together. Patience is going to go out the window if I can't stop thinking about tonguing her pussy. Clearing my throat, I focus again on what she said, and I can't help but chuckle. "What kind of DB makes his date pay?"

"*I know, right?*" She slaps my arm and nods emphatically, her eyes wide. "And yeah, laugh it up. It was *hilarious* when he burped in our waitress's face. And also when he dropped me off and asked me ever so eloquently if I 'wanted to fuck, or what.'"

The laughter dies in my throat, and I wish I'd known that when he dropped her off. Although it's probably better I didn't. The last thing I need right now is to spend the night in jail for assault and battery.

"Oh, you can wipe the macho, scorned man look off your face. I can take care of myself." She lifts the beer to her lips, takes a healthy swallow, then sighs as she rests the bottle on one bare knee. "Just wish I didn't have to suffer through that *and* pay for it in the end. Literally."

"That guy's an ass."

"No argument from me." She glances at me. "So what are you doing out here?"

I shrug. "Couldn't stand being inside anymore. Got tired of looking at spreadsheets and needed a break."

"Spreadsheets? Oh, for your parents' business? How's that going?"

I'm surprised she remembers why I'm here, with how much she's put into the act of pretending she doesn't care. "It could be going better. Though it could be going a lot worse, too, so I should count my blessings and shut the hell up."

"I think I've been to their shop before. Pretty sure we got my new skis there in high school."

I glance over at her with raised eyebrows. "I didn't know you ski."

While she doesn't laugh this time, she offers me a smirk, her lips curved up on one side and pure amusement in her eyes. "There's a lot you don't know about me," she says, returning my words from earlier. "And, yeah, I do. Growing up with two brothers and a military dad meant I didn't get handled with princess gloves. I can run with the boys any day of the week."

My assessment earlier of her actually doing shit and not spending her time just looking pretty was spot on. And if the reaction in my jeans is anything to go by, I really, *really* like it.

She tips her head back, swallowing the rest of her beer, then turns to me. "Thanks for this. And for the chat." She pauses and looks at me, then glances down at her lap as she fingers the hem of her dress. "The evening started off pretty shitty, but this made it suck less."

"Careful, Paige, that sounded suspiciously like you actually enjoyed your time with me."

Bumping her shoulder into mine, she says, "Don't get used to it." She stretches out her legs, then stands, and I should be a gentleman and not watch the way the hem of her skirt rides up even more before she can tug it down. I should be, but I'm not. "I'm going to head in, I think. You coming?"

Pulling myself away from the silky skin of her legs, I shake my head. "Nah. Every inch of my shoebox apartment is covered with shit for the shop. I can't look at it anymore tonight. I'm going to stay out here for a while."

Paige hesitates, shifting from foot to foot, and I'm trying to get a read on her, but she makes it damn hard. She's got a poker face nearly as good as mine. Finally, she says, "You can hang out at my place, if you want. I was just going to watch a hilariously awful horror movie, but I do have a couch that's not covered in paperwork."

She looks like a model, talks like a sailor, skis and who knows what else, *and* watches horror movies? Who *is* this girl?

I must hesitate for too long, because she quirks an eyebrow. "You know, 'watching a hilariously awful horror movie' isn't a euphemism for anything."

"Damn."

That pulls another laugh from her, and she turns her back to me and opens the door to the building. "Sorry, buddy. Just you, me, some really ratty clothes, and a bunch of blood and guts between us."

She leans against the open door. "Speak now or forever hold your peace."

I stand from the stoop, bottle clutched in one hand, and grab the door above her head. Leaning toward her until I can feel her breath on my lips, I glance between her eyes and her mouth, restraining myself from swooping in and capturing those lips in a kiss. A kiss I've thought about getting every day since December. A kiss she's withheld from me, for whatever reason. From the way her breath hitches, I don't think I'm too far off the mark thinking she feels the same. This should be fun. "I'm in."

TEN

paige

Why is it that whenever I'm around Adam, every single one of my brain cells runs for the fucking hills? It's like all common sense just totally bails on me. That's the only logical explanation, really. Because if I *did* have an ounce of sense left, I wouldn't have invited him into my apartment for the night. I also wouldn't have changed out of my dress and heels and into my pajamas, tossing my bra on the floor while I was at it, letting the girls just hang free. And I definitely wouldn't be sitting on the couch with him, so close his knee brushes my thigh more often than should be legal. It doesn't even matter that I have on yoga pants and that he's not actually touching my skin, because I already *know*. I know exactly what it feels like when his fingers brush against me, like tiny sparks are lit up under my skin.

Trying to get my mind off what his hands feel like all over me, I grab the remote and navigate to Netflix, pulling up my queue. "Okay," I try to say, but it comes out like a porn star moan, so I clear my throat and try again, hoping he didn't notice. "On the docket for tonight in the hilariously awful horror movie genre, we have *Big Ass Spider*, *Sharknado*, *Evil Bong*, or *Zombeavers*. Preference?"

Adam studies each of their summaries as I pull them up, like he's trying to pick an Oscar contender instead of the movie we're going to spend the next ninety minutes heckling. His brow is furrowed, his eyes scanning the details of each as he reaches up and scratches his jaw. The sound of his short nails scraping against his stubble echoes through the room, and I swear I feel those echoes in my body.

When he crosses his arms against his chest, the tattered sleeves of the deliciously thin T-shirt he's wearing wrapped tightly around his biceps, I've had just about enough of his unintentional sexiness. Really, there's only so much a girl can take. "All right, buddy. You're thinking way too hard on this. Just pick a goddamn movie."

He looks at me out of the corner of his eye. "It's a serious decision that can't be rushed."

I scoff and roll my eyes, tucking one leg under the other as I turn toward him. "You must be new to the hate-watch. You just have to go with your gut. First instincts, and all that. The only logical way to go is *Zombeavers*. I mean, the title alone guarantees a plethora of laughs. And that graphic? She has a beaver coming out of her beaver. Comedy gold."

"You do make valid points." He nods. "All right, *Zombeavers* it is."

"Glad you finally came to your senses." I turn on the movie and settle in to watch, very aware of just how close Adam is. Even worse, I'm remembering what happened the last time he was in my apartment... When he had me bent over the arm of the couch. How it wasn't impersonal like it sometimes can be in that position—like it usually is. Instead, he curved his body over mine, his chest pressed against my back, his lips at my ear whispering the dirtiest things while his fingers stroked my clit, pulling orgasm number too-many-to-count from my body.

Jesus, is it hot in here?

Adam snorts next to me, bringing my attention back to the TV and what's happening in the movie. I laugh when one of the characters scrolls through pictures on her phone, the images taking up the majority of the TV screen. "You know it's gonna be good when dick pics show up within the first five minutes."

"Definitely. Dick shots are really the only reason I watch horror movies, anyway." He says it with so much sincerity, I can't help the laugh that bursts free. Turning in my direction, he joins me, a smile curving his lips. His attention drops to my mouth briefly before he looks into my eyes again, and there is an undeniable heat behind his.

This just reaffirms how stupid I am. Adam and I are attracted to each other; there's no denying that. But being attracted to him because of what he can do to my body is one thing.

Being attracted to him because I genuinely *like* him is another thing entirely.

ELEVEN

adam

Before coming to Cade's place today, I wondered how it would be being around Paige after hanging out just the two of us—even though nothing sexual happened the night of *Zombeavers*. And while no one else probably notices the changes, I do. Paige is less guarded, more relaxed, bullshitting with me while Cade and Winter are paired up against Jase and Tessa to face off in a game of bean bags in Cade and Winter's backyard. Paige and I are taking on the winners, and even *that* is a huge step for her. Before, she'd find any and every excuse in the book not to even be around. And yet here she is.

"You see that?" She leans closer to me, the neck of her beer bottle clutched in her hand. Her voice is pitched low and serious as hell, but all I can think about is how sweet she smells. "You see how Jase can't throw if he's on the right? You have *got* to get that side to throw from, okay?"

Pulling myself from her sweet-scent inducing haze, I glance over at her, seeing her brows pulled down, her face set in concentration.

While I've been wondering if it's her shampoo or body wash making her smell so fucking good, she's been plotting world domination via Cornhole. "You know this is just a game, right? And not even a *real* game. Just one where we throw bags filled with beans toward a hole in a giant sloped ramp thirty feet away."

She spins on me, poking me in the chest. "Okay, look, buddy. This may not be a contact sport, but it's a *game*. And I do not go into games unless I plan to win. If you're not man enough to kick their asses with me, tell me now. I'll get Cade to be my partner."

"How do you know Cade and Winter aren't going to win?"

She snorts. "Oh, please. The score is 15-1. And Winter...I love that girl, but she can't throw for shit. Plus, she's at a disadvantage. We've all been playing this for *years*. I think this is her second time. She doesn't stand a chance."

"You know as well as I do that the score means fuck-all. It can be flipped in no time, especially when they try to get twenty-one."

"Don't think I didn't miss how you're not answering about bringing your A-game to this party. Don't hold me back, Reid."

"Wouldn't dream of it."

"Auntie Paige! Come swing with me!" Haley yells from her perch on the playset across the yard.

Paige presses her beer bottle to my chest, leveling me with a serious look. "You're my eyes and ears now, big boy. Find their weaknesses so we can exploit them. Don't fuck it up." She says it with such seriousness, she might as well be talking about a mission in Afghanistan, not a game of bags in the back yard. Then she beams a smile toward Haley and takes off in that direction. "Coming, Haley girl!"

Jesus, why does her talking to me like that get me hard? And now I've got two beers in my hands and can't even reach down to adjust the statue growing in my cargo shorts.

I try to focus on the game, watching for weaknesses or patterns from any of them, but all I can concentrate on is the sound of Paige playing with Haley, her laughter settling on my shoulders. If I thought I was fucked before when I only wanted to explore this attraction between us, it has nothing on the need coursing through me now to get to *know* her.

"Aw, shit," Cade groans when Winter's last toss misses the ramp completely, making Jason and Tess the winners. To Winter, he says, "It's okay, baby. Next time."

"Fucking *hell*." Winter kicks the side of the ramp, sending it off-center.

"Hey, hey, hey, don't take out your frustration on inanimate objects." Jase straightens the ramp again, lining it up perfectly.

"I could kick you instead," Winter says with a saccharine smile.

"Not again, baby." Cade walks toward her, grabbing her hand and tugging her to where I'm standing. "I had to listen to him whine about that bruise on his shin for a week."

"I was not *whining*. I thought she broke something!"

"I know you did, babe." Tessa rubs her hand along Jason's back before standing on her toes to give him a kiss, and the jealousy hits me like a freight train.

Seeing my best friends happier than they've ever been should make me happy. And it does. I'm not that much of a selfish prick, but I can't deny this overwhelming *want* consuming me as I witness them together. I've always felt the urge to be in relationships. To settle down. Getting married wasn't ever a *maybe someday* kind of thing like it was for my best friends. It was a foregone conclusion for me. I've entered every relationship I've ever been in thinking it might be the one. And when I figured out it wasn't, it ended.

So how the hell did I get here, watching my two playboy best friends settle down before me?

Once we were old enough, I stood by, content in my relationships, as Jase and Cade went through their phases, the two of them going through more girls in a few months than I did...ever.

And now? Now they're both in relationships, and I'm off to the side, coveting every goddamn minute of it.

"Your turn, man. Don't let Jase win or we'll never hear the end of it." Cade knocks me from my daydreaming with a slap on my shoulder. "Paige! You're up!"

Paige gives Haley one final push on the swing before jogging toward us. Her eyes are focused, like a soldier going into combat, but it's a total contrast to the rest of her. Her face is pure warrior—her jaw set, her eyes determined—but her body? All woman. Her long blond hair blows behind her as she runs, her full lips brushed in some kind of shiny pink stuff are pursed in concentration, and her simple white V-neck tee clings to breasts that bounce with each step she takes. And her shorts that are so fucking short they might as well be panties? They showcase long, solid, muscular legs that I want wrapped around my head again. How is this girl real?

"You ready, hot shot?" She takes her beer back before guzzling it and passing the empty bottle to Cade. Then she walks toward the game, glancing to make sure Haley's still occupied all the way at the other side of the yard. To Jason and Tessa, she says, "All right, it's game on, motherfuckers, and I'm not here to lose. Let's get this bitch started."

And I'm snared just a little bit more.

paige

How can Adam make tossing a beanbag look so goddamn hot? I don't understand it, but I certainly can't deny it. His arms bunch and flex when he tosses the bag across the lawn, and I'd love to be behind him to watch the muscles in his back move along with him. I also wouldn't mind seeing his tight little ass in those shorts. Again.

But it's not just the physical attraction I feel with him—

though that's there in spades. That's never been in question, but it was never more apparent than when I invited him in to watch a movie. I still have no idea what I was thinking. That I could sit next to him in the dark, feel the heat of his body next to mine, get lulled by the rhythmic rising and falling of his chest, and *not* want to climb into his lap and ride his cock? It was the longest ninety minutes of my life, and after he left, with nothing more than a strained goodbye, I got good use of B.O.B. Twice.

Besides the attraction, though, I actually *like* him. We just… click. We're more alike than I ever thought. Like right now, he pretends he's not as into winning this as I am, but the determined concentration on his face proves him wrong, as do his strategic throws. He's just as competitive as I am; he just doesn't voice it quite as loudly.

"Come on, baby, you've got this one!" Jase says as Tessa prepares to throw her last bag, the other three littering the ramp along with mine.

"No, you don't," I taunt. "Face it, Tess, you don't have jack. It's gonna land in the grass and then you'll fall behind, thus leading to Adam and me winning."

Tess laughs. "Shut it, bitch." She lines up her throw before pulling her arm back and releasing the bag in her hand. It sinks straight through the hole.

She fist-pumps and does an air high-five to Jason while I say, "Fuck."

"Gonna take more than teasing words from you to make us lose, girl."

"How about awesome throwing skills on my end, then? That work?" I ask her as I take my shot, sinking my bag right behind hers. We canceled each other out this whole round, neither of us gaining a point, but I can't even be bothered by it. Not when Adam turns his blinding smile on me and makes me feel like I'm sixteen all over again. Seriously. What is *up* with me and this guy?

"That's what I'm talkin' about," he says. And my stomach

is absolutely not flipping because of that grin being directed at me. Absolutely *not*. Those fancy burgers Cade made for us must not be sitting right with me.

"All right, babe, nice and easy," Tessa calls to Jase as the boys take their turn to throw.

I barely resist rolling my eyes. If I have to hear one more term of endearment from any of these sickly sweet couples, I might actually puke. It's been nearly non-stop all day, and I'm goddamn sick of it.

"Coming to you, baby," he says.

This time I can't resist rolling my eyes, just thankful nothing regurgitated into my mouth. "Enough with the chit-chat, fuckers. You wanna whisper sweet nothings, go into the house and take care of that shit. Otherwise, throw the damn bag."

"If I didn't know better, Paige, I'd think you were on a drought," Jason says. "Feeling a little neglected?"

I try to ignore the way Adam's shoulders stiffen. I also pretend I don't feel his gaze burning into me. I know if I look at him right now, I'll see everything written all over his face. That look that says, *I'll give you whatever you need. Anytime. Just say the word.*

Word. Word word motherfucking word.

Can't say that, though, so instead I keep my gaze focused on Jason and offer a sweet smile. "Not any more than Tess. She told me you had a little problem the other night. You know"—I lean toward him and stage whisper—"getting it up."

Tessa gasps beside me. "Oh my God, I did not! Don't listen to her, babe. We both know it's not true."

Doesn't matter if it's true or not, because Jason tosses and misses, and this time it's my turn to fist-pump.

"You wanna win by cheating, Paige? Afraid your skills can't hold up to ours?" Jase asks.

"Oh, please. This isn't cheating. I can't help it if your delicate man-ego can't handle a little ribbing. From what I hear, though, Tessa would like a little *more* ribbing, if you know what I mean."

Adam's laugh reaches me the same time the bag lands high on the ramp before sliding down and straight through the hole. Which means we just scored twenty-one, and as long as we can keep Jason from scoring, we're golden.

"Hell yeah!" I shoot a smile to Adam, wishing I could do more than offer him a lame thumbs up from my side of the yard.

"Shake it off, babe. Shake it off," Tessa says to Jason. "You've got this."

Doesn't matter how much she encourages, though, because he's still off his game. As he throws bag after bag, all of them missing the ramp, Adam follows suit, tossing the bags short so we don't bust.

"Last one, Jase," I say as he lines up his throw. "You know, I was totally kidding about that delicate man-ego, but apparently it's true."

"Ignore her, baby," Tess says. "She's trying to get in your head."

"Trying and succeeding." I grin at them both.

I silently curse Jason under my breath as he takes his last shot and groan when it sinks into the hole.

"Finally!" Jase shouts as Tessa does a dance next to me. "That's what I'm talking about."

"It's okay, it's okay," I say to Adam. "You just need to sink it again. That's all, and we win. Line it up and put it right in the hole."

Adam raises an eyebrow at me, his gaze burning into mine, and how did I never realize how freakin' dirty this game could sound? I tear my eyes away from him, afraid if I stare at him any longer, this frayed leash holding me back from him will snap, and I'll attack him in front of all our friends and make him do exactly what I told him to. Instead, I glance at him out of the corner of my eye as he takes his stance, lining up the shot while Jason continues to taunt him from their side of the lawn. Adam doesn't even flinch, though, and I watch with breath held as he releases the bag. It sails to my side and lands with a thump on the ramp, then slides down and into the hole, canceling their points and causing us to win.

"That's game, bitches!" I yell, running over to Adam and wrapping my arms around his neck before I've even had a chance to realize what I'm doing. He catches me and spins me around, his arms banded around my waist and his laugh puffing against my ear. It doesn't take long for me to realize what the hell I'm doing…and that all of our friends have gone silent around us. I can feel their eyes on us, on me specifically, and why wouldn't they be looking? Whenever I'm paired up with Jase or Cade, I offer high-fives when we win, not full-body hugs. The only thing I have going for me is that I somehow managed to refrain from wrapping my legs around him…barely. But, God, I want to. Remembering exactly what I'd feel if I did, Adam long and thick and hard for me, sends a shudder through my body.

I pull away, needing some space, but the look Adam shoots me tells me everything I need to know. It doesn't matter how much space is between us because that chemistry we have is always going to be there, like a giant hot pink elephant sitting right in the center of the room. And if I'm going to make it through this summer with him here, I've either got to figure out how to ignore it…or climb on for a ride.

TWELVE

paige

Growing up in the family I did, with my father being career military, it meant we moved around a lot. Twelve schools by the time I was fourteen, one of which was in Italy. I didn't mind it. I didn't love it, either, but there could've been worse things. My parents have always been happily—almost sickeningly—married. The exceptions in the love department, I always say. My brothers, though eight and ten years older than me, always had my back before they left for the police academy and the Army, respectively. And it wasn't like I was shy. You don't move around that much without picking up a few tips of the trade, and without getting really good at putting yourself out there. But that didn't mean I didn't have problems making friends. I didn't fit in with the girls, because while they wanted to play Barbies or do each other's hair, I wanted to be in the backyard with their brothers, playing baseball or soccer. And the guys? When I was younger, it was all about the cooties...can't play with a *girl*. And when I was older? It was all about the ass. If they were hanging out with me, it wasn't because they wanted to go hiking. It was because they wanted to fuck.

It all changed junior year when my parents and I moved back home—or as close to home as we could get. It was the one place we always came back to. The place my grandparents live. The place my brother Tanner became a cop. And, most recently, the place my oldest brother Dillon got a transfer to.

Even though this house isn't my childhood home, it's the closest thing I've got to it, and I love it. I love it *here*, where my family is. Where my friends are—ones who take me and accept me for the conundrum I am.

"Mom?" I call out as I walk through the back door, tossing my purse on the couch before I get attacked by my dog. I lean down to rub his ears while doing my best to avoid his slobbery kisses. "Hi, Buddy," I croon. "Hi, sweet boy. You're a good dog, aren't you? Did you miss me?"

"I'm in here, honey!"

I stand from my crouched position, and Buddy follows behind me as I head into the kitchen to find my mom going to town on a pot full of what I assume are soon-to-be mashed potatoes if the scent of roast is anything to go by. I walk over and wrap my arms around her from behind, squeezing as she pats my hands clasped over her stomach.

Stepping back, I reach out to pluck an olive from the salad she's already prepped and hop up on the counter, Buddy sitting on the floor at my feet. "Where're the boys?"

"They should be here any time. Tanner was helping Dillon do some unpacking. He wanted to finish up the kitchen before they came over."

I don't have to see my mom's face to know there's a huge smile on it. For the first time in fifteen years, she has all her kids in the same place, and she's loving every minute of it. Even if the circumstances surrounding my oldest brother's transfer aren't the best, she's happy he's home.

Before I can ask her how Dillon's getting acclimated, my dad pokes his head in from the garage. "Paige! Get your ass out here and let your old man beat you in some hoops."

Snorting, I roll my eyes and hop down from the counter. "You wish, *old man*." I don't bother asking my mom if she needs help with anything before I give her a smile and head out to find my dad, Buddy trailing at my feet. This is par for the course on Sundays at my parents'. Mom loves to cook and hates basketball. I'm sure she'd also like some help in the kitchen, but not as much as she likes things done a certain way...*her* way.

"Dinner will be ready as soon as your brothers get here, so don't all four of you get wrapped up in a game and forget to come inside." She stares pointedly at me over her cute red-framed glasses, the bangs of her short blond hair sweeping over her forehead.

"That happened *one* time..."

She laughs, knowing as well as I do that it's happened more often than not...and it'll probably happen tonight, too. Especially with Dillon back home.

My dad is already in the driveway, tossing free throws at the basket. He sinks more than he misses. He's good, but I'll never tell him that. He tosses another one as I walk out there, missing the basket by a few inches.

"You forgot your glasses, Dad. Need me to grab them for you so you can see? The hoop is that bright orange circle backed by the white board. You know, that thing you can't seem to hit?"

"Stop running your mouth, Punky, and get over here. Unless you're scared your old man will beat you?"

I bark out a laugh, pulling my hair back in a ponytail with the elastic around my wrist. "I'd have to be blind, deaf, and not have use of either of my arms for you to beat me."

"Them's fightin' words, little girl."

I step right up to him, not at all intimidated by the solid brick wall of man in front of me. He was in the Army for thirty years, and

I have no doubt that every one of his subordinates were scared as shit of him. He's six-feet-plus of pure muscle, even at fifty-five. He can take a man down with his bare hands. Knows which guns to use for maximum damage and minimum discovery. He can bench-press two of me and not blink an eye. He is a badass motherfucker…no denying that. But his subordinates have never seen him cry while watching *Marley & Me*, or listened as his voice got all gruff the day I graduated summa cum laude, or watched him dance with my mom in the kitchen when neither of them thinks anyone is watching.

"You don't scare me, gramps," I say, keeping my eyes on his so he doesn't expect it when I steal the ball from him, dribbling it over for a quick layup. I grab the ball when it bounces on the cement of the driveway, a couple feet from where Buddy is curled up watching us, and pass it to Dad, offering a grin. "That's 1-0."

"Only because you cheated."

He doesn't give me a chance to even sputter at that before he shoots from his spot on the driveway. Swish. The curses that fly out of my mouth would have sailors blushing, but they only cause him to smile. "Don't let your mom hear you talk like that."

"I don't see any moms out here. Just me and you, old man."

He passes the ball to me again, and we continue shooting and trash talking. This is my favorite part of the week. Sunday night dinners with my family, hanging out with my parents, and now both my brothers. By the time Tanner and Dillon show up, I'm a sweaty mess, but I'm also grinning like a fool, because I beat my dad.

"I call winner," Tanner yells out when he gets out of his car, Dillon stepping out of the passenger side.

It's been so long since Dillon has lived in the same city as us, years getting by on too-quick visits over holidays or when he'd come home briefly over leave, that I forget he's here to stay. I run over and throw my arms around his waist, squeezing him as tight as I can. He wraps his arms around me and presses a kiss to my head. "Hey, Punky."

"What the hell?" Tanner says. "Every time I see you, all I get is slapped upside the head, and this asshole gets a bear hug?"

Pulling away from Dillon, I raise an eyebrow at Tanner. "I just hung out with you the other night, and I didn't slap you once."

"Didn't hug me, either," he mutters with a scowl.

"Aw, are you feeling left out?" I go over to him, wrapping my arms around him in a hug and wipe my sweaty forehead on his T-shirt, laughing when he groans.

"Gross, Punky."

"Hey, you're the one who wanted some affection."

"Not when it comes at the price of your stink. Jesus, did you shower today?"

"I know it's been a while for you, but this is what victory smells like, Tan."

He looks to my dad, his jaw dropped. "You let her beat you?"

I punch Tanner in the stomach and dance out of the way before he can retaliate. "Oh, please, he didn't *let* me do anything. He's getting too old to keep up with the young-uns."

My dad sputters in protest as Tanner says, "Yeah, well, I'm not. You. Me. Rematch."

The side door from the garage into the house opens, and my mom pokes her head out. "Don't even think about it!" she snaps. "You can play more after dinner. Now get in here before everything gets cold." She shuts the door, and we all follow behind dutifully, Buddy included. My mom is tiny. Five-foot-nothing, and one hundred pounds soaking wet. I shot past her when I was in fourth grade. Still, when she gives an order, we all comply without question. She demands respect and, because of that, we all give it to her.

"I swear to God, she's got a camera out here," Tanner says under his breath. "How does she *know*?"

"She always knows," Dillon offers. "How many times did you try to sneak out in high school?"

"I don't know, maybe seventy?"

Dillon laughs. "And how many times did she catch you?"

"Seventy-one."

This time we all join in the laughter as we shuffle into the house, going straight to the dining room. Even though my brothers were both out of the house by the time I was ten, that still gave me ten years to learn the rules. And the rules in this house were if I wanted something to eat, I needed to take no prisoners and get in there right the fuck now. Because of that, I don't take a minute to go to the bathroom and freshen up. My spot's next to Tanner anyway, and he deserves to suffer through my stench after showing up the night of my date.

When talk moves to what we've all been up to this week, Tanner cuts in. "I went to Paige's place on Thursday night thinking we could hang out...brought her dinner, even...and she was all, you know"—he waves his hand in my direction with a disgusted look on his face—"girled up. Like, in a *dress*. Apparently, she had a date. And from the looks of what I was in the middle of, she's got more than one guy interested." He turns to me. "Don't think I didn't notice whatever was going on with you and neighbor guy across the hall."

The thought of Adam makes my toes curl and my legs clench together. It's an involuntary reaction. Just like everything I seem to do around him. I've thought about him way more than I should, especially since having him over for the movie and then the night at Cade and Winter's when I managed a full-body tackle, barely restraining myself from climbing on his dick.

And I absolutely do not need to be thinking about that right now. I also definitely don't need to be discussing my dating—which, let's be honest, is generally more about fucking—life with my parents. I glare at Tanner. "Really? You couldn't talk to me about this Friday night when I not only came over and watched *CSI* with you, but also brought you those burritos from that food truck downtown you absolutely freakin' love? Instead you thought it'd be a good idea to discuss it over dinner? With Mom. And Dad."

Mom snorts. "Paige, honey, I hope you didn't think we thought you were a blushing virgin whose dating life dried up after you moved out. We may be your parents, and we may be *so old*, but we're not stupid."

I drop my forehead to my hands and groan. "Oh my God, how is this even happening right now? How did we go from talking about the best cookware for Dillon to discussing my sex life at the dinner table?"

Tanner holds up his hands. "Whoa, whoa, whoa. I never said anything about sex. And Mom and Dad might not think you're a blushing virgin, but I sure as shit do. Back me up, bro."

Dillon's eyes stay focused on his plate as he cuts up some roast before taking a bite. "I'll be honest and say I've never once thought of Paige and sex in the same sentence, and I'd like to strangle each and every one of you for making me do so now."

Mom snorts. Dad coughs. Dillon shakes his head. Tanner looks appropriately chastised. All I can do is groan.

"You both have *seen* your sister, right?" Mom asks, amusement in her voice.

My brothers lift their heads and look at me, scrutinizing expressions on their faces. Tanner shrugs. "She looks like annoying Paige to me. The same one who would chase us around the yard and go dirt bike riding with us. Plus, she reeks, like usual."

"God, why can't you grow up?" I elbow him. "You're over thirty, old man. Start acting like it."

"Hey," Dillon cuts in. "If he's an old man, what does that make me?"

"Geriatric."

That earns a laugh from everyone but Dillon, who scowls at me until eventually cracking a smile. I love this. I've *missed* this. Except that's not entirely true, either. We've never really had it. While Tanner and I always make sure to be home for Sunday night dinners, Dillon's been stationed all over the world. The last time he was a regular figure at our weekly dinners, I was eight.

"How's the internship going, Punky?" my dad asks.

"Oh, it's awesome." I plaster on a bright smile. "Super great."

Tanner snorts. "'Super great'?"

"What? It is."

"Uh huh. Sure. So making all those copies is living up to your expectations? How about filing that paperwork? And making coffee runs? And refilling the staplers?"

My shoulders sag. "Okay, so it's not *exactly* what I hoped I'd be doing, but I've only been there a couple weeks. They'll come around." I glance at Tanner out of the corner of my eye. "They'll come around, right?"

He says, "Definitely," but he shakes his head, and I barely resist the urge to punch him in the stomach again.

Before I can act out my urge, Dillon asks, "What are you hoping they'll have you do?"

"I don't know." I shrug and stab some roast with my fork. "I knew I wouldn't be able to go to any crime scenes or anything, but I'd love to sit in on some of the meetings. See how they profile the suspects, that kind of thing. After five straight years of school with no summer breaks, I'm ready to be *doing* something. I just want to be in the field already."

"You'll get there, kiddo," my dad says. "Just have to put in your dues. Not every twenty-three-year-old already has their master's degree and a job on the horizon."

"I don't have either yet."

"But you will." Dad says it with such conviction, I can't help but smile. My parents have always encouraged me to be whatever I wanted to be. They didn't shun or coerce me when my interests veered toward what's most often thought of as *boy stuff*. Didn't try to enroll me in ballet when I wanted to play soccer. Didn't persuade me into trying out for cheerleading instead of the track team. And they never once told me I couldn't do anything. They also didn't try to cram me into their mold. My dad might have been career Army, but he never pushed that on any of us. Even on Dillon, who decided to follow in Dad's footsteps of his own volition.

"How about you, honey?" Mom asks Dillon. "Are you getting settled? Have you…have you heard from Steph?"

I love my mom. I really do. But, *Jesus*, she doesn't understand the meaning of boundaries sometimes. My dad clears his throat as Tanner and I shift awkwardly next to each other. I keep my eyes on my plate, both wanting to peek up and see my brother's face and dreading what I'd find there—because I know exactly what I'd find. I remember the exact look I'd find in his eyes, because I was there. When he wouldn't talk to anyone else about the reasons behind the divorce, he'd talk to me. Maybe—probably—because of what I'd already been through. I talked to him on the phone, Skyped with him whenever I could, as he dealt with the aftermath of what was done to him by that bitch who was once my sister-in-law.

"I'm getting settled fine. And no." Dillon's responses are curt, and my mom looks wounded by the tone of his voice. I can't exactly blame him, though. Sunday night dinner with your family, talking about your wife who not only cheated on you, but did so with your best friend…while you were deployed? Yeah, I'll pass.

Silence descends over the table. I can't fight it anymore, and I peek up at Dillon. Really take him in for the first time tonight. His blond hair isn't as closely cropped as it used to be, like he hasn't had the time or the desire to get a trim. His face isn't clean shaven like usual, instead sporting some scruff, and the bags under his eyes couldn't be camouflaged even if he borrowed some of my concealer. He looks…exhausted. Haunted. *Defeated*. My brother, one of the baddest badasses to ever walk the planet. The same brother who went through three tours in Iraq and Afghanistan and who bears the scars to prove it. And it fucking kills me to witness the aftermath of his wife's—*ex*-wife's—betrayal.

It's like living mine all over again.

Once again, I have to clench my hands into fists in my lap, trying to stifle the anger that bubbles up whenever I think of his cheating wife and his shitty friend. Seeing this...seeing him...is just another reminder, though. It's been almost a year since he caught that bitch screwing around on him, and he's still *devastated* about it.

More proof that love is for suckers and fools and has absolutely no place in my life.

THIRTEEN

adam

I stand off to the side on the putting green, leaning on my golf club as I watch the other two couples grope and make-out as we play a round of mini-golf. Fucking mini-golf. With five people.

Five.

Because Paige bailed on our little group outing.

I thought not seeing her over the week was a coincidence. Once again, most of my time has been spent at the shop, and I've been eating at my parents' when I can to placate my mom, who's still pissed I moved out. My assumptions all week were shot to hell when I showed up tonight and Tessa informed me Paige wasn't able to make it because she was busy with work.

Work. *Right.*

"Adam! You're up," Jase yells, snapping me out of my thoughts.

I dig my hot pink golf ball out of my pocket and put it on the green, then take my shot, sinking a hole-in-one. Normally I'd be thrilled with that outcome, but that means I have absolutely nothing else to focus on other than the direction my thoughts naturally go every time they're not occupied. Straight back to Paige.

"Hey," Tessa says as she comes up to me, smiling as she bumps her hip into mine.

"Hey." I glance up, noticing Jase is busy trying—and failing—to get his ball through the windmill obstacle. That would explain why Tess is by me now, since both couples have been using the putting green as if it were their own personal hotel room. Cade and Winter are making out by the little bridge right now.

"You okay?" she asks.

"Me? Yeah. Fine. Why?"

She shrugs and links her arm through mine. Staring straight ahead, watching her boyfriend fumble with his putts, then proceed to kick the green and swear a blue streak, she says, "I didn't know she wasn't coming until we pulled up, otherwise I would've told you."

"Who said I was hoping for anyone else to be here?"

Huffing out a breath, she gives me a tiny pinch on the underside of my arm. Tiny, but fuck, those hurt the worst.

"Ow! Jesus, Tess. Don't abuse me."

"Don't lie to me," she counters.

I stare at her, her eyes meeting mine in challenge, a single eyebrow raised. With a clenched jaw, I concede with a nod. "Fine. Yes, I thought Paige would be here. Mini-golf with two couples isn't exactly on my list of must-do activities."

"Aw, I'm sorry. Are we being horrible?"

Horrible? No. Obviously committed to each other and barely restraining themselves from going at it in a public place? Yeah… "It's fine. Don't worry about it."

She stands with me for a while longer, watching as Jase fails at mini-golf. "She'll come around," she finally says. Tessa squeezes my arm before dropping hers and heading over to Jason now that he's finally sunk his ball. Before she gets too far, she turns back to me. "Just keep pushing her. Don't give up, and don't give in. Not yet."

It sounds to me like she just gave me the green light, even though it's obviously not what Paige wants. With a raised brow, I say, "Thought you were her best friend."

"I am."

"And don't best friends usually look out for the other's best interests?"

She grins at me and winks. "What do you think I'm doing?"

ONCE I ARRIVE at the apartment building after mini-golf, I don't even pause before I bang on Paige's door. As soon as I was able to without looking like an asshole, I bailed and headed home with the sole intent to find out if she was telling Tessa the truth about what she was doing tonight, or if my suspicions are correct and she hung me out to dry because she wanted—or needed—to avoid someone. Me, specifically.

After I continue with another round of knocks—it's pretty hard to pretend she's not home when her car is parked right out there next to mine—she finally answers the door. And I know my suspicions of her avoidance are right. Her hair is pulled back in a ponytail, a sheen of sweat covering every inch of skin I can see—and it's a *lot* of skin thanks to the tank top and booty shorts she's got on—and streaks of dirt on her face. Work, my ass.

"What's up?" she asks, like she didn't totally ditch me and leave me to endure the wrath of two couples by myself.

"I can't believe you just…just…*left* me there. To suffer on my own. I thought we'd managed a form of friendship here."

She crosses her arms, the act doing nothing to help keep me from looking at her breasts in that flimsy piece of cotton. How this girl looks hot in a ratty tank top with dirt all over her, I'll never know, but she does it and she does it well. "Hey, bud, it's not my fault I've got all the brains in this duo."

I brace my hands on the doorframe and lean toward her. "I

thought about bailing, too, but I was being considerate, not wanting to leave you there with them by yourself."

She tilts her head to the side. "Oh. See. There's the difference. I'm not considerate."

That pulls a laugh from me, and her answering smile is worth the ninety minutes I suffered in the presence of two disgustingly in-love couples. I drop my arms and prop my shoulder on the frame, slipping my hands in my pockets. "So, really, why didn't you show up? Because I'm calling bullshit on your work story," I say, gesturing to her appearance.

She snorts and rolls her eyes. "I didn't show up for the same reason you bailed early. God, they make me wanna puke with all their lovey talk. *Baby* this and *babe* that." She pretends to dry-heave. "I seriously thought I was going to hork up my dinner last weekend during Cornhole. Honestly, they all still have names. They could use them once in a while."

"If I didn't know better, I'd say you were jealous."

Her mouth drops open, her hands falling to her sides. "Jealous. Jealous? *Jealous?*"

"Saying it a bunch won't change the meaning of the word."

"I know that, smartass. That was my incredulity at your accusation."

I shrug. "You can deny it all you want, but I know the truth."

"Oh, really? And what truth is that?"

"You want someone to call *you* baby."

If I hadn't been watching, I would've missed how she paused for a split second, her entire body going taut before she glares at me, shaking her head. "You're an idiot."

Her lips speak the words, but her body is telling me more than her mouth ever could. And I didn't miss the way she froze when I said that. And I definitely don't miss the spots of color high on her cheeks or the way she rubs her fingers over her thumbnails—a tell I'm not even sure she realizes she has. I wouldn't call it a nervous tic…

maybe *unsettled*. She did it almost constantly while we were watching the movie last week, and that's enough to coerce me into doing what Tessa said and push…just enough.

"Not a very nice endearment, but we'll work on it, honey pie."

She huffs out a laugh. "*Honey pie?* Are you serious right now?"

"No good? That's okay, I've got a whole pile of them to try out, cuddle bear."

She rolls her eyes, her lip curling. "Oh my God. You do realize we're not a couple, right?"

"That's what makes this so fun."

"We obviously have very different definitions of the word 'fun'."

"I don't know, it looks like you had some fun tonight," I say with a nod toward her appearance. "Go mud wrestling?"

"Rock climbing, actually."

I laugh, but when she just continues to stare at me, I say, "You—wait, are you serious?"

"Why wouldn't I be? You get a lot of girls who lie about going rock climbing?"

No. None, actually, but why should that surprise me with Paige? The list of her qualities that turn me on is too long to count, but this is just one more to add at the end of the ridiculously lengthy list. And once again, Tessa's words give me enough of a nudge to take another step.

"So I have a proposition for you…"

paige

I stare at him, not certain I heard him right, because seriously? I'm not sure if I should be insulted or turned on. If the hard points of my nipples and the tingling in my lady bits are anything to go by, I'm definitely the latter. But that shouldn't come as a surprise. Everything having to do with Adam turns me the hell on. He could probably walk around in a giant hot dog costume and I'd be all, "Let me ride your wiener!"

"I just want to make sure I have this right… You want to go on non-date date nights where we do the least romantic things possible to balance out having to spend time with the fixated foursome. Is that right?" It's like my dream dude fell from the sky and was delivered right to my front porch for my very own personal consumption. It's proof God loves me and wants me to be happy. But surely there's a catch. Maybe he picks his nose when no one's watching. Or maybe he secretly belches the alphabet just like Brent. The issue is, I think I'd even forgive him for it. And that is a goddamn problem of epic proportions.

Adam nods, his stance casual as he leans against the doorframe, his hands tucked into the pockets of his jeans. "That about sums it up, yes."

"And what would these non-dates consist of? Are we talking about movies?"

"Only if they're horror and only if we watch them while in ratty clothes we'd never wear in public."

Oh my God, can he see into my very soul? "Dinner?"

"If we must have sustenance, I imagine it'll consist of whatever we can throw together from our fridges, pizza, or the occasional swing through a Taco Bell drive-thru."

I narrow my eyes at him. "Did Tessa tell you about my love for Taco Bell?"

"She did not."

Okay. He can clearly read my mind. He's absolute perfection all wrapped up in the prettiest package of male specimen I've ever seen. Why is God testing me?

Someone clears their throat loudly on the landing, and I don't have to glance around Adam to know it's Mrs. Connelly from the apartment next to his. I know I should be nice to her—respect my elders and all that—because she's approximately one hundred forty-two, but the truth is she's a crotchety old lady who spends too much time with her nose in everyone else's business and not enough time doing things like learning how to be a decent human being. Rolling my eyes, I reach out and grab Adam's arm, ignoring the heat of it under my palm, how rock freaking hard it is, and tug him inside my apartment before slamming the door behind him.

"If you wanted to invite me in, all you had to do was ask." His smile is smug and it should look stupid on his face, but it's like my nipples are hooked up to his mouth via jumper cables, and every time he grins, they get a little jolt of electricity. Honestly, have my nipples ever been this hard for this long?

"If I didn't pull you in here, Mrs. Connelly would've stood out there, clearing her throat until one of us asked her if she was okay. Then she would've proceeded to tell us what horrible human beings we are because we didn't help her carry in her groceries on Sundays when she goes shopping or get her mail for her since we're already up there getting ours."

"You sound like you speak from experience."

I shrug and walk toward my kitchen, grabbing a bottle of water from my fridge. Adam came pounding on my door about thirty seconds after I walked in, and I'm thirsty as hell from working my ass off on the rock climbing wall. "I've lived here a while."

"Yeah? How long?" he asks from the living room.

After I've downed the bottle and tossed it in the recycling, I walk toward him, ordering myself to keep my eyes up. Eyes *up*, Bennett. Do not look at his ass. *Don't do it.* "It's been about three years, I think."

"You like it?"

I glance around my space and feel that happy sort of contentment that I spent a lot of my life searching for, especially after Bryan. It's nothing fancy. A single bedroom apartment with a living room, tiny kitchen, and even tinier bathroom. It's filled with the ever-popular garage sale chic, plus a few castoffs my parents or brothers tossed in. Mixed together with my eclectic taste in everything else, and it's a decorating clusterfuck. But I love it. I love my vintage *House on Haunted Hill* poster next to the world map my dad gave me, a rainbow of push pins decorating it. I love that my bright purple throw rug doesn't at all match the couch my parents had the majority of my teenage years before they upgraded. I love that I have my collection of horror movies and true crime novels on the beat-up bookcase Tanner found by the dumpster of his building. The one he helped me sand down and paint a bright, vibrant blue.

"Yeah. I love it."

He nods and walks over to the worn map above my couch, and I fail at the goal I gave myself. My eyes drift down to take in his sweet ass in those jeans. Jeans so threadbare, there are tiny holes by the pockets. They're small enough that all I see beyond them is darkness. But maybe that's because he's wearing black boxer briefs like he wore the night we slept together. I can't stop myself from thinking about walking over to him, unbuttoning his jeans and sinking to my knees to find out exactly what color they are.

"What do all the different colors mean?" he asks.

My head snaps up, and I don't have to look in a mirror to know I have guilt written all over my face. Jesus, he really *is* a mind-reader. When he raises an eyebrow and gestures to the colored pins stuck all over my world map, I breathe a sigh of relief.

Dragging myself away from thoughts of what kind of undies he's wearing, I glance at the map. "Red is me. Green is Tanner. Blue is Dillon. All the places we've lived. Yellow are the places my parents lived before they had us. Purple are the places I want to travel to someday."

He turns back to face the map as he studies it, and I make a conscious effort not to shift under his scrutiny. He threw me off guard, caught me when I wasn't thinking. My reaction to him knowing this information about me is stupid. It's just a map, names of places I've been and want to go someday, but it's *me* on that map. My past. My present. My future. Sharing that with him makes me feel…open. Vulnerable. In a way I've only ever allowed myself to be with one other guy. The only other guy who's ever held the power to devastate me.

"You've got me beat by a dozen," he says.

Clearing my throat, I force my voice to come out strong and am pleased when only the tiniest waver enters it. "Yeah? Where've you lived?"

"Just here and Colorado."

While I've never loved moving around so much, I also can't imagine only ever having lived in two places. I'm perfectly happy to stay where I am now, but I think a huge part of that contentment comes from having already seen a lot of the world. Not able to stop myself, I ask, "Are you content with that?"

"Yeah. I've never had the wanderer gene, I guess. I mean, I'd love to visit some of these places, but that's all. Visit and then come home. I can't imagine what it was like to live in Italy. I've always wanted to go there."

"To be honest, I don't remember much about it. I was pretty young, and we were only there for a year."

"Did that suck? Moving around so much?"

"It was all I knew. I don't regret it, but I also have no desire to live anywhere else now that I'm here." He doesn't have to know about my failed plans to move away for college and the boy who dashed said plans.

He stares at me in a way that makes me uncomfortable. He has that way about him. Adam doesn't casually glance at someone. He looks, really looks. But more than that, he *sees*. I force myself to stand still. To not fidget. To not show any more of myself than he's already wrung from me today. Hoping to divert his attention, I say, "You didn't tell me what else these non-dates will consist of besides movies and shitty food. I'm not agreeing to anything until you give up the goods, dude."

His eyes pierce me for another few seconds before he nods. "Okay, how about this? We take turns deciding what to do. You can even go first."

"You sure you want to do that?"

"I'm pretty secure I can run with the big boys no matter what you come up with." At my raised eyebrow, he tips his head, a smile curving the side of his mouth. "Big boys *and* girls. So does that mean you're in?"

"Oh, I'm in." I walk over and open the door for him, not even a little ashamed as I stare at his ass as he walks out. "We're on for next week. And Adam? Wear a cup."

With that, I shut the door and lean against it, ignoring the way my nipples harden once again at the sound of his breathy laugh through the door. Looks like B.O.B. is going to get yet another workout.

FOURTEEN

adam

"I think for what you're looking to use it for, this one is your best bet." I point at the mountain bike with front and rear suspension shocks. One of the new things we've started implementing this week is offering some of our inventory to the customers to try out before they buy. This guy's ridden five different bikes over the past couple hours, and he's gotten it narrowed down to two. "You like how it feels?"

"Yeah, it's definitely the most comfortable of what I've tried."

"Well, there you go. I think you have a winner."

He smiles and reaches to shake my hand. "I think you're right. Thanks a lot for all your help with this. I've been putting this off for months because I've been so overwhelmed any time I looked."

I walk him over to the cash register and ring out his purchases, adding on the new helmet and platform pedals. "No problem. That's what we're here for. And if you wanted to come back to check out the rock climbing guided lessons like we talked about, I stuck a coupon for half off your first one in the bag."

"Thanks, man. You'll probably see me back here this weekend."

As he walks out the front door of the shop, this weird sense of accomplishment settles over me. I'm not sure if it's because of that particular purchase, since I spent two hours with him to find the perfect bike for what he's planning to use it for, or if it's a mixture of what else is going on at the shop, but I can't deny it's there. I also can't deny it feels damn good.

After more than a month of doing nothing but crunching numbers, of forcing myself to stay in that too-tiny closet of an office and figuring out exactly how far into the red my parents were and how to get them out of it, I'm finally on the floor *doing* something. I forgot how good this feels, how accomplished I feel at the end of the day when I use not only my mind and my expertise on something, but my hands and my body, too. While working with numbers all day is satisfying, working in black and white with no shades of gray, I didn't realize how much I missed the other aspects of this job. I've missed this. Missed feeling how I do at the end of a day at the shop.

We're only days away from implementing the plan I came up with. Everything's already been put in motion. The rentals and classes are all listed on the new site Jason designed for us—for which I seriously owe him a truckload of beer in thanks since he refused payment. Both rentals and classes are scheduled to start on Saturday. The only thing the classes are costing the shop is my time, and since I'm working for free, we're not out anything. And we've actually managed some extra income from it on top of the fee we're charging for the lessons, because almost all of the people who've signed up are renting the equipment needed from here to see if the activity is something they'd like. And if they're not renting it, they're coming in to buy it.

If I can keep up this pace the rest of the summer, I actually have half a chance of getting my parents out of the hole they've dug themselves into. The projected profits from this weekend are triple what the previous weekends have been…for the past three years. And this is only the first weekend. Once word of mouth takes off and the people doing the rentals and taking the classes start telling their friends about it, who knows what could happen.

My mind spins on new and innovative ways we could do even more. Like expanding to offer more classes than the three we're starting with. And after I see how these do, I can look into offering a bigger variety, think about switching things to winter sports in the coming months, maybe offer ski or snowboarding lessons.

The thought stops me short—not because it's a bad idea, but because I won't be here to see it through.

If all goes according to plan, I'll be back in Colorado by the end of August, beginning of September at the latest. And if my projections are anything to go by, I might actually be able to get home sooner.

That should make me happy…leaving before I planned. Getting back to the life I put on hold in Denver. The life of routine and security. A life purposely so far removed from the one I had growing up just so I could avoid outcomes like the one I'm stuck dealing with now.

A life I'm only just coming to realize is a bit…boring. It's always been something I've wanted. Safety. Security. Predictability. And now? Now I'm not sure. All I'm certain of is I've had a blast these past weeks, being presented with challenges like I'm not in Colorado. Not just with the shop, but with Paige. Having someone push back, not bend to everything I say is a high I never thought I wanted. But I do. Want it. Want *her*. Badly.

And now, the whole goal I set out with this summer—to get my parents' shop back on solid ground again—is directly at odds with the goal I didn't even know I had: to get closer to Paige.

Seeing the shop succeed means maybe leaving town—leaving Paige—early. Possibly before we've even had time to start anything. Well, anything more than we've already started.

Doesn't matter. Doesn't change anything. I'm not going to let it. I'm sticking with my plan to get closer to her, as close as she'll let me, and then keep pushing a bit more, just like Tessa suggested. Not hard. Not enough to make Paige run scared, but enough to let her know I'm here and I'm interested. And she's not going to scare me away like she's managed to do with all the other guys who've come knocking.

And I'm going to start tonight, when we have our first non-date date. It was a stroke of goddamn genius, coming up with this solution. I'm not going to waste a single "date" either. Starting tonight, the game is on.

paige

Holy shit, I'm nervous. Like, butterflies staging a revolt in my stomach, oh-God-I'm-maybe-going-to-puke, epic level freak out, nervous. *Why* am I nervous? This isn't a date. In fact, I'm pretty sure this is the exact opposite of a date. Even the name Adam gave these… *events*…suggests that.

So what is *up* with all the anxiety?

While my brain knows it isn't a date, can understand the logic of having non-date dates with my former one-night stand and the guy who fingerbanged me in a bathroom, my stomach is all, *what the fuck, dude?* And my lady bits? Well. Let's just say they're most definitely revving up for the night at the mere thought of spending time with him.

But no, that's not it. Not *spending time* with him. Why the hell would I get all tingly at the thought of hanging out with him? No, it's because I'll be *seeing* him. He's like an all-you-can-eat buffet for my eyes, and I'm feeling one hundred percent lust for all his muscly goodness, that's all. And, really, only someone who was blind wouldn't feel some humming downstairs at the sight of him. He's so fucking hot, I'm pretty sure he's capable of making even straight dudes take a second look.

For my last night out with the douchebag extraordinaire, I wore a skintight dress, heels, and spent an hour on my hair and make-up, making sure they were just right. And tonight? When I'm actually looking forward to the plans? I spent a total of five minutes throwing shit on just to counteract everything going on in my belly and my underoos. I'm wearing the jogging pants that don't do anything for my ass and Tanner's old football T-shirt from high school that's at least two sizes too big for me. My hair is pulled back in a ponytail, and I actually scrubbed all make-up off my face after getting home from the station. I also wore my period underwear just to make sure I don't give into whatever this pull is that's always between us.

Except there's an annoying—and pretty fucking loud—voice telling me period underwear wouldn't stop me if I decided to go for it with him. In fact, I'm pretty sure *nothing* would stop me.

A quick set of knocks sounds at my door, and I don't let myself look in the mirror again before I answer it, because it's most definitely not a date and who cares what I look like? When I pull open the door, Adam stands on the other side, the handles of a duffel bag clutched in his right hand. I let my eyes take a quick path up his body, and apparently there's nothing this guy could wear that wouldn't be hot as hell on him. He's in basketball shorts and an unzipped hoodie over a T-shirt that's tight enough for me to make out the defined muscles in his chest, and all I want to do is peel off every layer and get to the prize underneath.

"You ready, snookums?"

The laugh bursts free before I can stop it, and it pulls a smile to Adam's lips. "Seriously? You're still on that kick?"

"Still? Oh, I'm not stopping until I find one you like. I've got a whole arsenal of them right here," he says, tapping his temple.

"Great. Can't wait."

"Your sarcasm isn't appreciated."

"Oh, well, if it's not appreciated, I guess I better not do it anymore."

"All right, smartass, are you ready or what?"

I grab my purse and step out into the hallway, shutting and locking the door behind me. "A better question is if *you're* ready. Did you bring your cup?"

Adam glances at me out of the corner of his eye as we ascend the steps and head toward the parking lot. "You're awfully concerned about me wearing a cup. Any particular reason?"

I obviously can't tell him that any harm that comes to his dick would be a damn shame because it's a glory to behold, so instead I shrug. "Just trying to protect your man parts for any future girlfriends." The words feel like acid in my stomach, burning all the way up my throat. Why would I say something like that? I don't want to see him with someone else, and I sure as hell don't want to think about him with someone else. Except I do. Late at night, after I've worn out B.O.B. and am trying to sleep, I can't stop the thoughts from coming to me. I have no idea why I torture myself so much, but I can't stop it.

From the little bits of information I've gleamed from Jase and Cade, Adam doesn't usually go for girls like me. So of course, I picture him with quiet beauties, the exact opposite of my obnoxious ass. His next girlfriend will probably be tiny. Like, so tiny, he can just tuck her under his arm and throw her around in the bedroom. And she'll probably be a brunette. Or a redhead. And she'll be a veterinarian or a pediatrician, not someone who gets excited at the idea of scouring crime scenes for evidence and examining blood splatter. She'll want to spend their nights together going for quiet walks on the beach and snuggling while watching *The* freakin' *Notebook*.

I can picture it just like it's a goddamn commercial for a dating website. Two perfectly beautiful people doing perfectly beautiful things. Perfectly beautiful and *boring* things. You never see couples in those commercials watching horror movies together. Or rock climbing. Or having a little friendly competition at the batting cages.

Whatever. It doesn't even matter if we're not a typical couple because we're not a couple at all. And I don't want to be.

"Any reason you're taking out so much aggression on my bag?" Adam asks. "Did it do something to you I don't know about?"

I don't realize I've ripped it from his hands and thrown it into the backseat of my car before slamming the door until he says something about it.

Jesus, Paige, get a goddamn grip.

"Sorry. Just getting amped up for our night. Woo!" I fist-pump, then climb into my side and wait for him to get into the passenger's seat as I start the car. The silence between us is heavy, so I attempt to steer the convo in a direction other than my irrational frustrations. "So is this killing you?"

He shoots a glance to me, brow furrowed. "Is what killing me?"

I reverse out of my parking spot and head out of the lot toward our destination for the night. "That you're not driving. You seem like the kind of guy who needs to do that."

"What kind of guy is that?"

"You know, an opening-the-doors, paying-all-the-time, mind-your-manners kind of guy. A perfect gentleman."

He's quiet for so long, I finally glance over at him, and I'm sorry I did. I shouldn't have. *Eyes forward, idiot!* But it's too late, because Adam's heated gaze is burned onto my retinas, no matter that I snapped my attention forward almost immediately.

And then he speaks and I'm afraid we're going to get into an accident, because I might actually be melting into a puddle in the battered seat of my Jetta.

"No. It's not bothering me." His voice is all low and gruff and fucking delicious. "And I think we both know I can be less than a perfect gentleman when it's warranted."

The words hang in the air between us, and it feels like all the oxygen was sucked out of the car, pulled straight from my lungs. Oh, I know, all right. I *know*. All I have to do is close my eyes and see him that night in December, his face set in concentration. He wasn't a perfect gentleman then. Not with his gruff words of demand against my ear or his panting breaths against the nape of my neck. Not with the tug of his fist in my hair, guiding me exactly where he wanted me to go. Not with the five tiny, finger-shaped bruises he left on the curve of my hip.

I don't answer him—find I *can't* answer. My mouth has dried up, all intelligent words fleeing my brain. But I don't have to speak at all. The responses from my body say more than my words ever could, and right now, my nipples are broadcasting like a flashing neon sign.

The silence descends over us, but it's not that comfortable kind of silence between two people who get along and can sit in the quiet. Don't get me wrong, we have that, too, but right now the silence is ripe with possibility and full of memories, and it's making it anything but comfortable.

Adam finally takes pity on us both. "Are you going to give me any clues about where you're taking me?"

I exhale a deep breath, grateful he's steered us back into appropriate territory. "You mean more than the fact that you need a cup?"

Huffing out a laugh, he shakes his head. "Yeah, about that… Are you sure I need to wear one?"

I glance at him as I turn right. "Considering I don't have a dick, I guess I can't be one hundred percent certain. All I know is if I were a dude and I had some jewels to protect, I wouldn't want mine just flapping around in the breeze at this place."

"Now you're just worrying me."

I laugh at his serious expression. "Did you bring one?"

"Of course I brought one. As someone with a dick, I can assure you I don't mess around when someone says I should protect it. The cup's in my bag you manhandled earlier."

"I wondered what that was for. What else have you got in there?"

He shrugs. "I don't know, a bunch of stuff. Spare clothes, knee wraps, gloves, that kind of thing. And, apparently, now a cup. You can poke through the bag later if the curiosity is killing you."

I slide him a glance out of the corner of my eye. "Don't think that gives you a pass to dig through my purse."

The look he gives me is pure horror, and I can't help but laugh. At him, not with him, because he still looks horrified. "Don't laugh. It's not funny. I'm not an idiot. I wouldn't even go into it if you asked me to get something for you. I have an older sister. She taught me all about purse etiquette. Namely, don't touch it. Ever."

I can't stop the grin from sweeping across my face. "She sounds like my kind of girl. Does she live here?"

"Nah, she's in North Carolina."

"That must suck. This is the first time my oldest brother, Dillon, has lived close since he graduated high school. It was rough not being near him." I glance at Adam as I stop at a stoplight. "Are you two close?"

"Close enough, I guess. Not like Cade and Tessa, though. Aubrey lives her life and I live mine, but we're there for each other when it counts."

I think about being there for Dillon when he was going through everything with Steph, and indignation boils in my stomach. Good. This is good. I need a reminder right about now, because it's easy to get lost in the attraction I feel for Adam. And it's even easier to get lost in the banter and ease with which we talk.

It's best to keep the topic on him. "You said she's older?"

"Yeah, by three years."

I shoot him a look. "Uh oh, we're both the babies. That means we're both going to throw fits until we get our way. Our non-date date tradition might end before it ever begins."

"I think we'll be okay."

I take the last turn and pull into the parking lot. "If you're sister's older, how come helping the family business fell to you?"

"I guess because I'm the one who stepped up. She's married with a toddler and is pregnant with her second. My nephew keeps her busy, and now with the baby on the way, she has her own shit to worry about. And I knew it wouldn't be a quick fix to come here and help out." He shrugs. "I could get away for a few months, so that's why I offered."

"Yeah, I've been wondering about that. Don't you have a job in Colorado? How'd you manage to get off for so long?"

"I'm lucky?" We both share a laugh. "The company I work for is a family-owned business, pretty small, and the owner is a friend of my family. He looks out for his employees, so his employees give a lot to the job. I've worked my ass off for him the three years I've been on at the company. Brought in some big accounts. Because of that, plus the history he has with my parents, he didn't have a problem letting me leave...unpaid, of course."

I laugh. "Of course."

It's then that Adam looks up and glances out the windshield before he smiles and shakes his head. "The batting cages, huh?"

"Ever been?"

He barks out a laugh and opens his door before stepping out. "Uh, yeah. You really don't know much about me, do you, ladybug?"

I roll my eyes at his nickname as I get out of the car and shut my door. "Like what?"

"Like the fact that I was MVP of my varsity baseball team in high school and got a partial scholarship to UNC—University of Northern Colorado—to play."

Sweet fancy Moses, did I do a potion for the perfect man and don't remember? Because the more I find out about Adam, the more I learn he ticks off nearly every box on my *Perfect Boy* list. If I had one of those. Which I do not.

I clear my throat. "Oh, yeah? No, I didn't know that. This little competition should be pretty easy for you, then."

"Competition, huh?"

"Yeah, I thought we could make it a little more interesting."

He narrows his eyes at me. "I'm listening."

"Pretty simple…it's winner's choice. Whoever hits the most balls."

"Okay, and when I hit the most?"

I roll my eyes at his show of confidence. "The *winner* gets anything he *or she* wants." At his cocked eyebrow, I clarify, "Within reason."

He walks around the car and meets me at the trunk, stepping so close I can feel the body heat emanating from him. He leans forward and I inhale the fresh, clean scent of him as his breath brushes against my mouth. "You sure you want to make this bet with me, sugar lips?"

The name is absolutely freakin' ridiculous, but my stomach doesn't think that when Adam's eyes drop to said lips and his tongue sweeps across his own. Those butterflies that were present earlier come back in full force, tiny little tornadoes in my belly, and no matter what pep talk I give them, I can't get them to settle down.

Forcing a bravado I don't feel, I say, "Oh, I'm sure. You gonna back out now?"

With a smile, he steps back. "Definitely not. Let the games begin."

FIFTEEN

adam

Paige is a hustler.

A hot hustler with perky tits and legs that go on for miles, but a hustler all the same. That's clear as she sends another ball flying—a triple, no doubt, if we'd been on the field. It's obvious this isn't her first time by the confident way she takes her stance, how her body twists when she swings. By the power in that swing, sending the balls soaring into the overhead net.

And it's hot as hell.

I've never been attracted to athletes before. Either that or I just never looked in that pool of women. Or maybe it's not athletes as much as it's just *Paige*. Somehow this girl has completely rewritten every preconceived notion of what I assumed I wanted in a woman. Erased them all and scribbled in every one of her attributes instead.

As much as it turns me on watching her, as much as I'd love nothing more than to just sit back and stare at the way her ass presses against those jogging pants every time she swings, I can't. Because I want that goddamn prize. A free pass to get whatever I want from her? Yeah, I'm going to do everything in my power to get it. And, no, I'm not above heckling. "You gonna start swinging for real pretty soon? Time's tickin'. I know we agreed to best two out of three, but every round counts."

She doesn't even turn around or acknowledge me with anything other than a brief, "Fuck off." And even how she says that—not hostile or even teasing, just Paige—turns me on. I think this girl could bring me a dead mouse and I'd get wood for her.

She swings again, connecting with the ball. The solid ping of it against the bat is one of my favorite sounds in the world. Because of that, I've got a war raging inside me. On one hand, it gives me this overwhelming sense of...*satisfaction*...to see her doing this. To see her succeeding at something that's been such a big part of my life...at something I've always loved doing, but haven't had anyone with whom to share it. On the other hand, I don't want to hear it at all right now, because I want my damn prize. She waved a red flag in front of a bull, tempted me with the one thing I haven't had from her, and I'm not stopping until I get a taste. I've sucked her nipples, bit her neck, pressed my tongue to her pussy, but I've never tasted her lips. And I want them. Badly.

The last of her balls for this round shoots out of the machine, and she, once again, connects with the target, sending it into the net. When she's done, she spins and walks toward me, pulling off her helmet as she goes, a face-splitting smile directed at me. She should look ridiculous with her hair mashed down to her head, a sheen of sweat on her forehead. Instead, she looks hotter than I've ever seen her. Even hotter than when she was in that red dress a couple weeks ago, and that's saying something.

"You're up, Reid. That's eight hits you've got to beat. Think you have it in you?" She passes me the bat.

"For what's on the line?" I lean toward her and watch with satisfaction as her breathing stops. Just ceases completely, her lips parting and her eyes going a little glazed. "Oh, yeah. I've got it in me."

With a smile, I step back and grab the men's helmet she brought. After I put it on, I shed my hoodie and step into the cage. I take a few practice swings, getting the feel for the bat. It's been a while since I've played, but I'm confident I can outdo her. I have to. "Ready."

"Roger that. Ball one, coming your way."

I listen to the whir of the machine winding up and get ready to swing.

"Oh, hey, your shoe's untied," she calls.

I glance down to see my shoelaces still tied, and the ball whizzes past me. Turning around, I glare at her, fighting against the tug at the corner of my mouth when she just grins. "It's gonna be like that? You sure you wanna play with the big boys, snuggle muffin? Things could get heated."

"I'm ready for whatever you can dish out, Reid."

She's going to be sorry she said that, but I don't say anything more. Instead, I twist back around and focus, put her right out of my mind as I swing and hit, swing and hit. By the time all the balls have been pitched, the score is close, but she beat me by one ball—the one that flew by when she diverted my attention at the beginning.

She's positively beaming as I step out of the cage. "Thought you were bringing it? If my calculations are right, that round goes to me."

With a nod, I concede. "It does. And it'll be the only round you win tonight."

"Big words for a loser."

I laugh, shaking my head at her as I hand off the bat and we switch places. "Just remember you brought this on yourself."

paige

I step into the cage, pleased as fuck with the turn of events. But it's still too close for my liking. Yeah, I won the first round, but only by one freakin' ball. And if I hadn't diverted Adam's attention at the beginning, I have no doubt that round would've gone to him. And that is unacceptable.

"Brought what on myself?" I glance back at him, and *God*, why did I do that?

Because at that exact moment, I get an eyeful of Adam stripping off his T-shirt, the act of him tugging the collar over his head bunching the muscles in his arms, his sculpted abs coming into view one two-pack at a time. And then he's just standing there in nothing but low-slung shorts and a sheen of sweat over the perfection that is his chest. My eyes don't know where to look first—the defined, broad shoulders? The cut arms? His pecs or freakin' eight-pack abs? That delicious V that disappears into the waistband of his shorts? Or the trail of dark hair that leads straight to what I absolutely am not going to think about? Snapping my eyes up to his, I see his stupid smug face grinning back at me, and I glare.

"Nice try, Adam. You think you're the first guy with a nice body I've seen? Gonna have to do more than that to get me off my game."

"Whatever you say, honey bunches. You ready?"

I face forward and give a quick nod, forcing myself not to look back. Taking a deep breath, I try to forget what he looks like standing there behind me, all dark-haired, muscled perfection. I try to concentrate only on the balls coming at me at sixty miles per hour, but it's goddamn hard. And it only gets worse when Adam steps into my peripheral vision, coming closer to the cage. He's standing off to the side so he doesn't get hit with stray balls, his fingers hooked in the chain-link of the cage. The stance is casual, but his intent is anything but. I know he has an ulterior motive. I'm not an idiot, and neither is he. When he stands like that, with one arm braced higher than the other, it does *amazing* things for his arms and his abs and, seriously, Ryan Gosling has *nothing* on him.

I miss four times in a row, and it's clear having him there messes with my mojo.

"God, can you go somewhere else?" I yell, taking another swing and missing.

"Something wrong?" I can hear the smug satisfaction in his voice, and I want to wipe that smirk off his face. With my tongue.

I growl at him, the fear of losing inching up my spine. I shouldn't have made that bet. I was an idiot, because, yeah, I was planning on having him doing something funny and beneficial to me—like baking me cupcakes while wearing that frilly apron my mom bought me as a joke. It would've been hilarious as fuck. But him? I know his winnings are going to be far more detrimental to my sanity than a frilly apron could ever be to his.

When the last ball comes sailing out and I miss—a-freakin'-gain—I stomp out of the cage and point the bat straight at him. "I'm calling DQ on that bullshit!" I'm not even sorry it comes out as a yell, causing a few of the others around us to glance our way.

He's the picture of innocence as he turns to face me, leaning back against the chain-link, his arms crossed, and my *God*, what kind of exercises does this guy do to get arms like that? Bench press houses? "What?" he asks. "I didn't do anything. Didn't even heckle you."

"Oh, no, I can handle heckling. What I can't handle is you being all"—I wave a hand in his direction, encompassing all that is his fuckhotness and make a disgusted sound—*"you know."*

"No, I'm afraid I don't know."

"Oh, please, you *totally* know."

"'Fraid not. Gonna have to spell it out for me, sugar plum."

"Look, dude, I'm not going to shower you with compliments over your fuckhot body, so try again."

He doesn't say anything, but the smile that starts slowly and then takes up so much of his face I want to kiss it off speaks volumes. Oh, it is *so on.*

"Fine. Just remember you brought this on yourself," I repeat his words from earlier. With that, I walk over to the bench that has all our stuff littered over the top of it. I pull off the helmet I'm wearing and set it on the bench. Then I reach down and grab the hem of my T-shirt, tugging it right over my head.

"I'm ready. Hit m— What the *fuck* are you doing?" His voice is like granite, hard and penetrating.

I shrug, not glancing at him. "It's hot."

"I don't give a shit if it's hot. You're not walking around without a goddamn shirt on." He glances around at the other cages. It's not terribly busy, but we're not the only ones out here. His jaw clenches as he spots a few guys a couple cages over looking at us. "Put your shirt back on, Paige."

"I have a sports bra on, *Dad*. This is way more than I wear at the beach."

"We're not at the beach," he bites out.

"Nope, we're here to hit some balls, and I'm starting the machine, so you better get ready to swing, big boy."

He snaps his mouth shut, his eyes glaring daggers into me, and I really didn't think this whole thing through. Because now, not only am I staring at a half-naked Adam, but I have one less layer covering me to hide my reactions to his body... How was I supposed to know he'd get all...territorial about me? And that I'd *like* it?

Without saying another word, he turns around, his attention on the machine, and starts swinging with a single-minded focus. It's a thing of beauty to watch. There's no denying it—Adam knows his way around a bat and ball. And, God, the way his back and shoulder muscles flex with each swing, the glimpse of his abs as he twists, the powerful clench and release of his leg muscles...holy mama. Batting cages were a really fucking bad idea.

By the time the last ball comes to him, I'm huffing on the bench, arms crossed and lasers attempting to be shot out of my eyes into his general direction. All his focus paid off, because he takes that round, making us even. He comes out of the cage and walks toward me until he's standing right in front of where I'm sitting on the bench, his helmet held in his hand.

I can feel his eyes on me, but I don't dare look into them. Don't dare look at his body, either, so I glance up and stare just off to the side, past the delectable muscles in his arms.

"You have any idea how difficult it is to swing with a hard-on?" he asks, his voice all low and scratchy and delicious.

I swallow, forcing my eyes not to drop to the front of his shorts and get another peek of what I already know he's packing. "Can't say I do, no."

"Yeah, well, it's really fucking difficult."

"Hey, don't blame me. You're the one who started stripping first. I warned you I'd retaliate."

He huffs out a laugh, lifting his hand to run through his hair, and I finally allow myself to meet his gaze. His eyes are focused, intent, and he looks…hungry. And determined. The combination is hot as hell if the wetness in my panties is anything to go by.

"If you think I didn't get hard until you stripped off your shirt, you haven't been paying attention, Paige." He drops his helmet, then rests his hands on either side of my hips on the bench, trapping me there as he leans toward me. "But just so you know? I'm not losing tonight." His eyes flit down to my lips, and I part them in response. "And I'm going to get my prize."

SIXTEEN

paige

Turns out Adam can tell the goddamn future.

To his credit, he's not being smug about his win. In fact, as soon as he hit the last ball to put him in the lead, he stopped. Just turned and walked right out of the cage, balls still flying out of the machine. He grabbed his shirt and yanked it on before thrusting mine at me, then grabbed all our shit off the bench and jerked his head toward the parking lot.

And now here we are. Me in the driver's seat, pouting, waiting…wondering. And he's seated on the passenger's side, *not* looking smug.

"Are you saving your gloating for when we get back to the apartment, or what?"

He slides me a glance out of the corner of his eye. "I don't gloat."

"But you will collect on your winnings."

"You're damn right I will."

The confident way he says this, his voice a little gruff, has all my best places clenching and throbbing with need. Damn them. I have to swallow before I can speak. "Are you going to tell me what it is yet?"

"Not yet, no."

"Why the hell not?"

"Because I'm afraid if I tell you now, I'll take it, and I'm still a little pissed at you for stripping down in front of two dozen other people. It won't go how I need it to."

"How do you need it to go?"

"Slow."

"And if you do it now…?"

"Not slow. Or particularly nice."

Who knew Adam had this side to him? I sure as hell didn't. And from his reactions, I'm not sure he did, either. The thought sends warmth through me when it shouldn't. Warmth at the thought that I might be the first girl he's felt like that for. Like I might be the *only* girl he's felt like that for.

"Fine, if you're not going to tell me yet, you need to do something else to cheer me up. I'm a very sore loser. I need to look through your murse."

"My what now?"

"Your *murse.*" I shake my head and roll my eyes. Men. "You know, your man purse."

The look he shoots me is pure outrage as he reaches around and grabs the said murse out of the backseat and places it in his lap. "This is not a murse. It's a duffel bag. A *manly* duffel bag where I carry manly things."

"Like a cup for your junk."

"Exactly."

"Which you didn't even use, by the way."

"And thank fuck for that. Would've been uncomfortable as hell in the state you put me in."

Why does him reminding me of it turn me on even *more?* "Quit stalling and hand over the goods, Reid. You promised."

He does so without comment, passing the nylon bag into my lap. With a giddy smile, I unzip it and yank it open, relieved when it doesn't smell like sweaty socks and dirty underwear. Somehow I knew he'd be like that…clean. Tidy. Makes me want to remind him when he wasn't like that. When he was dirty and messy and hot as hell.

I start tossing stuff out into his lap. First an extra pair of shorts, then folded up socks, some weight lifting gloves. "Boring, boring, boring." I was hoping he'd have something good in here. Something I could taunt him with. Like a bottle of hairspray or face lotion. Something feminine in his manly duffel bag. But then I don't even care that he doesn't have anything like that in here, because I come across what can only be described as something from another planet. I pull out the cup, still in the packaging, and stare at it before bursting into laughter. "Holy shit, it looks like something an alien would wear over their face. See?" I ask, pointing at it, then holding it up in front of my face. "Like, their nose here and it strapped around their head?"

He raises an eyebrow at me, and I can tell he's trying to fight a smile. "I can assure you I've never put one of these anywhere near my mouth."

"Looks like you've never worn one, either," I say, gesturing to the plastic package.

"It's been a while. And I didn't exactly think to bring my cup home with me when I was packing for this trip."

"How do you…" I turn it over in my hand, look at it from all directions, and shake my head. "I don't even know how this works."

"Want me to show you?" And there's the Adam I'm familiar with. The one who's easy going and flirtatious. Not the one who's intense and a little possessive. Funny thing is, both his sides get my motor humming.

I ignore his question and continue looking at it, before opening the plastic and pulling out the cup. It looks small. Way too small to hold what I know Adam has tucked away in his pants. And holding him while he's hard? Forget it. He'd need three. At least. "How does it all, you know, fit?" I gesture with the cup toward his lap.

He laughs, but it comes out strained, and he closes his eyes, resting his head against the seat back. "You're very good for my ego, sweet cheeks. My restraint only goes so far, though, so unless you want to get naked in the backseat, I suggest you start driving."

"The sooner I start driving, the sooner you're going to collect on your winnings."

With his head still resting against the headrest, he turns to look at me. In his eyes there are a thousand unspoken words. Most of them dirty. "Don't look so nervous. You're going to like it, Paige. I guarantee it."

That's exactly what I'm worried about.

HE HASN'T EVEN done anything yet, and the anticipation is freakin' killing me. What the hell is he working at? I can't figure it out. Unless he was telling the truth when we were sitting in the car outside the batting cages. Maybe he really does need to get himself under control so he doesn't crack.

Adam doesn't crack often. And by often, I mean *ever*. That much is certain.

In the short trip to our apartment building, he's relaxed in degrees, little by little, until he's perfectly at ease as we walk down the steps inside, standing on the landing between our doors.

I'm a little tired of this waiting game, to be perfectly honest. It's making me jumpy, flustered. I just want to get it over with. I have no idea what he has in store for me, but I'm anticipating the worst. What the worst is, I don't know. I haven't been brave enough to even allow myself to contemplate it. With a bravado I don't feel, I say, "Time's up, buster," then I occupy myself as I fish for my keys in my bag. "It's now or never."

I don't even feel him moving close, not until his breath whispers across my lips as he says, "Now."

Startling, I glance up and he's *right there*. Stepping into my space and causing me to retreat until my back presses against my door. "What..." I internally curse myself at the breathless quality of my voice, then swallow and try again. "What did you decide you want?"

He's quiet for a minute, his eyes assessing me in a way that makes me nervous. "That's a loaded question if I've ever heard it. I want it all, Paige. Don't for a second think otherwise. But since you're not ready to give me that, I'll settle for something else. Something you've managed to keep from me."

This man has licked my breasts, my thighs, the space between. He's had me on my knees, on my back...has taken me in the most primal ways, so I'm having a really hard time figuring out what I've kept from him. But when his eyes drop to my lips, I know. *I know.* The thought causes me to suck in a breath. How is that possible? How can I crave him as much as I do and not even know what his lips feel like against my own? How do I not already know the taste, the texture, the pressure of his mouth?

And how I have lived without it?

"Last chance to back out." He's so close. Less than an inch of space between our parted mouths. His eyes are connected with mine, so dark despite the pale blue of his irises. Desire has him in a chokehold. Desire for *me*.

Reaching out, I grab his hips and pull him against me. Feel the power of his arousal straining in his shorts. "I don't back out of bets."

The corner of his mouth kicks up. "If that's what you need to fall back on to let me taste those cocktease lips of yours, take it. I'll give you a hundred bets if it gets your mouth on mine."

I open my mouth to respond, but he's already there, his parted lips pressed against mine, his tongue sweeping inside. On a groan, he presses against me harder, rotating his hips and pushing me flat against the door, and I can't hold in a whimper. Adam kisses me like he can't get enough. Like he wants to devour me. Like he *owns* me. That should turn me off. It should make me want to shove him away and slam the door in his face. It shouldn't make me want to melt into a puddle at his feet. Shouldn't make me want to hook my leg over his hip, climb him like a tree, and rub up against him until we both come in our pants like a couple of horny teenagers.

He sucks my bottom lip into his mouth, then trails his lips down, nips at my chin, licks up the column of my neck. "You know how many nights I've stayed awake thinking about these lips?" He tugs on one with his teeth. "How many times I've stroked my cock to the thought of them?"

I shouldn't ask. I shouldn't ask. I shouldn't— "How many?" Goddammit.

"Too many." He closes the space between us again and slants his mouth over mine. His hands cradle my head, his thumbs pressed to my chin, guiding my mouth open even farther so he can take the kiss deeper as he rotates his hips against me.

I've been kissed a lot. And I've been *kissed.* The kind that make you breathless and giddy. The kind that make you want to rip your clothes off and fuck right where you stand. So then if I've had those kind of kisses before, how can Adam make it feel like he's the first? Like he's the only one who's ever done this to me? The only one who ever *could.*

The strokes of his tongue slow, gliding against mine gently, until they stop completely. Then he presses three soft, chaste kisses on my mouth and…steps back?

"Wha…" Jesus, I can't even *talk.* The only thing holding me up right now is the door and the knowledge that I would look like a damn fool if I sank to the floor like I really want to.

"Night, pooh bear." He turns around, pulling his keys from

his pocket and unlocks his door before stepping through it without a backward glance.

What. The. Fuck.

I reach up, pressing my fingers to my lips, and shake my head. I couldn't have been the only one feeling that, right? That wasn't just me getting pulled under by the kiss of my whole goddamn lifetime. But what if it was? God, what if he's in there right now, thinking I'm just an okay kisser? Well, fuck that.

"Don't think this means these non-dates are suddenly kissing dates!" I yell at his door as I finally find the strength to slip the key in mine and unlock it...after three tries. "And, FYI, that name was stupid!"

I hear his chuckle through the door as I slam mine. The only thing that settles me a bit, calms my nerves, is that it sounded strained...pained. And I do something I know I shouldn't, but even knowing that, I can't stop the train of thought...

I let myself imagine what it means if Adam felt exactly what I did, and that's why he walked away.

SEVENTEEN

adam

Standing in front of my parents at the shop, going over the new website in detail, is not the time nor the place to be remembering what Paige's lips felt like against mine last night. What her body felt like pressed all up on me, her hips rolling and seeking what I knew she wanted...what we both did.

Except I didn't give it to us. Instead, I walked away like a goddamn idiot.

But I knew if I didn't, if I went into her apartment with her, pulled her down on the floor and guided her to ride me, it'd feel great in the moment—it'd feel fucking *awesome* in the moment—but when all was said and done and I walked out her door, we'd be right back to square one. She'd shove me aside, shove me away, and all the progress we've made would be for nothing. And I'm not interested in playing this game forever. It's obvious she wants me, but she's fighting it. Listening to Tessa's advice, I'm going to push her just enough, then let her get the rest of the way on her own. And if her frustrated shouts at my door last night after I walked away are any indication, she's slowly getting there.

I force my thoughts away from Paige, because the last thing I need is to get wood with both my parents standing within five feet of me.

"Can you go back to the doohickey, honey?" my mom asks, pointing at the laptop screen. "You know, the one that shows all the stuff."

I resist from rolling my eyes, but it's damn hard. We've been looking at the site for forty-five minutes, and she still doesn't have a clue how it works. And forget about updating it—it might as well be in Japanese for all the sense it makes to either of them. Keeping it up-to-date will definitely fall to my shoulders. At least while I'm here. Probably after I'm gone, too. "It's a website, Mom. Every part of it *shows stuff.*"

Her spine snaps straight, and it doesn't matter that I'm twenty-five and an adult, I get the same *oh shit* feeling in my stomach at knowing I've stepped over the line that I did when I was thirteen. "Don't get smart with me, Adam Christopher. I don't know all this techie speak you do."

Blowing out a breath, I deflate against the counter, rubbing my fingers against my forehead. I'm taking out frustrations on my mom that she isn't the cause for. "You're right. I'm sorry. I'm just a little stressed."

Mom tuts and rubs my back while my dad looks on, shaking his head, but he's trying to hide a smile. Growing up, it was the two of us a lot of the time, going off on our own to do *guy stuff.* And during many of those outings, he stressed how far an apology went with my mother. Whenever I'm in the doghouse, I'm quick to say I'm sorry.

"See? I've been telling you you've been working too hard. Haven't I been telling him that, Calvin?" Mom doesn't wait for Dad's reply before she continues, "And you look like you've been losing weight. Have you been eating now that you're out on your own again?"

I want to remind her that I've spent ninety-nine percent of the past seven years living on my own, but a sharp shake of my dad's head has me pressing my lips together. Smart man. "Yes, Mom, I've been eating."

"Not *my* food, you haven't. I'll bake you some pies and bring them over tonight. You need some fattening up."

"You don't have to do that."

"I know I don't have to, but I want to. Let me do something. Please. I've been feeling so useless around here, can barely keep up with all the changes you're making to the business." She holds up her hand to stop me before I can say anything. "Changes we need, I know that. But still, I don't like feeling like I'm worthless. I need to *do* something. Let me bake you some pies." Having perfected the mom guilt long ago, she adds, "Plus you've been living there for *weeks*, and we still haven't seen it."

There's a reason for it, too. If my mom sees the crackerjack box in which I live, she'll have a coronary. Probably break down sobbing right there in the minuscule space between my kitchenette and bathroom, wailing about how this pitiful shoebox was better than being home? Being with *her?* No, thank you.

I glance to my dad for help, and the only response I get is raised eyebrows. It's a look I've seen dozens of times from him. One that says, *you got yourself into this, you can figure out how to get out of it, buddy.* Clearing my throat, I say, "I've been so busy I haven't been able to unpack everything, and I don't want you to see it like that. How about I come over tonight instead? I've been craving your homemade lasagna. I know it's a lot of work, but—"

"Of course!" She beams at me, clasping her hands together. "Lasagna and homemade garlic rolls. And blueberry pie...no, chocolate torte. More calories." She pats me on the stomach then walks over and feeds some of the receipt paper from the register, ripping it off before grabbing a pen and scribbling down a list, presumably for the grocery store.

My dad gives a nod of approval at how I handled the situation, and I breathe a sigh of relief. He's a man of few words, until it comes to his wife. If I made her sad—or worse, *left* her sad—I'd get reamed up one side and down the other by him.

The bell above the front door rings, and I step out from behind the counter to greet the new customer, leaving my parents at the cash stand. When I get within viewing distance, I freeze. Suck in a breath between my teeth. Even though her back is to me, I'd know that ass anywhere. And all those thoughts I pushed away when I was with my parents come back full force. There's not a second of those five minutes when I had Paige pressed up against me I don't remember. And now she's here, right in front of me, and I want a repeat.

"Paige? What are you doing here?"

She whirls around like she's been caught with her hand in the cookie jar, her eyes darting all around the store before taking a sweep of me, then settling somewhere over my left shoulder. And even though I should be focusing on her face, on the almost…guilty…look she has, I can't. Because all I see when I look at her is her face right before I kissed her last night. How her eyes fluttered closed a second before I pressed my lips to hers. How her hands grasped my T-shirt, like she wanted to make sure I didn't go anywhere. The greedy way her tongue slipped into my mouth…and that dreamy, glazed look in her eyes when I pulled away? Got me so fucking hard. Remembering it isn't helping me in that area, either.

Paige clears her throat. "Oh, hey, I didn't expect to see you. This is your parents' shop? I didn't know." Her words come out too fast, all jumbled together. Paige is usually smooth, collected. The only other time I've heard her like this was when she was trying to convince me her old neighbors were meth heads and cat hoarders.

And then I remember her telling me she's been here before, buying skis in high school. She's lying so hard, I'm surprised her pants aren't on fire. I narrow my eyes at her. "You didn't know," I repeat.

"Nope." She shakes her head for good measure.

I stare at her for a moment, then glance pointedly at my work polo, at the embroidered letters on my left pectoral. The ones that say *Reid Sporting Goods* in a big, bold font, and look back at her with a raised eyebrow.

She darts her eyes everywhere, ping-ponging them anywhere but me, then she spins around and faces the display in front of her. "Well, anyway, I need some gloves." She stares intently at the merchandise on the wall.

I step closer to her, positioning myself so we're standing side by side. "Gloves."

Huffing out a breath, she turns and shoots daggers at me with her eyes. "Why do you keep repeating everything I say? It's annoying."

"Because everything you say is fishy as hell."

She sniffs, turning her head away. "I have no idea what you mean, but I need some gloves. That's why I'm here. At this store I didn't know was your parents'. For rappelling gloves."

I narrow my eyes at her. With the way hers keep darting away from me and back again, it's like I'm watching her wage a war with herself right in front of me. She wants to look, but she's forcing herself no to. It seems a hell of a lot like the entire reason she came here was to see me. If that's the case, I might be further ahead in my plan that I ever thought.

Time to test that theory. "And you needed them at"—I glance at my watch—"five-thirty on a Tuesday."

"Yes," she snaps. "Look, dude, are you going to help me with the gloves or not?"

Considering the time, that means she came straight here, immediately after work. Almost like she couldn't wait to see me until we inevitably ran into each other at the apartment building tonight. The thought nearly brings a smile to my face, but I know that wouldn't sit well with Paige, so I clear my expression entirely. I'll let her play it how she wants. For now.

"Okay, well, we've got a few options for your hand size." She looks startled that I'm not pushing harder, but I ignore it as I grab the three best pairs off the wall and pull them out of the packages so she can try them out. "You rappel fairly often?"

"Yeah."

"Then I'd probably go with these." I hand her the most durable ones. Bonus that they're not the most expensive, especially since I'm pretty sure she already has a pair at home.

She slips her hand into the right one at the same time my mom walks toward us with her head down, looking at her list. "Adam, do you want a salad tonigh— Oh, dear, I'm so sorry. I didn't know we had a customer." My mom smiles and glances at Paige, then does a double take, her finger pointed in Paige's direction. "Wait, I remember you."

Paige shakes her head and rushes to say, "No, I don't think so."

My mom laughs and steps closer. "Honey, with a face like yours, I'm sure most people don't forget you. Weren't you here last month for new gloves?" Mom frowns. "Did they rip?" She tuts, shaking her head. "That's completely unacceptable. You bring those back in here, even if you don't have your receipt. Adam'll get you set up with a new pair."

"Oh, no, you don't have to do that. It's fine."

"It absolutely isn't." Mom's tone is firm. "We don't sell shoddy merchandise, and I want to know which kind they were." She glances at the gloves on the wall, her eyes scanning each as if trying to remember, then she reaches out and plucks a single glove out of my hand—the match to the one Paige's currently trying. "It was these, wasn't it? Such a shame. They used to be great quality. But you know, these companies now, they're trying to take shortcuts. Anything they can do to make an extra buck, even at the expense of the customer. Well, I won't put up with it. If that's how they're going to start producing their products, good for them, but *we* certainly won't be selling them anymore."

"No, no," Paige says, almost tripping over her words. "They didn't rip. I, uh, lost them. Or they were stolen. Probably stolen."

"Stolen."

She glares at me because I've just repeated yet another thing she's said, but I'm not buying her story for a minute. She comes here immediately after work, less than twenty-four hours after the kiss that could cause riots, pretends she doesn't realize this is my family's shop, and now she's got some tale about how her last pair was stolen? Not fucking likely.

"Yeah, *stolen*. At the gym." She nods and tucks her hair behind her ear. "Right from my bag, if you can believe it."

"I can't actually."

"What some people do, right?" The laugh that falls from her lips sounds strained.

"What gym?" I press.

My mom has been watching the verbal volley between us with narrowed eyes, but at my last question, she finally steps in. "What gy—honestly, Adam, why does it matter? Let the poor girl get her gloves." She turns her attention to Paige. "I'm so sorry about him. Talking to gorgeous girls doesn't usually affect him this much. Must be just you," she finishes with a wink. Then she turns to walk away and says, "I'll make the salad. You need your veggies, too."

Paige waits until my mom is out of sight, then says, "You talk to a lot of gorgeous girls in here, do you?"

It takes me a while to figure out where she's going with this, and then I remember my mom's comment. I can't keep the grin off my face. "Aw, pookie, it sounds an awful lot like you're jealous."

She sputters. "Hah! Jealous. Pfft. Like I would be jealous. I'm not jealous. I don't even know what it feels like to be jealous, that's how often I get jealous. Which is never."

"Pretty sure it's whatever you're feeling right now."

Glaring at me, she holds out her hand. "Give me my other glove."

Instead of handing it over, I lean closer and listen with satisfaction as her breathing hitches. "Why'd you really come here, bunny? We both know you've got a pair of gloves at home—probably a couple if you go as often as I think you do." Cocking my head to the side, I can't keep the satisfaction out of my voice when I ask, "Did you come here to see me?"

She scoffs. "What? No. Why would I do that? If I wanted to see you, I could just wait until you got home. Which I don't. Want to see you."

"Uh-huh."

"*Whatever.* You're being very rude to your customer. I'm trying to spend money here. On gloves. That I don't have." She snatches the box out of my hand, then waves it in front of my face. "So if you'll excuse me, I'll just go pay for these." She spins around and walks to the cash register, and I'm left standing here, this time not able to do anything about the smile that overtakes my face.

This might not take as long as I thought.

EIGHTEEN

paige

I slam my hand down on the stapler harder than necessary, then snatch the packet of paper away and stack it on top of all the others, before repeating it all over again. I've been doing this for the past twenty minutes, and even though my hand aches from the abuse, the aggression still isn't doing anything to calm me down. I've been wired, edgy, ever since yesterday after work. Actually, if I'm going to be honest, I've been like that since Monday night, when Adam kissed the ever-loving shit out of me and then…just…just…turned around and walked away. Just left me there. Wanting.

Clever little bastard.

I know what he's doing. Thinking that if he makes me crave him enough, I'll give in to the not-so-subtle hints he's given me that he wants us to hook up while he's here for the summer. And the really awful part is that I've actually been…considering it. But it's just hooking up; it doesn't mean I have to change my life for him. Would it really be that bad? Having someone like Adam at my beck and call sexually while at the same time hanging out with a pretty awesome guy and participating in activities I normally have no problem doing solo—both in and out of the bedroom?

It's like I don't even *know* myself anymore.

Going last night and seeing him and his stupid smug face at the shop—that, yes, I totally knew was his parents', sue me—and hearing his stupid smug voice, that wired, edgy feeling that's been choking me has morphed into irritation and frustration. *Sexual* frustration. B.O.B. isn't even working for me anymore. Which brings me here, to beating up a defenseless stapler while at work. Whatever. It totally had it coming.

A few people walk past, coughing not-so-subtly in my direction as I pound away at the stapler, but no one's been dumb enough to approach me. That is, until I hear the scrape of a chair and glance up in time to see Jared, a newer cop, flip it around and sit down, his arms folded over the back.

"Hey, Paige."

I grunt out a greeting, barely looking at him as I slam my hand on the stapler again.

"Whoa, what'd that stapler ever do to you?" he asks with a chuckle.

While all I want to do is level him with a glare, maybe hiss at him to get the hell out of here and let me be a brat all by myself, I know I can't. This is my place of business now. And, yeah, I'm just here for an internship, as so many people have pointed out, but it's so much more than that. There are two other interns who are working in this department, all of us vying for the single open position available at the end of the summer, and neither of them are doing jack. They might as well be jerking off all day for all the good they're doing while they're here.

I snort when I think about how much good I'm actually doing while stapling these packets together. *Heaps, Paige.* Lifting my eyes to Jared, I take a deep breath. "Sorry. Just a bad day."

He shrugs. "Understandable. We all have those." He braces his feet in front of him and leans forward, bringing the chair to rest on only two legs. I hate when guys do that. "Maybe I could do something about that. Let me take you out for dinner tonight."

I smile but shake my head and grab another stack of papers, gently stapling them. Which is not at *all* satisfying. "Thanks for the offer, but I'm not going to be very good company."

"Friday, then. Or Saturday. Or next week."

Something in the tone of his voice has me looking up. He's still leaning toward me in his chair and has a hopeful look on his face. Hold the phone. Flirty smile? Check. Open body language? Check. Blatant freakin' come-on? Check, check, check. Holy hell, am I so far off my game that I don't even realize when someone asks me out on a date anymore?

"Like, a date?"

He laughs, but it sounds uncomfortable, and runs a hand through his hair. "That's what I was hoping, yeah."

I look at him—scrutinize him, really. He's good looking, I guess, if you go for that well-put-together-without-looking-like-they're-trying vibe. He's got longish light brown hair that I'd normally think about gripping in my fingers while moving his head how I want it when we kiss. His eyes are a dark, chocolate brown, and by this time, I should be thinking about what they'd look like peeking up at me from between my legs.

Problem is, I'm not.

He's got a nice body and he's tall. Not super tall, from what I remember, but taller than me, even when I wear heels. He smiles when he realizes I'm checking him out, and a dimple pops out. A freakin' *dimple*. And yet…nothing. There is absolutely zero interest on my end. All my relevant lady parts might as well be in hibernation for all the attraction they're showing. In fact, I think there might be negative attraction, because the thought of going out with this guy puts a boulder in my stomach. Especially when I think about how

Adam would look if he saw Jared picking me up for a date.

Goddamn Adam.

This is all his fault. Him and his stupid voice and those rough hands and his perfect mouth and that *kiss*. God, how have I never been kissed like that before? More importantly, how did I go this long not even realizing he and I hadn't yet? But I know why. Because sex isn't intimate for me. It's rough and sweaty and satisfying, but I never want to cuddle afterward and press a sleepy kiss to the guy's lips before I pass out. Sure, sometimes I make out with a guy before we sleep together, but other times…not so much.

But now…now all I can think about is how Adam rocked my world that night in December, and that was *without* his kiss. The same kiss that made me hustle into my room and fumble on my nightstand—let's be real, it's a waste of time to even put B.O.B. in a drawer at this point—and then go to town on myself, imagining the entire time it was Adam who was getting me off.

He must've drugged me. That's the only logical explanation. Just slipped something into my mouth along with his tongue. Something that makes me think about him nonstop. About that kiss and his body pressed against mine, his cock hard and insistent against my stomach, and I want it lower, lower, lower, until he's so deep inside me, I can't remember where I end and he begins.

Jared's grin widens when he notices my parted lips and my, no doubt, flushed face, probably assuming it's all because I was checking him out. At least he has a healthy dose of self-esteem. Still…it's not going to happen.

Shaking my head, I straighten another set of papers before stapling them. "I'm sorry, Jared, but I don't think that'd be a good idea."

"Aw, come on. We'd have fun."

"I'm sure we would, but if it's a date, the answer is still no. I don't date people I work with."

He laughs like what I said was the funniest thing in the world, but the sound trails off when he realizes I'm not kidding. "But you don't even work here. Not really."

"No? What am I doing now?" I wave the packets in his face and withhold a cringe, because, yeah, stapling papers in a police station is *such* important work.

"Come on, you can't be serious. You're an *intern*. And the internship is only for another two months, anyway. Then you're gone."

His absolutely certainty that I won't be the one to get the job at the end of this shouldn't sting, but it does. I don't know why I'm surprised. For the most part, the people here have been tolerable. No doubt a great deal of that friendliness is the fact that Tanner is my brother, and if you fuck with me, you fuck with him. Even with that silent threat, I'm sure there's office cooler talk that I'm not privy to. Jared just proved that. He's been friendly to me since my first day… too bad it took me so long to realize he wasn't doing it because he thought I could do the job. He was doing it because I'm just another pretty face, another perky ass. Looks like I get to add one more fucker to the list of people who've underestimated me.

I shift toward him, hooking my finger over the back of the chair he's still leaning forward on two legs. "I plan on being here for a long time, and even if I weren't"—I apply pressure to the chair and watch with satisfaction as he scrambles to his feet to avoid falling on his ass—"I don't date condescending assholes. How's that?"

His handsome face twists with an ugly sneer. "Whatever. You never would've gotten this internship if it weren't for Tanner. Not to mention"—he gestures to my general proximity—"all this."

I'm going to assume he means because I'm a living, breathing human being, and not just one with tits and a nice ass. "Well, this has been fun. Good luck getting a date." I take the stacks of papers I've just finished and walk away.

So far, I've been satisfied sitting back and letting everyone settle in, but I'm done. No more tiptoeing around and not pushing to get my hands a little dirty. I'm done being underestimated.

And if I want the single job they're offering at the end of this internship, I need to step up my game and show everyone I'm in for the long haul. And I deserve to be here as much as—*more than*—anyone else.

WHEN TESSA SHOWS up at my apartment, letting herself in after my text instructing her to do so, she tosses her purse on the counter and marches over to where I am. She plops down on the couch, crosses her legs, and tucks a throw pillow in her lap. "Okay, what's up with the emergency girls' session? I had to promise Jason some pretty dirty things to get out of our family night. He got roped into a tea party with Haley instead."

I blow out a heavy sigh and turn my head to look at her from where I'm sprawled out. "I think the saddest part of this whole situation is that I don't even care to know what those dirty things are."

Tessa's eyes go exaggeratedly wide. "Oh my God. Who are you and what have you done with my best friend?" She reaches out and clutches my shoulders, shaking me while fake crying. "*Where's Paige?*"

I swat her hands away, then reach for another handful of caramel popcorn—which I don't even *like*, if that tells you how far I've sunk in my pity party. What I wanted was a caramel/cheese mixture, just like the kind Cade got me hooked on when Tessa and I visited him in Chicago last year. Well, they don't sell the Chicago Mix in freakin' Michigan, so I'm stuck with this second-rate bullshit, and I'm pretty butthurt about it. I shove the not-Chicago Mix in my mouth and speak around a grotesque amount of food. "Oh, you're *hilarious*. I'm broken and you think it's funny."

She laughs and rolls her eyes. "You're not broken. Now, tell me what's going on."

"Well, it all started about seven years ago when I moved here and met you…"

"*Me?* I'm the root of the problem?"

"Yes, that's what I'm saying. If I hadn't moved here, we wouldn't have met. If we hadn't met, I wouldn't have eventually met Adam and therefore my life wouldn't exist in this weird alternate universe right now where I care about things like how many gorgeous girls Adam talks to and I turn down hot—albeit douchey—guys who ask me out on a date because all I can think about are brief, and—all things considered—pretty freakin' PG kisses against my front door."

Tessa is quiet for a minute, her mouth opening and closing. "I…don't even know where to start."

"How about we start with figuring out how to fix me? *Fix* me, Tess."

She reaches out and takes a handful of popcorn, eating her pile one kernel at a time. I mean, honestly, who does that? "Okay, let's rewind…someone asked you out on a date?"

I make a disgusted noise in my throat and shovel more caramel corn in—inhaling it the way you're supposed to. "Yes. Did I ever mention Jared to you? One of the newer cops who's been to headquarters a few times?"

"I don't think so."

"*See?* That's what I'm talking about! This guy is hot, Tess. Like, fap fodder hot, and I didn't even tell you about him, because *I didn't notice.*"

"Honey, you need to focus. Hot guy asked you out. And you said no…" she trails off, gesturing for me to continue.

"Yes, I said no. And the thing is, I said no even before he turned into an epic douche who was only being nice to me because of my tits. And do you know *why* I turned him down?"

"No, but it'd be awesome if you could tell me so I can stop feeling like you're speaking Hungarian."

"Because of Adam. Sweet, gorgeous, funny, adventurous… *irritating, frustrating, jerkface Adam!*"

"Whoa, dude, no need to scream in my face. *I'm* not Adam."

I throw myself back on the couch and mumble, "Sorry," around another mouthful of food.

"And what's this about Adam talking to gorgeous girls? He did that in front of you?" Tessa's eyebrows are drawn down, like the very thought of perfect Adam doing anything so assholish is preposterous. And the thing is…she's right.

"I went to Reid Sporting Goods the other day to get some rappelling gloves."

"Didn't you just get new gloves last month?"

"Whatever, I do what I want! God, why is everyone hung up on that? A girl can have more than one pair of gloves, okay?"

Tessa reaches over and flicks me right in the forehead. "Stop yelling at me and continue with your story."

"Sorry," I say. *Again.* Par for the course when I get worked up about anything. I bitch. Tessa flicks. I apologize. Lather, rinse, repeat. "Anyway, I was at the shop, and Adam totally knew I just went to see him and he was, like, grilling me about it, you know? Just waiting for me to crack and spill my guts and admit I was there just for him. And then his mom came over and witnessed it and said something to the effect of, 'Sorry he's acting like this. He can normally talk to gorgeous girls just fine,' and then…I don't even know what happened. I asked him if he talked to a lot of girls there and he smiled that smug-ass smile and asked me if I was jealous and then I acted like an idiot and paid for another pair of the exact gloves I already own and left. And I've been avoiding him since then because I'm afraid I'm going to climb right up his delicious body the first chance I get."

She's quiet as she eats another single kernel of popcorn. Then, "Well, I've gotta hand it to you. You don't do anything halfway."

"Not helping."

"Okay, okay. Do you remember when I started having all those feelings for Jason, and you sat me down and told me to buck up and try something new?"

"Yeah."

"Would it be so bad if you tried something new with Adam?"

My spine straightens. "I don't do relationships, Tess, you know that."

"I didn't say it had to be a relationship. No one is suggesting you plan your life around Adam like you did with Bry—"

I hold up a hand to cut her off. "I'm mad enough. Probably not a great idea to discuss him right now."

"I'm just saying…it doesn't have to be all or nothing. What's wrong with a little extended between-the-sheets time with two consenting adults?"

I stare at her like she's grown another head. "You're seriously suggesting I engage in an on-going friends-with-benefits situation with your brother's best friend?"

"Apparently, yes." She leans forward to grab another handful of popcorn. "Look, there's obviously something there between you two. Everyone saw it the other night at the house, me included. Stop thinking so much and just go with it."

She's right. I have been overthinking everything with him, which is so far off my usual M.O. it's not even funny. I think the problem lies in the fact that even though I've been with my share of guys, I've never had to think about any of them. They were just… there. To waste some time with. To satisfy an itch.

But Adam is more than that. I actually enjoy spending time with him, and that it happens when he's not touching any part of me is equal parts exhilarating and terrifying.

NINETEEN

adam

We still on for tonight or are you going to continue ignoring me?

I shoot off the text to Paige, glancing at her door before I let myself into my apartment. I spent the past nine hours working my ass off, prepping for my first guided classes this weekend and unpacking a shipment that showed up mid-afternoon. Pretty much the only thing I want to do is sprawl on the couch with a cold beer and some mindless television... Unless I have the chance to see Paige, then all bets are off. And I don't even care if that makes me sound pussy-whipped.

I strip off my work shirt and toss it in my hamper, then move on to unbutton my jeans with my phone pings with an incoming text.

Full of yourself much? I'm not ignoring you. Maybe I just haven't been home.

I chuckle as I type out a response.

So that shadow I saw moving behind your peephole was your roommate?

Whatever, creeper. Find something better to do than stalk my peephole.

Challenge accepted. Are you in or what? Shorts and tank top if you are.

Even if these aren't technically dates, I can't deny that planning them has been fun as hell. Fun and also a good reminder of exactly how much I like doing this kind of stuff—physical activities that engage my body as much as my mind. And doing them with a member of the opposite sex is just the icing on the cake. I realized earlier today I've never so much as gone on a bike ride with any previous girlfriends, let alone gone to the batting cages or any of the other activities I have planned, and that bothers me. I never realized what I was missing.

Originally, I was going to take Paige paintballing tonight, but a frequent customer stopped in at the shop and told me he was playing sand volleyball tonight. There are always games after the winners are announced where anyone is welcome to jump in and play, so I figured we'd take advantage of the hot temps and do that instead.

When Paige doesn't respond for a couple minutes, I toss the phone to the couch, then strip the rest of the way before walking into the bathroom and cranking on the shower. Kind of pointless to shower before sand volleyball, but considering I spent the majority of my day lugging boxes around from the shipment, I'm not exactly fresh and clean. The only time I want to be sweaty and dirty around Paige is when we've worked to get there together.

After a quick shower, I hear my phone ping as I'm drying off. Wrapping the towel around my hips, I head to the main room and pluck my phone off the couch.

Yeah, I'm in. Be there in 5.

That must've been the second alert that sounded when I was getting out of the shower, because I don't even have time to pull on a pair of boxers before there's a knock at my door. I think about calling out for her to wait and throwing something on…but this will be more fun.

I pull the door open just as the second knock sounds.

"Took you long eno—" Paige's snarky reply cuts off when she looks at me, her eyes darting all over my exposed skin before pausing to look at where the towel hangs off my hips. Her lips part, and a flush works its way up her neck to her cheeks.

"Sorry, you caught me before I could get dressed."

She finally lifts her gaze and narrows her eyes at me. "You don't sound sorry at all."

"Yeah? Neither do you."

She huffs and crosses her arms, and I realize this may have been an epic disaster in the making, because Paige listened to me. She's dressed in a fitted tank top, the straps of her hot-pink sports bra peeking out at the top, and a tiny pair of running shorts, her long, toned legs on full showcase. Jesus.

"Are we going, or what?"

Clearing my throat, I drag my eyes up and will my semi to go down. Not much I can conceal with just a towel. "Yeah, just let me get changed." I hold the door open for her. "You can come in, if you want. I won't pull out my dick and slap you in the face with it or anything."

She doesn't offer a response, just shakes her head, but she steps into my apartment and walks ahead of me to the living-slash-bedroom. I grab some clothes from the closet and make my way to the bathroom, quickly pulling on a T-shirt, boxer briefs, and a pair of basketball shorts. After running a hand through my wet hair, I head back out to find Paige looking around.

She jerks her chin toward the monstrosity my parents loaned me. "Nice couch."

I can't tell if she's being sincere or not. "Thanks. It pulls out."

"It...what? Are you trying to be pervertedly clever right now?"

"Uh, I have no idea what you're talking about, so I'm definitely not being clever, pervertedly or otherwise."

"'It pulls out,'" she mimics, her voice pitched low. Then she points a finger at me as she says, "Don't you dare whip your cock out right now. You promised there'd be no cock slapping."

Chuckling under my breath, I step closer to her and watch as pleasure and apprehension battle each other in her expression. "Not until you ask." I lean forward until our faces are only an inch apart. "Are you asking, Paige?"

She scoffs. "You wish."

Her breath puffs against my mouth, and I can't keep my eyes off her lips...can't stop from remembering what they felt like against mine. I want that and a hundred other things. Again and again and again. "I'm not going to deny that."

She stares at me, her eyes darkening even further, and then she clears her throat and averts her gaze. "Where are you taking me?"

I step back and grab a couple bottles of water before tossing them in my duffel bag along with some towels. "I have a customer who plays on a sand volleyball league. He said after winners are announced, anyone can jump in and play. You up for it?"

"I'm up for anything you can dish out, Adam."

I smile as I hold open the door for her, gesturing her out ahead of me. "Be careful what you say, cuddle muffin. Or I might start calling you on it."

paige

Whereas my first planned non-date date took place at the innocuous batting cages, Adam goes balls to the wall and brings his A-game straight out of the gate. There's absolutely no way he didn't realize exactly what watching him play sand volleyball would do to me.

We're playing against each other, so I have a perfect view of him on his side of the net. Especially when halfway through the game, he reaches back and tugs off his shirt before tossing it to the side. Okay, so maybe it's a little hot out here with the sun beating down on us, but honestly. How many spikes does one player need to go for? He's just showing off now. I get it, buddy, you can jump high and you have all these manly muscles that flex in your abs and arms when you pound the ball down on the other side of the net...

The whole situation is doing bad things to my self-control. As in, I have none. It's gone. Has left the building. I'm pretty sure if we weren't surrounded by all these people, I'd go over and lick the sweat off his chest. And I wouldn't even be sorry about it.

Even with my hair pulled back into a ponytail, it's hot as hell out here, and considering all the other girls playing are in their sports bras or bikini tops, I don't think anything about following suit. And anyway, it serves Adam right to get an eyeful of me like this when he gave me the smorgasbord that is his body.

When I catch his eyes focused on me after I've tossed my tank top to the side, see his jaw clenching, I smile and flutter my fingers at him in a wave. Then I mouth, *What? It's the beach.*

The other players are occupied, chatting and laughing with each other as the guy on my team gets ready to serve, so Adam leans closer to the net. "Don't play this game unless you're ready to face the consequences."

I cock my head to the side. "And what would those consequences be?"

"Not having this"—he flicks his finger between the two of us—"happen on your timetable." I should be turned off by how he speaks with such confidence. He says it like it's a foregone conclusion, insinuating I'm fighting a losing battle. That it's *him* allowing me to maintain whatever laughable amount of control I've managed thus far. And that thought is scary as hell because...oh God, what if he's right? What if I haven't even *seen* his A-game? Holy shit. What if this is Adam *holding back*?

The thought sets me on edge the rest of the game, and I miss so many passes, it's embarrassing. I can't concentrate, though. Not when I think about having all that restrained want focused directly on me. God, what kind of combustible chemistry would we have together if he held nothing back?

Adam goes in for yet another spike, scoring the winning point for his team, despite my teammate falling to the sand to try and save it. And it should say something that I'm so distracted about what's going on between Adam and me that I don't even care that I lost.

"Good game, cookie," Adam says, walking over to me and offering his hand for a high-five.

I laugh at his nickname, not even bothering to get mad at them anymore, and slap my hand against his. "You too." I can't help my eyes from straying to his body. His delectable muscles are covered with sand and sweat. When I look back up at his face, his expression is a mixture of smugness and arousal. Rather than telling him I have a way to get him all cleaned up, and it involves the both of us stripping down and spending a lot of time in the shower, I say, "We're going to get your car filthy."

He stares at me for a minute, and I swear to God it's like he can see right through me when he does this. His eyes flick down to take me in as I use my discarded tank top to try and brush some of the sand off my body. He clears his throat. "I brought towels to put over the seats. Or in case we wanted to use the outdoor showers over by the clubhouse." He tips his head in that direction and cocks his eyebrow in silent question.

It's an innocuous question. We're in public, for fuck's sake. Out in the open with dozens of other people. It's not like he's going to fuck me up against the wall in the view of everyone else. Still…that doesn't keep me from thinking about it. Or wishing it would happen. Which is probably why I make the foolish choice and say, "Showers, please."

But, really, the chance to watch water sluice down a half-naked Adam? I'm not an idiot.

He nods and heads in the direction we need to go. He bumps

his shoulder into mine. "Thanks for coming out tonight. I had fun."

"Me too." And I realize I mean it. I'm not just bullshitting him. I'm also not just talking about enjoying the fact that I have eye-candy readily available to me when we go out. There's no denying we get along great—both in and out of the bedroom. He challenges me in a way guys usually shy away from. I've had guys interested in me sexually, and I've had guys interested in my sporty side, but I've never had someone who was interested in both. And I…like it. Love it, actually. Which is probably why I'm so hesitant to do anything with him again. I click more with him than I have with anyone since… ever. Needing to take my mind off that, I say, "Guess I need to think of something for next week to top it."

"I was going to take you paintballing tonight until this opportunity presented itself. You can steal it if you want."

"Oh, please, I don't need your castoff ideas. I can do just fine on my own. Or did you forget about last week?"

His eyes burn twin paths down my body, until he locks his gaze on my lips. "No, Paige." His voice is low and gruff. "I think it's safe to say I didn't forget about last week. I've thought about that kiss every night before I go to bed…and every morning in the shower." He leans closer. "You gonna give me another tonight?"

I force my voice to be steadier than I feel, because I'm pretty sure Adam just told me he jerks off to thoughts of kissing me. "Don't push your luck, buddy."

"We'll see…"

The outdoor showers are set off to the side of the building, and, thankfully, they offer a bit more privacy than I was anticipating. There are four of them in a row, the surrounding walls high enough where you don't have to look into the eyes of the stranger showering in the stall over. The last stall is the only one unoccupied. When we get to it, Adam looks inside, then back to me with a raised eyebrow.

"We're not *actually* showering," I say. "I trust you have enough self control not to attack me when you see me watering sand off my legs." I hang my tank top on the hook by the opening and step inside the stall to turn on the water, yelping at how cold it is. It might be hot as balls outside, but that doesn't help the shock of ice-cold water hitting my bare skin.

Adam's deep, rumbling laugh reaches me as he steps inside, hanging his shirt next to mine, and I don't take a minute to think about what I'm doing before I grab the spray hose off the wall and shoot it directly at him. He sputters as it hits him right in the face, then lower to his chest and stomach. I can't hold in my laughter at the shocked look on his face, and I double over, the spray hose falling to the ground.

Mistake number one.

He wastes no time snatching it up and gripping it like a weapon. "You really shouldn't have done that, cupcake."

Sobering up immediately, I shoot to a standing position and hold my hands out in front of me while I retreat backward. "Come on. It was just a little fun. You don't have to—" A stream of freezing water hits me right in the face, and I cut off, sucking in a shocked breath and sputtering as I bring my hands up to block the spray.

He points the water to the ground. "Tell me you were wrong to do that, Paige."

"Not gonna happen."

He shoots me again, this time not stopping until he's covered every inch of my body, the blast of ice pulling the breath right out of me. "Wrong answer. Say it."

"Never!"

He stalks toward me, the spray directed at the bottom of the shower stall, but I know that's going to be short lived. "You're not really in a position to deny me"—he lifts the hose and sprays my ankles—"so say it. Say, 'I'm sorry I was a bad girl, Adam. I didn't mean to get you all wet.'"

I gasp and gesture to my body. "What about *me*? I sprayed you once. You've hit me three times with that sucker, one of which soaking me head to toe! Are *you* going to tell *me* you're sorry for getting me all wet?" I continue walking backward as he advances on me, but the floor is slick from the water, and combined with the plastic of my flip-flops, it's only a matter of time before disaster strikes.

I slip but Adam's there before I ass-plant on the shower floor, his arm like a steel band around my back as he hauls me up against the front of his body. And *holy hell*, I thought guys were supposed to shrink when exposed to cold water? Whoever came up with that theory was a big fat liar, because the part of Adam that's currently pressed against my hip is anything but small.

I'm barely breathing as he leans toward me, our noses so close I can feel his breath ghosting across my lips. When he speaks, his chest rumbles against mine, and the girls perk up even more than before, not even ashamed as they get harder, my nipples straining toward him. "In the interest of being honest, I'll never apologize for getting you wet. And I will *always* mean to do it." The only thing I can do is stand here on my tiptoes, pressed to his body with my hands resting against his bare chest. It's taking all my willpower not to dig my nails in and...*mark* him. And that urge only increases when he closes the distance between us, his lips glancing over the corner of my mouth, across my cheek, until they're right next to my ear. "Did I get you wet, Paige?"

And that's it. I'm done. Game over. He wins.

I grip his face and bring it to mine, fusing our mouths together. Adam groans as he drops the spray hose and engulfs me in his arms. He hauls me closer to him, stepping back to sandwich me between his body and the shower wall. Tilting his head, he uses the hand not wrapped around my waist to move my head, urging my chin down so he can take the kiss even deeper. Twining my arms around his neck, I try to pull him lower or yank myself higher, but nothing is working. When I hook a leg over his hip, Adam growls—fucking *growls*—and grips the backs of my thighs before lifting me and hauling me up against him, and *oh yes*, that's exactly what I need.

"Christ, Paige, you're fucking killing me." He nips at my bottom lip, then swipes his tongue over it. "How long are we gonna keep playing this game?"

I suck in panting breaths as Adam's lips feast on my shoulders, down into the scoop neck of my sports bra, and God, I want him to go lower. I want him to rip away this piece of cotton covering me so he can take my nipples in his mouth. The only thing stopping me is that we're in public with barely any privacy. And that seals the deal for me. If we were home, in my apartment or his, this wouldn't be a question. He'd already be inside me.

Grasping his stubble-roughened cheeks, I pull his head up until his eyes connect with me. Against his lips, I say, "We're not. Take me home."

TWENTY

paige

I thought the feeling would fade on the drive home. Abate somewhat. I worried it would get awkward. That the burning inside me would lessen when I had enough time to actually think about what we were going to do, and it would get weird when we got home and I wasn't into it anymore.

Well, we're home and I'm fumbling with my keys to open my apartment door, and I can't get him inside—the apartment or *me*—fast enough. It doesn't matter that I had fifteen minutes to do nothing but think about what the hell we were doing. Turns out, my brain is a bit of a hussy, because all I thought about was how good it felt the last time I slept with Adam, and how much better it'll be now after all this build up.

Apparently he feels the same way, because he takes over, brushing my hands out of the way and unlocking the door before forcing it open. And then his arm is under my ass, easily hauling me off my feet and up against him so our mouths can connect. Vaguely

I hear the door slamming in the background before Adam walks us farther into my apartment, but I can't focus on any of it because I'm too swept up in the way his tongue slides against mine, the way he carries me so easily through my living room.

It isn't until I hear the sound of the shower turning on that I realize he's brought us into the bathroom, and I reluctantly tear my lips away from his. "This isn't the bedroom. What are you doing?"

"Taking a shower. We didn't exactly get washed off, because *someone* wanted to play."

"Oh, sure, blame me. You were the one who—" I cut off in a gasp as Adam's hand cups my breast, his thumb flicking over my already hard nipple through the material of my sports bra. "God, why are we still wearing clothes?" I push away from him so he can set me down on my feet, and then it's a flurry of discarded clothes as I strip him and he attempts to help me do the same.

"Jesus, how the hell do you get this thing off?" he asks, tugging at my sports bra after he's already divested me of my shorts and panties. "It's glued to you."

"Yeah, well, that's your fault. It wouldn't be so bad if it wasn't soaking wet," I say, trying to tug it over my head, but I'm trapped in a cotton prison.

Adam makes a satisfied noise in his throat and takes advantage of my arms being confined over my head by the soaked cotton. Reaching out, he traces gentle circles around my nipples with his finger, and I pause my efforts, arms crossed over my head as he plays with me.

"You know how hot you look, standing here completely naked with your hands bound over your head?" He leans in, brushing his mouth over my chest, licking a line straight up between my breasts. "I could do anything to you right now, and you couldn't do a damn thing about it."

Sweet sparkling Christ, if he keeps talking like this, I'm going to come before he even touches my clit. I start working harder to get the drenched cotton off me while he continues to torture the ever-loving shit out of me. When I finally tug off my sports bra enough to free my arms, I toss it to the other side of the room and wrap my hand around his cock, thick and hard and straining for me.

"I wouldn't mind binding your hands, either." I squeeze his shaft, and he reciprocates, pinching my nipples between his fingers, pulling a low moan from me.

"In the shower, Paige." He reaches down and pulls my hand off him before turning me around and slapping my ass. "We didn't get in here last time, and you better believe I'm going to enjoy every minute of it."

Does he know I've been thinking about it, too? It must show on my face, because he smiles and stalks toward me until I'm in the small tub, the warm spray at my back. He reaches around me and grabs my body wash, squirting some in his hands, then lathering them up. Watching him watch me is nearly enough to make me come. His eyes are…hungry. Bouncing to every inch of my skin on display as he follows the path his soapy hands take. Over my shoulders, down to my breasts, my stomach, then between my legs. His touch is fleeting, though, quiet whispers when I need a megaphone. I roll my hips, trying to entice him to go right where I want him, and make a frustrated noise when he doesn't.

"You need me, Paige?" he asks, his voice a low rumble, and he's all I can hear…all I can see. His tall, hard body is in front of me, blocking out everything else, his arms banded around me. He runs his hands up and down my back, rinsing the soap from my body, and while it's sweet, almost reverent, I don't want either of those right now. I want fast and hard and a little dirty.

Standing on my tiptoes, I nip at his ear. "Reach between my legs and find out."

His chuckle is pained as he drops his forehead to my shoulder. Then he turns his head and brushes his lips along my neck. "If I do that, I'm going to want to fuck you, and I didn't bring a condom in with me."

"Why didn't you say that? Let's hurry and get the fuck out of here." I fumble behind me and grab the body wash, intending to squirt some in my hand and reciprocate. Instead, he snatches it from me and washes himself in thirty seconds, rinsing before he turns the water off. He yanks the shower curtain open and grabs one of the two towels I have hanging on hooks. With quick strokes, he wipes me down, squatting on the floor and lifting each of my legs to dry them before standing up and wrapping the towel around me. After the other is secured around his hips, I don't have time to step out of the tub before I'm airborne as he lifts me into his arms and carries me into my bedroom.

Amusement in my voice, I say, "I could walk, you know."

"We'll get there faster this way."

"Aw, you in a hurry?" I trail a finger down his chest, chasing a water droplet, and smile when his eyes meet mine.

He lays me down in the middle of my bed, my legs hanging over the side, and braces his hands next to my shoulders as he lowers his face to mine. "Considering you've put me in a constant state of blue balls since I've been back home and no amount of jacking off will alleviate them? Considering I've thought of little else than what it's like to be buried inside you? Yes, I'm in a hurry. "

It isn't like it's been a secret, how he's felt. He's been open and transparent about it since he got back, but hearing him say it so directly loosens something inside me, and I melt further into the mattress. Reaching out, I snag the towel from his hips and toss it somewhere across the room, eyeing his cock as it bounces free. Fuck Jason and his Hall of Fame dick...if anyone could get in there, it's Adam. He's long and thick, pre-come beading at the tip of his flushed head. Swiping my thumb to gather the wetness, I wrap my hand around him. "What are you waiting for, then?"

He groans and closes his eyes, pumping his hips into my waiting fist. After a few thrusts, he stops and moves out of my grasp.

"I'm in a hurry to fuck you, Paige, but that doesn't mean I'm going to rush straight to the moment I sink deep inside you." He flicks my towel open, letting it pool at my sides, exposing me to his hungry gaze. Then he leans down, cupping my breasts, his thumbs brushing over my nipples before he descends and sucks one tip into his mouth. The pressure is feather light, just the faintest brush of his tongue over my peak, but it nearly sends me shooting off the bed.

I reach out, grab his shoulders and try to pull him closer to me. "Oh God. Harder. Suck them harder."

Instead of doing what I ask, he pulls away completely, and I let out a frustrated groan. He waits—doesn't move or speak—until my eyes flutter open. "Don't tell me how to get you ready for my cock. I remember exactly what you need to have you dripping. So lie back and enjoy it."

Glaring, I snap, "I'm not enjoying anything right now, because you're being a dirty, rotten teas—" I cut off in a gasp as his mouth closes over my nipple and he sucks hard at the same time his hand travels over my stomach, fluttering from hip to hip until lowering it and swiping a single finger through my slit. "Oh God, I lied. I'm sorry. Don't listen to me. I'm enjoying this. I'm enjoying this so fucking hard."

His chuckle heats my chest as he breaks away from my breast, his lips trailing all over my body—a hundred different places, and yet never where I want him—until he drops to his knees on the side of the bed, his broad shoulders braced between my spread legs.

I prop myself up on my elbows and look down at him, watch him tracing a finger through all my wetness, his eyes focused on my pussy. "Do you know how much I wanted to lick you in the shower? How bad I wanted to get on my knees for you?"

I fight the urge to grab his head, shove him forward and tell him to get busy, because I remember the last time I tried that, he took everything away. Instead, I grip the sheets to keep my hands from delving into his hair. "Why didn't you?"

He looks up at me, his normally pale blue eyes darkened with lust. "Because I don't want anything to dilute the taste of your pussy. I've dreamt about this every fucking night since December. Now throw those legs over my shoulders so I can get to work."

He doesn't even give me a moment to comply before he does it for me, tossing my legs over his shoulders and lowering his mouth to me. He moans after the first swipe of his tongue, the sound getting lost with mine when he fuses his mouth to me, devouring me whole. My arms shake with the effort of holding myself up, but I refuse to drop back on the bed, because watching Adam with his face between my legs is just about my favorite view in the world, especially when he lifts those eyes and looks right at me as he continues to work me over with his magical tongue.

A whimper escapes my mouth when he pulls away, grabbing one of my hands and placing it on the back of his head. Puffs of air whisper across the wetness he's coaxed from me. "Show me how much you love it when I lick your pussy," he says, his voice gravely and low. "Shove me where you want me, pull my hair, whatever you need. I can take it." He drops his mouth to me again as he reaches up, engulfing my breasts with his hands, pinching my nipples between his fingers. Holy shit, I'm almost there. He's had his mouth on me for less than a minute, and I'm already about to come.

"Oh God, Adam." I pull him tighter to me, sliding my fingers into his hair and clutching it hard in my fist. His answering groan shoots straight through me, and I drop my head back on a moan. "Fuck, I forgot how good you are at this."

He removes one of his hands from my breasts and trails it down my body, over my stomach, the outside and then inside of my thigh, until he reaches exactly where I want him to be. I can't tell anymore if it's his tongue or his fingers that are driving me crazy—probably both—but I don't care. Whatever he's doing, I need more of it.

"Don't stop, don't stop, don't stop," I chant, my body arching closer to him. "Oh *God*."

And then he slides two fingers inside me at the same time he sucks my clit into his mouth, and I'm gone. I arch off the bed, a scream ripped from my throat, as I come all over his tongue. Adam continues pumping his fingers into me, his tongue slowing as he wrings every last drop of my orgasm from me.

I'm still trying to catch my breath when he sets my feet on the floor and leans over me, his mouth wet from making me come. "Don't move."

Huffing out a laugh, I mumble, "Like I could..."

He leaves the bedroom and walks in a moment later. I glance toward the doorway in time to see him roll a condom down his length, and I never thought I'd be sad at the thought of getting fucked, but I really wanted him in my mouth.

"What's the pout for?" he asks as he hovers over me, his hands resting on either side of my shoulders.

"Just wanted to reciprocate."

The smile starts off slow, creeps over his face until it's swallowed as he lowers himself and kisses me. "Next time," he says against my mouth. "I can't wait anymore to be inside you."

He presses our foreheads together as he grips his cock with one hand and slides it up and down before rubbing it back and forth against my clit, watching every bit of what he's doing to me. When I arch toward him, groaning, he makes a satisfied noise in his throat, and if I were in any kind of coherent state, I'd give him shit for it. As it is, I'm barely a functioning human being while I wait for him to fill me. He takes one more pass through my slit before lowering his cock to my entrance and pushing in. Even though he made sure I'm positively drenched, he pumps in and out slowly, until he finally works his whole cock inside me, and I'm reminded just how fucking huge he is. And exactly how perfectly we fit together. "*Fuuuuck*."

He blows out a laugh, his mouth resting against mine, before he traces my lips with his tongue. "Christ, you feel so good."

With excruciating slowness, he pulls out of me and pushes back in, doing this a couple times until I reach around and grip his ass, digging my short fingernails into him. "I know you're sort of getting off on being in charge here, but I'm going to need you to move faster before I hop on top and take what I need."

He chuckles and pulls almost all the way out of me. "Are you doubting I can give you what you need, Paige? I know we were only together the one night, but I thought we did this enough then that you'd remember exactly what I can do to you." To punctuate the statement, he pushes all the way in, swiveling his hips in a way that puts him in contact with my clit at each pass. He hums deep in his throat, lowering his head to brush his lips up and down my neck before scraping my skin with his teeth. "See? Your pussy's already squeezing my cock. And I haven't even started."

And then, holy hell, he *starts*. He pulls back, slamming his hips into mine, and his hands are everywhere. Gripping my hips and pulling me to him, reaching up to cup my breast, trailing down my stomach until he can circle his thumb around my clit, and I don't even have time to register I'm about to come before I'm exploding around him, my hands clutching at his forearms.

He grunts through my climax, thrusting into me as he continues teasing my clit. "You feel fucking perfect, coming around my cock." His hips work faster, thrusting into me with abandon, as he slips his other hand around my neck and into my hair, pulling my head toward him and capturing my lips in an all-consuming kiss.

I slide my tongue against his, gripping his shoulders as I wrap my legs around his hips, pulling him into me at the same time I lift my hips from the bed. We break away from the kiss on a moan, Adam's forehead dropping to my chest. I lick the shell of his ear, then whisper, "Feel how deep inside me you are?"

"Shit, Paige, you can't— Christ, you're gonna make me come. Fucking *hell*." He groans as he pushes in as deep as he can, holding himself still as his cock jerks inside me. I run my fingers up and down his back as he shudders against me, his breath harsh puffs against my breasts.

After a few minutes of silence, only the sounds of our labored breathing filling the room, I say, "Well, I guess we both know what happens when we've got six months of build-up between us."

He chuckles as he lifts his head enough to look down at me. "That's not just months of build-up, buttercup. That's us. Give me a minute and I'll prove it to you in round two."

TWENTY-ONE

paige

A couple days later, I'm getting ready to leave the station for the day as Tanner steps into my...well, office isn't exactly what I'd call this corner I've been shoved into, but it is what it is.

"Hey." I glance over at him as I pack up my stuff. "I take it you got the call from Mom, too?"

He takes his phone out of his pocket and turns the screen toward me, showing me the seven missed calls and multiple texts. "Uh, yeah, you could say that."

I blow out a deep breath and reach down to grab my purse. "I get that she's worried about Dillon and how he's handling everything, but harassing him is only going to piss him off."

"And that's where her great master plan comes into play. If she harasses him through us, she can feign innocence."

Snorting, I roll my eyes and stand, following Tanner toward the elevator. On our way there, Jared passes us, offering Tanner a head nod. "Hey, man."

Tanner returns the greeting but doesn't stop to chat, for which I'm eternally grateful. I've managed to avoid the asshat since our last encounter, and it's been a strategic move on my part. Mostly because I'm not sure I can control my tongue around him, and I don't want to do anything to jeopardize my chances at that full-time position.

Pushing the button to call the elevator, Tanner slides a look to me. "What's the scowl for?"

"What scowl?"

"The one you just wiped off your face. The one that suddenly popped up when what's-his-face showed up."

We step into the elevator, thankfully the only two people in here, and he pushes the button for the main floor. "I think you mean Jared. Or, as I prefer to call him, *that asshole.*"

He narrows his eyes at me and crosses his arms, planting his feet shoulder-width apart. Uh-oh, I've evoked the pissed off cop stance. "Okay, what'd *that asshole* do?"

The elevator doors open and I wave him off as I step out and head toward the front doors. "Nothing you need to worry about."

Tanner easily keeps stride, and I don't have to look at him to know he's got his Protective Brother face on, angry glower and all. "The fuck it's not. If he's done something to you, I need to know about it."

He extends his arm, pushing the main door open for me, and I slip my sunglasses on as we make our way to our cars. "I promise you, you don't."

"Punky…"

"You make it really damn hard to be a grown woman, you know that? I don't need my brothers to come to my rescue all the time. I can do that shit just fine on my own." We get to my car and I settle back against it, crossing my arms as I stare at him.

"If you took care of it, what's the harm in telling me about it?"

"Because I know you, and I know you won't drop it."

"Jesus Christ, Punky, just fucking tell me!"

"Oh, okay. Since you asked so nicely…"

"You are such a brat."

I reach up and pat his cheek. "And you love me for it." Tanner doesn't even crack a smile, and I roll my eyes. "Fine. But you are not doing anything to him, got it?" I stab my finger to his chest until he concedes with a nod. "He asked me out. I said no. His delicate ego was damaged, and he said I'm only here because of you."

"That *asshole*."

"See? Told you."

"I'm going to—"

"Do nothing."

"But—"

"*Nothing*. I'm serious, Tan. He really thinks the only reason I have an internship here is because you called in a favor, and you doing anything to him for what he said would only prove his point."

He clenches and unclenches his jaw, his arms crossed against his chest. He's pissed, and I know this is absolutely killing him not to be able to do anything about it. But finally, he relents with a nod. He reaches around and opens my door for me, waiting until I get in before he braces himself on the top of the car and leans into the open space. "Just for that, it's my choice for dinner tonight."

"You are such a baby, do you know that? *I'm* the one it happened to."

"Yeah, and not letting me do anything about it is like cutting off my balls. I'll grab José's and meet you at Dillon's in twenty."

"Yeah, yeah, yeah. You better get me extra guac. I'll swing home and get stuff for margaritas."

"Sounds like a plan. See you in a bit." He steps back and shuts the door for me, waiting until I pull away before he heads to his car.

He'll probably deny me my extra guacamole out of spite, just because I won't let him doing anything to Jared. Tanner knows as well as I do that I'm right—it really would cause more harm than good if he did. The best revenge I can possibly get is to work extra hard, busting my ass and inching my way toward that permanent position.

Since the day that interaction with him went down, I've spent my time going above and beyond. I'm done holding back and waiting to do what they tell me to. I'm stepping in, asking if I can be involved in things they'd never normally think to allow interns to be pulled in the loop on. And I managed to make a friend with one of the detectives. All it took was figuring out fresh baked snickerdoodles were her favorite, and I was in. One delivery to her desk and a strategically timed question, and I'm sitting in on the meeting they're having tomorrow morning while the other interns continue collating papers, alphabetizing files, and jerking off.

I don't mind working hard for what I have, and I'm going to prove that.

TANNER AND I pull up at the same time to Dillon's small bungalow. I wait outside my car until Tanner walks up, several bags in his hand. I slide him a look. "Did you get me extra guac?"

He leads the way up to the front door, then turns to me. "I didn't want to."

"I *knew* it."

"But then I realized you were right."

"I'm—what?"

He smiles and pounds on Dillon's door. "You're right. It's not going to do anything if I say something to that asshole about it."

I open and close my mouth several times. "Wow. I'm actually speechless." Bumping my hip into his, I say, "I think this is what maturity looks like."

"Don't get too excited. Just because I agreed not to say anything to him about you doesn't mean I'm not going to make his life at the station a living hell." The smile he gives me is like a kid in a candy store, and I decide I need to pick my battles. Besides, I wouldn't be totally against *that asshole* getting some shit work for the next who knows how long.

Tanner raises his fist to knock again at the same time it swings open, and Dillon stands there, leaning against the door, exasperated look on his face. "Let me guess…Mom sent you."

"What? No," I say at the same time Tanner says, "Definitely not."

"Uh huh." Dillon levels us both with a look. "So she hasn't been blowing up your phones like she has mine?"

"She, uh, may have called once or twice." I shrug, but Dillon doesn't make room for us to come in. "Whatever, dude, she called us. It's hot as balls out here and your a/c feels like fucking heaven. Plus I have margarita fixins, and this one"—I jerk my head toward Tanner—"got José's. Now let us in, you grumpy bastard." I don't wait for him to extend the offer before I shove my way through, jabbing him in the stomach with my elbow while I'm at it.

"Our sister, she's so docile and ladylike…" Dillon says to Tanner.

"Yep…a regular Mrs. Brady."

I flip them the bird as I head into Dillon's kitchen and set down the margarita fixins. Thanks to Tanner coming over a couple weeks ago and helping Dillon get this room unpacked, it's in a better state than the rest of his house, but not by much. Everything is… sterile. There are no pictures, personal or otherwise. No small touches. Even in Tanner's place, which is Bachelor Pad Central, he's got some candid shots up of the family and him with his friends. That thought sends a sharp pain through my heart, realizing the one friend with whom Dillon would have pictures—the one who was his best friend for as long as I can remember—is no longer in his life.

Hoping it encourages Dillon to talk to us, I make the margaritas extra strong, then balance all three in my hands and bring them into the living room where the boys are already set up on the couch. A buffet of Mexican food is set out on the coffee table in front of them, but no plates.

Setting down the glasses, I say, "Jesus, do I have to do everything around here? Lazy bastards..."

"We love you, Punky!" they call in unison.

I come back out, throwing paper plates at their heads before I sit in between them and start dishing up before either of them can. "You love me so much, you'll let me have first dibs on all this glorious, glorious food."

They grumble behind me but don't argue, and I smile as I dish up before settling back into the couch. With how strong I made the margaritas, it doesn't take long to get a buzz going. And it takes me exactly that long to realize I maybe shouldn't have made mine quite so heavy on the tequila. I always overthink shit when I'm buzzed...focus too much on things I should just let be. Namely, Adam.

God, I can't even think his name without getting tingly. And he was right...that explosive chemistry between us had nothing to do with the build up and everything to do with...*us*. He did exactly as he told me he would, too, and proved it to me in rounds two *and* three. I was so exhausted after that, I didn't even realize he fell asleep with me until I woke up to my alarm and the smell of bacon. I walked, bleary-eyed, out to the kitchen to see him standing there in nothing but his black boxer briefs and the frilly apron my mom got me as a joke, cooking bacon.

And the really fucked up thing? I didn't know whether to laugh or jump his bones. So I did what I do best...I pushed him away. I inhaled the food, then shoved him out the door, thanking him for the grub and the orgasms.

An elbow in my ribs jolts me out of my thoughts, and I glare at Tanner. "What the hell?"

"What's the matter with you?"

"What do you mean?"

He and Dillon exchange a look over my head. "Besides the fact that you've been quiet the whole time, we're watching *CSI* and you haven't pointed out the thousand things wrong with it. In fact, you haven't even pointed out *one*."

"Yeah? Well, maybe this is the one show they got right."

"Oh, please, you know as well as I do they didn't follow protocol in collecting that evidence!"

I wave him off. "Whatever, dude, we're not here to talk about me. No more avoiding." With that, I shoot a pointed glance at Dillon who rolls his eyes and crosses his arms.

"I'm not a child. I'm a thirty-three-year-old man. No one has to come check up on me. Jesus Christ."

I bump him with my shoulder. "She's just worried about you. We all are. How are you, really?"

"I'm…" He trails off, scrubbing a hand down his face. "I'm getting there, okay? That's not perfect, but it's all I've got. It would go a lot easier if you'd both lay off. And if you'd help me convince Mom to back off a bit."

I glance over at Tanner, and he tips his head in a nod. Turning back to Dillon, I say, "Okay."

Dillon exhales a breath for what seems like the first time all night. Then he grabs his plate and goes to town on his chips. "So why'd you zone out? That's not like you. I know how much you love hate-watching."

I snort but shake my head. "Oh, no. You don't get to evade and then make me talk."

"Come on. It'll get my mind off everything."

I narrow my eyes. "Oh, that was low." But they're both big talkers and they'll run screaming if I tell them what was going through my mind, so I shrug. "Fine, I was thinking about this guy who spent the night—"

"That's enough!" Tanner yells at the same time Dillon shoots up from the couch and practically runs to the kitchen.

"Anyone need another fuckin' margarita?" he asks. "Yes? Yes."

I tip over on the couch, falling into a fit of giggles. That was too easy.

    If only everything surrounding Adam was that way.

TWENTY-TWO

adam

This, right here, is exactly why I've always stayed away from casual sex. This whole, should I call, shouldn't I call bullshit is tiring, especially when I spend the entirety of my working day thinking about it. I hoped sleeping with Paige would abate the incessant need I feel toward her. That backfired big time. Since the other night, I've actually thought about fucking her *more* than I did before, which I didn't think was possible.

"Fuck it," I mutter and pocket my keys, then head to her door and knock. After a few seconds, she answers, clad only in a pair of miniscule shorts and a sports bra. I don't know where to look first, so I look everywhere, my gaze sweeping over her body, pausing on my favorite parts—the swells of her breasts, the toned softness of her stomach, the curve of those drool-worthy hips—as I let out a groan. "Are you trying to kill me?"

She laughs and turns around, giving me a spectacular view of her ass. Since she left the door open, I take that as invitation and walk in as she pulls a bottle of water from the fridge. She turns to look at me over her shoulder. "Get over yourself. Not everything is about you, you know."

I lean against her counter and cross my arms. "I'm fully aware. If it was, you'd already be in my lap."

She doesn't respond to that statement, but she doesn't have to say anything for me to see the effect my words have on her. Her nipples tighten against the bright blue cotton of her bra, and her cheeks flush. At least I have my answer as to whether or not she's thought about me since the other night. It's hard to keep the smug grin off my face, and from the way she rolls her eyes, I don't succeed. At all.

I tip my head toward her. "You going somewhere?"

"Yeah, but you wouldn't be interested."

Quickest way to get me interested in something? Tell me I won't be. "No? Try me."

"It's just yoga. Like I said, not your thing."

"How do you know?"

Hands on her hips, she narrows her eyes at me. "Are you telling me you've done yoga before?"

No. "Yes."

"And you like it?"

I have no idea. "Yeah, it's good for, you know..." I gesture vaguely to my body.

"Uh huh." She walks past me, the sweet scent of her filling my nose, and it takes all my strength not to inhale. Goddamn, this girl has me by the balls. I follow behind her as she goes to her bedroom and then bends over by her bed, pulling something out from underneath it. I can't pay attention to what it is, though, because all I can see is her ass in those tiny shorts pointed directly at me. She stands and gathers her hair back into a ponytail, arching her back, and I don't know where to look first. While I'm taking in the visual buffet that is her body, a flash of purple behind her catches my attention, and my eyes narrow on it. Is that…

"Why do you have a dildo on your nightstand?"

She glances at me as she finishes her ponytail, then slings a long, cylindrical bag over her shoulder. "I don't have a dildo on my nightstand."

"No?" I point toward the offending object. "That giant purple thing with the attachments and curved head isn't a dildo?"

"No," she says as she breezes past me and into the living room. "It's a vibrator."

She says it like it's the most ordinary thing in the world to have on one's nightstand. As if I said, "Oh, I see you have the new Stephen King novel…" instead of talking about a sex toy. I'm torn between grabbing her and throwing her on the bed and showing her exactly why she doesn't need that stupid vibrator in the first place, and begging her to use it while I watch.

I trail after her into her living room. "What the fuck do you need a vibrator for?"

"A girl's got needs, Adam."

"Thought I took care of those needs pretty damn well the other night."

"Yeah? You telling me you haven't jerked off since you were here?"

Well, she's got me there.

"That's what I thought. Girls like to come, too."

"Oh, I remember, babycakes. And I think you remember exactly how much I can make you come, so do me a favor…" I walk over to where she's leaning against the back of her couch and cage her in, bracing my arms on either side of her.

"What's that?"

I trail my nose up the column of her neck and satisfy in the way her breathing changes, the way her hands tighten on the fabric of her couch. "The next time you want to reach for your purple friend, walk across the hall and knock on my door. I'll give you what you need."

I pull away and stand to my full height, backing off enough so I can take in her flushed cheeks and parted lips. She looks like she's two-point-five seconds away from jumping my bones. But then she narrows her eyes and stabs her finger into my chest. "I know the game you're playing, and it's not going to work."

"What game is that?"

"The Let's Make Paige Forget She Wanted To Go To Yoga And Fuck Instead game." She traces her fingers over the embroidered letters on my work shirt, and that only exacerbates the problem in my pants. "It's not going to work, but you're welcome to join me, even though it's not our usual night. You know, since you love it so much."

It takes me longer than it should to clue in to what she's saying, and that she isn't inviting me into her room for some purple playtime. Not only have I not talked her into sex, but I've also somehow made it impossible to say no to yoga. Her voice has just enough of a taunting edge to let me know she's ready and willing to call me on my shit, which means I'm stuck doing fucking yoga, because if I bail, she'll know I'm lying.

On the plus side, at least I'll get to watch her in those two minuscule articles of clothing, bending and contorting into all kinds of fuckable positions. I hope yoga's easier to do with a hard-on than the batting cage was. With a nod, I say, "Sounds good. Let me go change."

"You'll probably want as few clothes as possible," she calls out to me before I can get to her door. "It's Bikram yoga."

When I glance back at her, her smile is bright. Even not having ever done a yoga class in my life, I have to sell the equipment at the shop, so I know enough about it to realize I just fucked myself over so hard. As if pretzeling myself into those positions wasn't going to be difficult enough, I now have to do it in one hundred-plus degrees.

I'm so screwed.

PAIGE LOOMS OVER me, a smile on her face, her skin shining with sweat. It's hot as balls in here. Or maybe I'm not even at the yoga studio anymore. Maybe I've died and this is hell. Seems entirely plausible based on the past hour.

"I'm impressed." She extends a hand to help me up. "You actually managed to keep up pretty well."

I wave off her hand and close my eyes, concentrating on breathing in this sauna. "I think if I get up right now, I'll die."

She laughs. "Thought you did this all the time."

I open my eyes just enough to see her squatting next to me. "You had to know that was a lie."

"I totally did, yes."

"Why the hell didn't you call me out on it at your apartment?"

"Why would I do that when this is so much more fun?" Her grin is big and obnoxious, but I can't even be mad at her, because it feels damn good to make her smile.

"Yeah, real fun. You could be witnessing my death right now. Laugh it up, puddin'."

She rolls her eyes. "Oh Jesus, here we go…"

"What's that supposed to mean?"

"It means I have two older brothers, so I'm well versed in the Man Hurt."

"What the fuck is the 'Man Hurt'?"

Gesturing to me, she makes a disgusted sound in her throat. "This. You. All of it." Pushing to stand, she shakes her head as she looks down at me, hands on her hips. "You're a disgrace right now. It's hot yoga, not climbing Mount freakin' Everest. Stop being such a testicle and stand up."

"Stop being a—what the hell are you talking about?"

Crossing her arms, she looks down at me. "It's me waving my feminist flag. I'm tired of inaccurate portrayals society feels are acceptable."

"Wait…is this your way of calling me a pussy?"

"No, this is my way of calling you a *testicle*. Pussies can withstand a lot more than your wimpy balls. How did that become a saying, anyway? It's not even a little bit accurate."

I snort and slowly peel myself off the floor. "Must've been started by a man."

"That's what I'm saying." She appraises me as I stand up, wincing as I do so. "You okay to walk home? You're looking a little flushed…" She's fucking *gleeful*. I'm going to be hearing about this for weeks.

"Careful, cuddle butt, or I'll show you what I wanted to do instead of yoga tonight and prove just how okay I am when we get home."

Her lips part as her gaze drops to my chest and the A-shirt plastered to my skin thanks to the heat and the workout. Even though I had enough confirmation the other night, it's still good to know she's as attracted to me as I am to her. A low laugh rumbles out of me, and she snaps her eyes back up to mine, affecting nonchalance as she shrugs, but she can't hide the desire in her eyes. And I don't want her to.

Reaching out, I brush a stray piece of hair away from her face, tucking it behind her ear and trailing my fingers down the damp skin of her neck. Running my thumb up and down her throat, I lean toward her and lower my voice enough so the other people walking around can't hear it. "If you need something from me, all you have to do is ask. You know I'm more than happy to give it to you. Any time, remember that."

She shrugs me off as she rolls her eyes and turns on her heels to walk out, but not before I see the interest there. I follow behind, grabbing the mat I rented and leaving it at the front desk. Even though it's June and the temp is in the high 80s, it's still cooler outside than it was in that death chamber. We start off in the direction of the apartment building, having walked since it's only a few blocks from home.

"So does this mean we're skipping our next non-date date night, since we hung out tonight?" she asks after about a block of silence.

I glance over, trying to get a read on her. I can't tell from the tone of her voice which answer she's hoping for, so I decide honesty is probably the best way to go. "I don't want it to mean that."

She stares at me for a minute, then drops her gaze to the cracked sidewalk. "Okay, sure." She shrugs. "Besides I have something awesome planned."

"Oh, yeah? What?"

"Ah-ah, you're not getting it out of me. Surprises, remember?"

With a nod, I agree. "Good. I'd hate to miss out on something awesome just because of my stupidity in agreeing to come tonight."

She laughs. "At least you can admit it."

"You know what the worst part of that was?"

"What's that?"

"I didn't even get to enjoy watching you bend over and contort into all those positions. I was too busy trying not to die."

Bumping her shoulder into me, she grins. "Maybe next time you'll get better and you'll be able to watch."

"Or…" I draw out the word and turn to her, "maybe you can give me a private show instead."

Feigning ignorance, she taps her finger on her lips. "A private yoga class? Sure, I guess we can do that."

"A private *naked* yoga class. Where you do all the positions from my lap."

This pulls a laugh from her. "Sounds to me like you're just trying to get fucked, Adam."

"Can I let you in on a secret?" I ask, leaning toward her. Her eyes are bright and teeming with interest as she nods. Dropping my gaze to her lips, I say, "There will never be a day I'm *not* trying to get fucked by you." Before she can pull away, I slip my hand around her neck and turn her to me, forcing her to stop right there on the sidewalk outside our apartment building.

She opens her mouth to say something, but I cut her off, sealing my lips over hers. She tastes like a mixture of salty and sweet, a combination of her exertion and the lip-gloss she always carries with her, and it makes me groan into her mouth.

It doesn't take as long as I figured it would to coerce her into the kiss. Or any time at all. She melts into me, resting her hands on my chest as she opens her mouth, sliding her tongue against mine. Trailing my hand down her back, I palm her ass and tug her toward me, grinding her against my cock, but it's not enough. It never is with her.

I drop kisses on her cheek, her chin, then I lick a line straight up the column of her neck. Against her ear, I say, "Your place or mine?"

It feels like an eternity of silence, her body tense under my roaming hands, before she finally releases a breath. "Yours."

With her ass still in my hands, I squeeze, then give it a tap. "Get moving, then, unless you want to go in over my shoulder."

"Yeah, like you would—" She yelps as I crouch in front of her and lift her in a fireman's hold, jogging up the front walk and into the building.

"You should know better than to taunt me by now, sweetums."

"I can't believe you actually did this. I hope you know everyone can see my ass cheeks like this."

I reach up and palm the back of her ass, blocking the view from anyone looking. "There's no one here to be worried about. Except Mrs. Connelly." I raise my voice as I turn my head toward our nosy neighbor's door. "And she's watching anyway."

Paige vibrates against me as she laughs, and I rush her inside my door, then set her down and work to get these layers off her. "Goddamn, why are you always wearing these contraptions when I'm trying to get you naked?" I tug at her sports bra, finally getting it up and over her head, then reach for the back of my A-shirt when Paige slides her hands up my abs to my chest, lifting the shirt as high as it can go.

"Because we usually fuck after some sort of physical activity. You have a thing for sweaty girls, Adam?"

"Just one sweaty girl," I say, peeling her shorts off, then stand to palm her pussy. Slipping my middle finger through her slit, I groan. "Fuck, you're already soaked. This for me?"

She's panting, her fingers clutching at the kitchen counter behind her. "No. It's for the yoga instructor."

"Yeah?" I dip a finger inside her before pulling out and tracing her clit with the wetness. Her legs are shaking from the effort of standing, and I can't stop the smug smile from sweeping across my face. "You thinking about him right now?"

"Mhmm." She nods, her eyes fluttering closed, and I pull my hand back enough to give her clit a short, hard slap. Her eyes fly open as she gasps.

With my lips brushing against hers, I say, "You don't think of anyone but me when I'm standing in front of you, got it? My fingers. My mouth. My cock. I'll give you any of them you want, but you only think of *me*."

She nods, her eyes rolling back when I give her my fingers again, slipping two inside her while grinding my palm on her clit.

"Spread your legs wider, Paige." She complies immediately, then lets out a long moan as I go deeper, hooking my fingers and stroking the spot that makes her scream.

"Oh shit." She drops her forehead to my chest.

I brush my lips against her bare shoulder. "You're close already, aren't you?" As if in response to my question, her pussy flutters around my fingers, and I let out a low groan. "I can't wait to get inside you again. Is your pussy as hungry for my cock as he is for her?"

"*God*," she moans. She releases the counter from her grasp and reaches up to cup my face, tugging me closer to her. "Kiss me," she breathes against my lips, but doesn't wait for me to comply before she takes what she wants, slipping her tongue into my mouth. She strokes it against mine at the same time her hips rock faster against my hand. I finger her deeper, grinding my palm against her clit harder, and then she's groaning into my mouth and clenching around my fingers as she comes.

"That's it, sweet girl. You got some more for me?"

She's still panting, trying to catch her breath from her orgasm. "Why don't you do some work and find out?" she sasses back.

I slip my fingers from her, then shed my shorts before grabbing a condom from my wallet. As I'm rolling it down my shaft, I say, "Turn around, Paige. Brace your hands on the counter."

She does as I ask, looking at me over her shoulder. Her eyes are glazed, her lids at half-mast. Her mouth's flushed and parted, and standing there, the long indent of her spine trailing into her tilted up ass, just a glimpse of her breast as she turns toward me, she's the sexiest thing I've ever seen. I step up behind her, bending my knees enough to tease her with the tip of my cock. I slide it back and forth, strumming her clit until her head falls forward and her legs are shaking, and then I find her entrance and reach up to grasp her ponytail, tugging her head back at the same time I thrust deep.

A choked gasp falls from her lips as she grapples for something to hold onto, gripping the counter in front of her before she reaches back and digs her fingers into my ass. "Oh God, Adam."

"That's right. It's me fucking you so good, isn't it? Say it."

"Fuck," she gasps, her mouth open and eyes closed as I pump faster into her. Tugging her hair harder, I skim my nose up the column of her neck and take her earlobe between my teeth.

"Say it." Gripping her hip, I pull her back to me, then slide my hand up over her stomach until I cup one of her breasts, pinching her nipple hard enough to get her attention. "*Say it.*"

"Oh God, yes, it's you. Fuck, it's you. *Holy sh*—I'm going to come. Oh God, I'm going to co—" She cuts off in a long moan as she lifts her ass even more, trying to get me as deep as she can.

Reaching down, I grab her leg behind her knee and brace it on the counter, spreading her open for me so I can push deeper. I slip my hand down to brush against her clit, and her moans never cut off as I thrust harder, faster, fingering her into another orgasm as mine consumes me.

Thrusting into her as far as I can, I drop my forehead to her shoulder. "Fuck, Paige. *Christ.*"

As she contracts around me, her pussy squeezing every last drop from me, I realize it was utterly useless trying to avoid having anything happen with her. I wasted months deluding myself into thinking this was only a one-night stand. This is different with her. It's not just the sex, though it's undeniably the best of my life. It's *her*.

And even though this summer was only supposed to be a three-month sabbatical from my life, I can't help but wonder if this isn't supposed to *be* my life and the one I have in Denver is the real placeholder.

TWENTY-THREE

paige

Considering I've been best friends with Tessa since before she got pregnant, it's safe to say I think of Haley like a niece. She is in all the ways that matter, and I love her to pieces. I also love hanging out with her. Because of that, I should be jumping at the chance to do so, since Tessa's in a bind. Instead, I get this weird pit in my stomach at the thought of not being able to hang out with Adam on our designated non-date date night.

"Come on, Paige, please? Becky cancelled. It won't be for too long—a couple hours, tops. I know you're probably busy with internship stuff, but *please*."

I blow out a sigh. I'm being ridiculous right now. When have I *ever* flaked on my best friend because of a guy? Uh, never, that's when. At the same time, I don't want to leave Adam hanging since it was his night to plan. "No, no, I get it. It's okay. Umm…let me just check with Adam quick, okay? I'm sure it'll be fine." The line gets quiet, and I pull my phone away from my ear to make sure I didn't drop the call. "Tess? You still there?"

"Yeah…"

"What's with the silence?"

"Nothing."

"Don't play that. What is it?"

"You have to check with Adam…" she trails off, the question clear in her tone.

"Well, I mean, I don't *have* to, but this is the day we always hang out."

"Mhmm…"

My spine stiffens at her tone. And the fact that I can read everything I need to from that inflection. What the hell am I doing? Checking in with a guy to see if I can watch my best friend's daughter… I don't want to be that person. The one whose existence revolves around a guy. The one who changes her whole life because of a guy. That's *not* me. Not anymore. "Whatever, it's fine. I'll do it. I just have to swing by my parents on the way and feed and let Buddy out, because they're not going to be back until late. That cool?"

"Yes, totally. Thank you, thank you! I'll see you when you get here."

I hang up with her, then shoot a text to Adam.

Sorry for the late notice, but I have to cancel.

Once I send it off, I change into a pair of shorts and a tank top, then grab a few of my sparkly nail polishes Haley wanted to try the last time she was here. I toss them into my purse and head to my apartment door, opening it to see Adam standing there, fist raised to knock.

"Hey," he says, glancing down at my outfit. "I thought maybe you were sick or something…"

"No, but Tessa's sitter is. She and Jason have some banquet thing tonight for his work, and she's desperate. I told her I'd watch Haley. Sorry I have to cancel." I step out into the hall and lock my door behind me.

He tosses his keys in the air. "If you want company, I don't mind coming with. I haven't seen Haley much since I've been back, anyway."

I should say no. There's no way this is going to go unnoticed by Tessa when we both show up. And especially after our phone call, she is going to have a dozen questions for me, and she'll pounce as soon as possible. But the thing is…I really do have fun with Adam. And it'd be kind of rude of me to ditch him completely since we had plans…

"You sure? I have to swing by my parents' on the way and feed my dog."

Instead of answering me, he just turns and leads us up the steps. "You have a dog?"

"Yeah, Buddy. We got him when we moved here. My parents didn't want him, but I begged and pleaded until they finally relented. I can't have pets here, though, so they're taking care of him until I move somewhere I can take him."

"What kind is he?"

"Um, we don't know, really. He was a rescue. But he's the cutest thing. You'll love him."

Adam walks us to his car, opening the passenger door for me, and I don't comment on it. I just slide in the seat and buckle up before directing him to my parents' house. It isn't until I'm standing at the door, key in the lock, that I start to worry maybe this was a bad idea. The only guy I've ever brought home was Bryan, and that was in high school. As an adult? Never. Adam's already met—okay, only in passing—one of my brothers, and now he's about to get a glimpse of me I've haven't given anyone else in a very long time. Too late to back out now, though, so I push through the door, squatting down to greet Buddy when he runs toward me.

"Hi, Buddy, hi." I scratch behind his ears and croon, "Have you been a good boy?"

Adam shuts the door behind us. "This is 'the cutest' dog you were talking about?"

"Yeah, isn't he adorable?"

He laughs and I turn around to look at him in question. His laughter cuts off abruptly. "Wait, you're serious?"

"What do you mean? Yeah, I'm serious. He's so cute, right?" I turn back to Buddy. "Yes, you are. Just the cutest dog, ever."

"Have you *seen* your dog?"

"What kind of question is that? Of course I've seen him, idiot."

"I'm just wondering, because that scraggly mess of fur in front of you is the ugliest thing I've ever seen. Jesus."

I gasp and shoot a glare at him. "Shut up. He can hear you, you know."

He shakes his head and reaches down to pet Buddy. "It's time someone told him the truth. You've probably been telling him how pretty he is for years. Time for him to be a man about it and own the ugly."

I stand and head into the kitchen to fill his Buddy's dishes. "You're awful, you know that? Just cruel."

"*You're* awful. You're the one who mentioned your *adorable* dog and how much I'll love him. I was picturing, like, a pug. Or even a golden retriever. Not a dog who looks like he's been scrounging around in back alleys watching drug deals go down."

I sniff and turn my head away from him, snubbing him the best way I can. I'm quiet as I get Buddy's dishes filled with food and water and go outside to play with him for a while. I throw his ball and he chases after it, but instead of bringing it back to me, he goes right to Adam, wagging his tail as he sits at Adam's feet, waiting for him to throw it again. How can he not think that's cute? Seriously.

Adam chucks it far, and Buddy tears off after it, then Adam steps closer to me, bumping his shoulder into mine. "You're not really mad because I said your dog was ugly, are you?"

I ignore him, crossing my arms over my chest and waiting

for Buddy to bring me back the ball. Except when I lean down to get it from him, he once again brings it over to Adam. Who laughs. Bastard.

"See? I told you he'd appreciate being told the truth," he says as he tosses the ball again.

"Whatever, you're a jerk." I head into the house, not looking to see if either of them are following me. They can have each other. I can't believe Buddy turned on me...taking up with the enemy.

A few minutes later, the patio door slides open, and Buddy lopes up to me, climbing on the couch and putting his head in my lap. "He probably told you to do this, you little traitor," I whisper as I scratch his ears.

"If I drop myself in your lap, will you do that to me?"

"I'll shove you off of me so you land on your ass on the floor."

Adam smiles, then comes and sits on the other side of me, propping his arm over the back of the couch behind me. I try to maintain my ire, but it's damn hard. Especially when he leans closer and whispers, "I'm sorry. Thanks for bringing me here and showing me your absolutely adorable dog."

I roll my eyes and grumble, "Don't push your luck, you little liar."

He laughs. "I can't do right by you. If I call him ugly, you get your panties in a twist about it. If I call him adorable, you call me out on lying. So how about, instead of talking about your dog, I kiss you instead."

"You wha—"

He doesn't let me finish before his lips are on mine, his hand cradling my jaw as he kisses me. It's soft and sweet, just the barest whisper of tongue, and man, he's good. So good I need to watch myself around him, because Adam Reid is one smooth motherfucker, and I melt into him way too easily. Something I cannot allow myself to do.

adam

With the way Tessa's eyebrows shoot up her forehead when she answers the door to find Paige and me both standing there, I'm going to go out on a limb and say this is unchartered territory for Paige. Though I think a lot of what we've done together is unchartered, and the thought that she's doing things with me she wouldn't with other guys makes me want to puff out my chest and strut around, maybe throw her over my shoulder for good measure and take her to my lair to have my way with her. Seriously…what is *up* with these possessive feelings I have around her?

"Uh, hey, guys," Tess says, stepping back to let us in. "Haley's in her room, getting her ponies ready for a horse show."

"She better have saved me Rainbow Dash. She knows how much I love that one." Paige kicks off her shoes before scurrying down the hall to where Haley's room is. "See you guys later. Have fun!"

And she's gone.

"That girl is the master of avoidance," Tessa mutters.

Jason laughs as he steps up behind her. "Hey, man, I didn't know you were coming with Paige."

I shrug and tuck my keys in my pocket. "Didn't really give her much of a choice."

"Excellent work, Adam," Tessa says with a grin. She looks to where Paige disappeared, then steps closer to me and lowers her voice. "I know I told you to push with her, but I gotta ask…what do you think is going to happen here?"

"Here? Uh, I figured we'd play with Haley until you got back." I shoot a glance between her and Jase and see matching curious looks on their faces. "I'm not going to fuck Paige in the hall outside Haley's bedroom or anything, if that's what you're worried about. I think I have enough self restraint to keep it in my pants."

Jase coughs out a laugh, and Tessa turns bright red before

fumbling in her purse, refusing to look at me. I think Paige is rubbing off on me, because all my tact seems to have vanished.

"Thanks, man. Appreciate your restraint, because doing something like that would be just…awful," Jase says with a smile, and Tessa reaches out to punch him in the stomach, glaring at him.

"What I meant," she says, "is at the end of the summer. You know, with Paige…"

With those few words I'm reminded of what I've, thus far, managed to put out of my mind. I'm trying to spend this summer doing something I've never done before—live in the moment. I'm trying to not be so rigid in my plans and see where it gets me. But I can't deny the thoughts have crept up, wondering how Paige and I could possibly make this last past September. Even though I know, without a doubt, she'd run screaming in the other direction if I even mentioned it.

"At the end of the summer, I go back to Colorado, Paige stays here, and we both keep living our lives." I pointedly ignore the look Tessa gives me, as well as the worried glance she slides to Jason. "You guys have to be there at seven, right? Better get going."

"Yeah," she answers, hooking her purse over her shoulder and shooting me with another worried glance.

Jase rolls his eyes and slaps her ass. "Get a move on, baby. They'll be fine." He holds the door open for her to step out and says to me, "Don't drink my booze and don't fuck in my bed. See you in a couple hours."

I laugh, shaking my head and shutting the door behind them, then follow the sound of Haley's giggles to find her and Paige set up in Haley's room, a huge-ass horse stable set up on the floor in between them.

"Adam!" Haley yells, then shoots up from her place on the floor and rushes toward me. It only took one unintended head butt to the junk for me to learn really damn quickly to always be ready for a full-on speed attack from the little gremlin. I crouch and catch her in a fireman's hold like I have every other time since the ill-fated head butt. She laughs and grips the back of my shirt as I spin her around several times before setting her on the floor and watching her stumble with dizziness.

"Hey, shrimp. Whatcha playin'?"

"Ponies! And we saved you one. Auntie Paige said you'd like the pink one because pink's your favorite color and even though pink is usually *my* favorite I said you could have it because Paige said you'd cry big fat crocodile tears if you couldn't have it and then none of us would have any fun."

"Is that right?" I look past Haley to see Paige sitting there, the picture of innocence. She shrugs and grins, mouthing, *What?* as I take a seat across from her. Picking up the pony Haley set aside for me, I say, "I don't know about big fat crocodile tears, but I do enjoy pink. In fact, I *love* pink." I lift my eyes to Paige and smile. "And Paige definitely knows exactly why."

"Why, Auntie Paige? Why's he love pink?" Haley grabs her pony and starts brushing the blue hair, her attention focused on Paige.

"Um...uh..." She glares at me when Haley's attention is diverted to the ponies again, and I mouth, *What?* then grin.

Taking pity on her, I get Haley's focus on something else, diverting her attention away from the line of questioning we definitely don't need to traverse. She's easily distracted, telling me about her summer with Miss Melinda before she starts kindergarten in the fall.

An hour later, she's curled up between Paige and me on the couch, getting ready to watch a movie, the questioning in her bedroom long forgotten. I only hope she doesn't mention it to Jase, because I'll never hear the end of it.

"What's on the docket tonight, shrimp?"

"*Frozen!*" she yells—seriously, this girl has one volume and it's Drunk Frat Boy—as she bounces in her seat, working the remote to turn on the movie. "Have you seen it, Adam?"

"Can't say I have."

"You're gonna *love* it. Jay pretends he doesn't like to watch it, but I see him singing *Let it Go* every time it's on. He's such a fibber."

I laugh. "You know what? You're right. He told me he likes that one the best." I point to one of the girls on the movie case.

"I knew it!"

It doesn't take long for the movie to capture her attention. Which is always nice for some quiet, but that's exactly what I don't need right now. I glance over at them, seeing her and Paige with their heads pressed together, both focused intently on the TV.

As much as I try to watch the movie and ignore the niggling in my stomach, I can't. It hasn't gone away since Tessa asked me what I was going to do at the end of the summer. I've tried to put it out of my mind, to not think about it while I enjoy the time I have here with Paige, but sooner or later I'm going to have to. My time is coming to an end faster than I'd like, and that's not changing. Whether Paige likes it or not, we're going to have to have a talk about where we stand…about where we want to go.

And if she thinks she can stick around with me.

TWENTY-FOUR

paige

I leave the station with a scowl on my face. Like usual. That asshole Jared has made it his goal in life to piss me off. The last couple weeks, he's been hanging around headquarters more and more, chatting up the other two worthless interns while tossing perfectly timed sneers in my direction. He's trying to throw me off my game. Too bad it's not going to work. I've got my in.

Detective Dodd has taken a liking to me. I don't know if it's because I'm a girl and there aren't a whole lot of us around this place, or if it's because of the snickerdoodles I keep her in supply with, or if it's just because I know my shit and I work hard. Or, hell, maybe it's a combination of all three. Whatever it is, she's gone above and beyond to help me get a leg up for the full-time position available.

Today, she had me verifying the leads she received on a case she's working while those other two jerk-offs stood around and BSed with half the department. And they look at *me* like I'm the one who didn't actually work to get an internship here.

The whole thing pisses me off, and I stay pissed off the entire ride home. I pull into my spot and get out, huffing while I go and slamming my car door harder than I mean to, but it feels damn good.

"You look like I feel. Rough day?" Adam's voice rings out in the otherwise deserted parking lot, and I startle.

Clutching a hand to my throat, I spin around and see him walking toward me, his messenger bag slung over his shoulder. "Jesus, you scared the shit out of me."

"Sorry. You must've been lost in your fit of rage."

That manages to pull a smile from me, and I answer his original question. "Yeah, you could say that. You too?"

"Yeah." He tips his head in the direction of the apartment in silent question, and we walk in together, Adam holding the main door for me. When we get to the landing in front of our apartments, he says, "I know we're supposed to go on some epic adventure tonight for our non-date date, but do you think we can…not?"

Disappointment flares in my stomach and spreads until it's all I can feel. Trying to hide it, I tuck a strand of hair behind my ear and nod. "Oh, sure. Yeah. I've got stuff to do tonight, anyway, so—"

He reaches out and grips my shoulder, stopping me from turning toward my door. His thumb sweeps along my collarbone, and I force myself to stand still and not shiver under his touch. My restraint only goes so far, though, and goosebumps prickle all over my skin. From the curve of Adam's lips, it's obvious he sees them. "I meant just not go *out*. Not cancel all together. Maybe we can watch another horrible movie? Order some pizza?"

While I could really go for some physical activity to get some of this aggression out, I can't deny how good it sounds to just veg on the couch with a stupid movie. I also can't deny how relieved I am that he still wants to hang out, even if I'd never actually admit that. "Yeah, okay. My place?"

He nods and his eyes drop to my lips. "I'm gonna drop this stuff off, change, and take out my contacts. I'll be over in five."

Quirking my mouth up on the side, I say, "Do you want to kiss me, Adam?"

Breathing out a laugh, he steps closer. "I always want to kiss you, porkchop."

"Good one," I say as his body presses against mine.

"Thanks, I thought so, too." His lips brush against mine with each word, and then he seals our mouths together, kissing me like he wants to forget everything about his shitty day but that. He slides his tongue against mine, his hand cupping my neck and tugging me closer to him, even though the only way I could possibly get any closer would be to climb up his body. When the hard length of his cock pushes against me, instead of pressing against me harder, he pulls away, brushing a couple brief kisses on my lips before taking a step back. He turns around and unlocks his door, glancing back over his shoulder, a smug smile on his face when he sees I'm still frozen in place.

That snaps me out of it, and I glare at him. "Oh, you think it's cute when you dickmatize me, do you?"

"When I what?" he asks around a laugh.

"When you"—I wave a hand in the general direction of said dick—"you know, use your cock for evil."

His lips curve up on one side. "Sugar britches, kissing you is never evil, and everything I do to you with my cock *definitely* isn't evil."

"Uh huh, likely story." I spin around and unlock my door, then call out, "Just for that, I'm getting green peppers on the pizza."

He groans as I shut my door and laugh all the way into my bedroom, tossing my bag and purse in the corner. I quickly change into a pair of yoga pants and a tank top, shucking my bra along with my work clothes. Walking into my living room, I pull my hair up in a messy ponytail, then grab my phone and find the number for the pizza place. I order a veggie with extra green peppers...on half, because I'm pitiful and cave. Damn him.

Last time we had pizza together, I didn't know about his little aversion to the peppers, and watched, amused, as he took a bite not knowing they were on his slice…and then proceeded to gag from the taste. Literally gag.

I'm still laughing from the memory when Adam walks through my door a few minutes later.

"What's so funny?"

"Just remembering the last time we had pizza. You know, when you were so manly about those green peppers." I look at him over the back of the couch, a huge smile on my face, and I don't have time to do anything when he vaults over the top of it like in some kind of freakin' action movie—seriously, I didn't even know that happened in real life—and plops down next to me before he attacks. Digging his fingers into my ribs, he's relentless as he tickles me. I shriek, shoving him away with my hands and trying to get my legs up high enough to push him away with my feet.

"Adam, oh my God, *stop*! I'm going to pee!"

"Should've gone to the bathroom before." He doesn't let up, but instead seems to double his efforts. His fingers are everywhere—every single inch of my body that's ticklish, he's found. And exploited.

"What do you want?" I ask through gasping breaths. "I'll give you whatever you want, just stop!"

"Nice try. I'm not falling for that."

Through my laughs, I manage, "How about a BJ?"

Just like that, his fingers are gone, and he swoops down to give me a kiss. "Pleasure doing business with you, muffin. I'll let you know when I want to collect."

There's a knock at the door, presumably the pizza, and Adam leaves me flat on my back, still catching my breath, while he answers the door. I blow the stray pieces of hair out of my face, exhausted from laughing so hard and struggling against him. I'll have to remember a beej gets me out of trouble with him—that's definitely good information to have.

While Adam takes care of the delivery guy, I head into the kitchen and grab plates and a couple beers from the fridge. When I get into the living room, he's standing in front of the TV queueing up a movie.

"How's *Sharknado* sound tonight?"

"Fucking awesome." I set the unopened beers down on the coffee table and get a slice of pizza—non-green pepper—for Adam and set it on the plate in front of his seat, then grab a piece for myself. I curl up on the couch, plate in my lap, as he comes over and sits next to me, reaching over to twist the cap off my beer before doing the same for himself.

When he glances down at his pizza, he looks over at me with a smile, then slips his hand under the leg of my yoga pants and caresses my ankle. He doesn't say anything, but he doesn't have to. He's smug as hell about me ordering the pizza how he likes it, and it's written all over his face. Just for that, I'm going to have to slip a lone pepper onto one of his pieces when he goes into another room. And I'm also not going to tell him how hot he looks in his glasses right now. That'll show him.

It doesn't take us long to finish off the pizza—and I mean finish off the pizza. Cheese and carbs are no match for me. Leaning back on the couch, I groan, rubbing a hand over my belly. "Oh my God, I'm so full. Why'd you let me eat all that?"

"I like having use of both my hands, thanks."

Laughing, I shove his thigh with my foot, then groan when the movement jostles my stomach. "Oh God…it hurts. It hurts so bad. I swear to God, it's like Thanksgiving."

"So you couldn't eat anything else right now?"

"Are you high, dude? I'm dying over here. No, I can't fucking eat anything else."

"That's too bad. I guess I'll give that Chicago mix popcorn to someone else."

"What?" I shriek as I fly to a sitting position.

Adam reaches down and grabs something from the side of the couch, and oh holy shit, he got me my beloved popcorn. I snatch the tin from him, tearing off the lid and peering inside. "Forget Thanksgiving; it's like Christmas!"

Despite my protesting stomach, I grab a handful and go to town on the cheesy caramely goodness. I guess this means he's forgiven for his smug face from earlier.

It isn't until an hour later that I realize I never explicitly told Adam about my love for Chicago mix. Which means he's paid attention to pretty much everything I say, reading between the lines and picking up on hints I'm probably not even aware I'm dropping. But even if I had mentioned it, that's beside the point. Because he still thought ahead and went out of his way to order this online and have it shipped here for the sole purpose of making me happy.

A niggle of worry sets up camp in my stomach. Suddenly this whole thing with him is starting to feel like more than two people who go out on non-date dates. This is starting to feel a hell of a lot like a relationship.

One I never wanted.

TWENTY-FIVE

paige

I jolt awake in the middle of the night, heart racing, a heavy weight on my chest holding me in place. I struggle against it, shoving it off me, and then scramble out of bed and turn on the lamp on my side table.

Once the room is illuminated, I see Adam sprawled out on my yellow sheets, his gorgeous, muscled back on display as he lies on his stomach, one arm shoved under his pillow, the other reaching out over my side of the bed.

Jesus. I have a side of the bed. I used to sleep sprawled out in the middle, going wherever the fuck I wanted to, and now *I have a side of the bed.*

That thought only makes the panic unfurl faster, my heart pounding like a drum. I can't back away fast enough, get *away* fast enough, but where can I go? This is *my* apartment.

Adam groans, shoving his face in the pillow, then peeks at me with one eye cracked open. "What the hell, pumpkin? It's three in the morning. Come back to bed."

Oh God, even when he's half asleep he calls me those stupid, sappy, ridiculous nicknames that I secretly love. And he lets me lie with my head in his lap while we watch movies and never puts up a fight when I ask him to play with my hair. And he ships in my favorite popcorn just because he somehow became aware of the fact that it's my favorite, and he likes to make me happy.

It's all too much.

Talking to Tessa the other night on the phone…having Adam over to my parents' home, regardless of the fact that they weren't there, then hanging out with Haley, just the three of us crowded on the couch. And then tonight, staying in when we were supposed to go out and get all dirty and competitive and—

"We didn't even have sex tonight!" I yell at him. I must look ridiculous, standing here in my panties and tank top, hair a mess on top of my head, pillow creases on my face, yelling about the lack of sex.

"Um…" Adam rubs a hand down his face. When he rolls over and sits up, the sheet pools around his waist. And I hate that I know the color and brand of his boxer briefs without even being able to see them. I hate that I *pay attention* to those details. "Do you *want* to have sex? I'm up for it whenever, but just for future reference, there are other, less shouty ways to suggest that."

"No, I don't want sex!" God, why can't I stop this annoying screeching thing my voice is doing?

"*Okay…*" he draws out the word like he's talking to a crazy person. And he is. God, I've lost my damn mind. "Do you want to sit down and tell me what you *do* want? Because I'm flying blind here, doodle bug."

"Oh my God, how do you come up with all those? And why did you buy me that popcorn? I never asked you to! And we didn't even go out tonight, and I ordered you pizza without green peppers, and then we fell asleep on the couch and dragged our asses to bed and *did not even have sex!"*

"Paige, I'm trying really hard to follow you, but I—"

"I never wanted a relationship!"

He snaps his mouth shut and stares at me. Just stares at me. I'm breathing heavy, my palms clammy and sweaty, my heart racing too fast, and he's the picture of calm.

"What did you think we were doing this whole time?" he asks after a too-long silence.

"Not that!"

"Well…" He reaches over and grabs his glasses from my side table—Jesus, he's got his glasses on my side table, like they belong there, and I hate how much I like that—and slips them on before he runs a hand over the stubble on his jaw. "I hate to tell you this, but just because you don't put the label on it doesn't mean that isn't exactly what's been happening."

"What? No. No, that's not—"

"It is." He slides his legs over the side of the bed and reaches out for me, grabbing my hand and tugging me forward between his knees. He runs his hands up and down the outside of my thighs as he looks up at me. "And it doesn't have to change anything if we *do* put the label on it. We still go out and have a good time, kicking each other's asses."

"You mean me kicking your ass," I cut in.

He smiles, one side of his mouth kicking up higher than the other. "We still hang out at your place or mine when we don't feel like going somewhere. We still have sex because we have fucking amazing sex. And, yeah, sometimes we don't have sex, and that's okay, too. The only difference that comes with the label is maybe I don't have to ply you with ice cream to get you to come over. And maybe I introduce you as my girlfriend when we're out."

Oh God. I think I might puke. Right here on uber hot, glasses-wearing Adam. The jumbled mess in my brain has migrated to my stomach, every cell in my body ready to bail. I haven't been someone's girlfriend in years. *Years*. But Adam doesn't know that. He knows I don't do relationships, but he doesn't know why. And he's not ever—

"I changed all my college plans for the last guy who called me his girlfriend and then he fucked some other girl in the front seat of my car at a pep rally." Jesus*fuck*, are my mouth and my brain at *all* connected tonight?

I keep my eyes focused somewhere over his right shoulder. I don't want to look at him. Don't want to see the pity and the revulsion there. But I look anyway, and Adam...isn't looking at me any differently than he always does.

"I'm sorry that happened to you, but I hope you know me well enough now to know I'd never do that to you. Besides, I hate pep rallies."

Somehow, even in the face of me having the ultimate freak out and exposing my most vulnerable moment in history to the one person I wish didn't know anything about it, he manages to make me crack a smile. Funny how every bit of that is thanks to the same guy.

He slides his hands up until his thumbs run along the edges of my panties, and his fingers tuck under my ass. "Do you want to talk about it?"

I shake my head and rest my hands on his shoulders. I can safely say I'd like to never talk about it again, especially with him. "No."

He nods. "Good. Time to pay up on your promise from earlier."

"My prom—"

"You were whining about not having sex. Well, I'm about to change that. And we're going to start with your mouth on my cock." He scoots back on the bed, his head up by the pillow as he props his arms behind it.

Adam just lies there staring at me, waiting. He's giving me an out. Letting me focus on something other than what all this means to me. Can it really be this easy? Can I really get past this anxiety I have at the thought of being in a relationship with him, even if that's exactly what we've been doing?

Having the label on it *does* change things, whether Adam thinks so or not. But I can do this. I can, because he's only here for another few weeks, and then he's going back to his life in Colorado, and that'll be it for our relationship... Frozen forever in a perfect summer fling.

I glance down and see him hardening already in his boxers, and start to climb up on the bed before he stops me by holding up a finger. "Panties and tank top off."

Pursing my lips, I slide him a look. "Bossy..."

His answer is a quirk of his eyebrow, so I tease him a bit, turning around and pulling the tank top off, then lowering my panties while bending over in front of him. When I glance back at him, it takes all of my willpower to force my legs to hold myself upright. Adam's got his underwear shoved down under his balls, his fist wrapped around his cock while he stares at me.

"Give me your mouth, Paige."

My body moves of its own accord, climbing up on the bed and settling next to him. Leaning over, I wrap my hand around his fist, using his fingers to squeeze his shaft as I bend forward and lick up the come beading on his flushed head. Adam's groan spurs me on, and I suck the tip into my mouth, glancing up at him to see him staring at me. Watching me. His lips are parted, his eyes focused on me behind those sexy-as-fuck glasses, and I close my eyes to block out everything but the feel of him in my mouth. It's silly, but after our talk, after everything that just happened, I'm afraid if I stare at him too long I might actually lose a piece of myself to him.

He moves his hand from around his cock and slides it into my hair, letting me take over, my fist chasing my mouth up his length, then down again. I get into a fast rhythm, my tongue flicking the underside of his cock at each upstroke while I caress his balls with my other hand. When his hips are lifting off the bed, trying to get himself deeper into my mouth, trying to work his cock into my throat, I pull off completely, and he curses, relaxing back on the bed.

"Careful, kitten, payback is a bitch," he says through heavy breaths.

I chuckle and tighten my grip on his dick, pumping slowly as I lean down to lick his balls, suck them in my mouth. So focused on making Adam lose his mind, I startle when I feel his fingers at my thigh, trailing a line up until he cups my pussy in his hand.

His answering groan and the way he slides his fingers through me makes me respond in kind. "Jesus, you're wet. This turning you on, sucking my cock?" His fingers dance over my clit, slide into me. Instead of answering him, I suck him deep into my mouth, moaning as he keeps playing with me. "Bring that ass up here. I need a taste of your pussy." He grabs my thigh, tugging me around until I'm straddling his head. All the while, I suck him deeper, harder, and then his mouth is on me, and I can't think about anything but how amazing he feels.

While he hooks a finger inside me and flicks my clit with his tongue, I suck him as deep as I can. His cock head bumps the back of my throat as his groan vibrates against my pussy.

I pull my mouth off his cock long enough to say, "Oh God, I'm gonna come. Don't stop. Keep doing th—" I break off on a moan. The climb starts all the way down in my toes, cranking higher and higher and higher until I'm teetering on the edge, and then all at once, it peaks and breaks. Waves rush over me as I engulf Adam in my mouth again, and his hips piston up off the bed before he grips my thighs hard as he comes, shooting into the back of my throat.

When we've managed to coax every ounce of our orgasms from each other, he kisses my inner thighs, then rolls me off him. I stay flat on my back, eyes closed in utter contentment. I can't see him, but I can feel him shifting on the bed until I sense him hovering over me.

"I hope you're not done," he says. "Because I'm just getting started."

adam

I should've anticipated Paige's freak out before it happened. And truthfully, I was. Whether or not I wanted to admit it, I was waiting for the other shoe to drop. And drop, it did.

Even though she didn't say it out loud, I could see her justifying our arrangement in her mind. Justifying being okay with this whole thing because I'm only here for another couple of weeks. She's writing us off as an extended hook up, and I have to remember that. She just proved that it can't be any more than that with her, and I have to get damn comfortable with it. I don't have another choice.

Paige blinks her eyes open at me, looking well and thoroughly fucked, even if I haven't had my cock in her tonight. Yet. "Just getting started? Pretty sure I just felt you come down my throat." She laughs and glances down, and I know the second she spots my already half-hard dick, because her laugh cuts off abruptly and her wide eyes snap up to mine.

Leaning down, I run my nose along her jaw, then down the length of her neck. "Turns out he doesn't need a lot of downtime around you. Was your pussy feeling a little neglected tonight? Is that why you needed sex so bad? Show me what you do when that happens."

"What?" Her hands are resting on my biceps, her voice breathy.

"When you want sex and you don't come get it from me, show me what you do."

"I still don't—"

I lift up, hovering over her again. "Get your purple toy, Paige."

I lower myself and nip at her bottom lip. "I want to watch you fuck yourself with it."

She stares at me for a minute, her eyes flitting between mine, her lips parted. A flush works its way up her neck to her cheeks, and I don't have to be a mind reader to know she's thinking about me watching her use it. And she likes it. "Oh God, I'll come before I even turn it on."

"Good." I push off the bed and stand off to the side. "And then you'll come again when it's inside you. And then you'll come again when I pull it out and put my cock in there instead. You wanted sex tonight? You're gonna get it. Now grab the toy."

For a moment, she doesn't move, and I almost think she's going to deny me, but then she scrambles over to her side table and pulls out the battery-operated cock she thought was a good substitute for me. We might only be together for the short time I'm here, but I'm going to do everything in my power to make sure everything she uses after I'm gone will pale in comparison to the real deal.

When she's got it, she lies back on the bed, her head on the pillows and her legs bent and spread, feet propped on the mattress. "I've never done this before," she whispers, tentatively running the head of the vibrator through her slit, looking more vulnerable than I've seen her.

I grip my cock hard, because the thought that we're doing something she's never done before makes me want to come like I'm buried deep inside her. Makes me want to shoot all over her stomach and breasts, mark her even more. My voice is gruff when I say, "Good, me neither."

That seems to relax her, and she spreads herself open with one hand, all that perfect pinkness peeking out at me, and guides the vibrator over her clit, then lower, before repeating it all over again.

"You've got the prettiest pussy, you know that? All pink and swollen and fucking delicious. I'd have you for every meal if I could."

Moaning, she bites her lip, shuddering as she watches me

while tormenting herself with the head of the vibe. And that's exactly what she's doing—tormenting. I can see it in her eyes. In the way her body shakes as she barely touches herself.

I grip my cock hard, fisting it in a punishing hold, just enough to keep me on the edge, but not enough to push me over. "You gonna turn it on?"

She shakes her head, her eyes fluttering closed before she opens them and drops her gaze to the fist I've got wrapped around my dick. "Not yet."

Watching her get herself off is better than watching porn. *Jesus.* Seeing her tease her clit, how she brings herself almost to the point of coming, her entire body taut, then pulls back, removing the vibrator from her pussy completely until she's relaxed once again. And then she does it all over again.

Finally—*finally*—she slips the vibrator inside her, and I watch with rapt attention as the curved, purple head disappears into her pussy, her lips spreading wide around it. Paige moans and closes her eyes, pressing a couple buttons, and then a whirring starts up and her entire body jolts.

"Oh fuck," she breathes as she pumps it in and out.

"That's not as thick as I am, is it? Not as long either. Does that satisfy you anymore?"

"No. Not since I've had you." That's the most honest she's ever been, revealing something she'd probably have kept to herself if she wasn't already half lost to pleasure.

"You wish that was me inside you instead, Paige?"

She whimpers out a breathy, "Yes," and I have to force myself to stand there. To not give her what we both want and let her get herself off this way first. I grip my shaft, pumping slowly as I watch her. I want nothing more than to match the fast pace she's set on herself, but if I do, I'll come in about three-point-seven seconds, and I'm not coming again until I'm buried deep inside her.

Paige continues to fuck herself hard, one of her hands going up to trace her nipple before she tugs it between thumb and forefinger. Her eyes are closed, her near constant moans telling me she's close. And, Jesus, I need her to be. I want to be inside her right fucking now. Want to show her how much better it is with me than it is any other way she can get it.

She opens her eyes and stares right at me, cock in hand, watching her get herself off, and then she does. She keeps her eyes connected with mine as she moans, body arching off the mattress, and I can't wait another second.

I fumble with a condom and roll it down my shaft as I climb on the bed. Kneeling between her spread legs, I brush her hand away before pulling the vibrator out of her. She's still shuddering from her orgasm as I hook her legs over my elbows, opening her wide for me, and drive home. Paige moans deep, reaching up to grip my face and bring our mouths together. She slips her tongue between my lips, sliding it against my own, as she lifts her ass off the bed to meet my unforgiving thrusts.

Pulling back to breathe, she slides her hands down my neck and over my shoulders. "God, Adam, *shit…*"

"This is what you wanted, isn't it?" I sit back on my knees and grip the backs of her thighs, holding her down while I pound into her harder. "My cock. Not just to come, but to come from *my* cock."

"Yes, yes, yes," she chants, her head restless on the pillow, eyelids fluttering closed as she clenches at the sheets, at my thighs, at anything she can to get purchase.

"Keep your eyes open, Paige. Watch me fuck you. See who's about to make you come."

She does as I say, her eyelids fluttering open.

"Who do you want to fuck you? Tell me."

"You, Adam. God, it's you…"

I thrust into her faster and faster, circling her clit until she's coming around me, pulling my orgasm from me and taking me with her. Her answer makes me crazy…wild…even if I know the honesty behind it is only temporary. As soon as the afterglow wears off, her walls will be back up again, keeping herself safe from anything more that could happen between us.

The only way this is safe for Paige is the one way it's not safe for me. Even still, I'm in. In this with her, for as long as I can get her. For as long as she'll let me be.

TWENTY-SIX

adam

A couple weeks later, I'm at my parents' house for dinner. So far, requesting elaborate dinners from my mom has worked in keeping her from asking to come to my place. Considering my time is dwindling more and more each day, I might actually escape this without her ever having to set foot there.

"Adam, honey, how are things going at the store? Be honest with us," my mom says, shooting a worried glance at my dad as she picks at her dinner.

"They're going good, Mom. Really good." I wash a bite of meatloaf down with some milk. "The profits have been growing steadily every week. The rentals are the biggest moneymakers, at least at this time of year, so we'll want to look at maybe expanding the selection. But I just crunched the numbers today, and if we keep going at this pace, you're on track to be in the black again by February."

When I finally glance over at my mom, she's got her hand over her mouth, and her eyes are brimming with tears. Quickly trying to reassure her, I say, "February really isn't that bad, Mom, all things considered. I know it seems like a long time, but with the amount of debt stacked against us, it's a strong improvement."

Shaking her head, she waves me off, then gets up and walks away from the table, heading into the kitchen, and I look to my dad with panic. "What the hell did I do?"

He chuckles and scoops a bite of meatloaf. "Not a damn thing." He shakes his head as he looks at me over the rims of his glasses. "You've been on this earth for twenty-five years, and you still can't tell the difference between your mother's tears?"

I shrug. "Tears are tears."

"Not with her. Your mother cries for every emotion. Empathy, sadness, happiness, anger, frustration...you name it, that woman sheds tears for it."

"Yeah, okay, so what were these?"

"Pride."

"What? Why?"

He shakes his head and points his fork in my direction. "Because of you, idiot."

"Gee, thanks, Dad."

"I don't know if you're being humble or just stupid."

"Apparently just stupid."

"Come on, Adam. Everything you've done here for us? You've single-handedly pulled us away from bankruptcy when you didn't have to. When you probably *shouldn't* have. We're your parents, and yet we're the ones who needed saving. You have a life in Colorado, and you dropped everything, dipped into your savings to be able to take three months off work just to help us." His voice gets a little gruff, and he looks away, clearing his throat. "We're just thankful. More than you can ever know."

I swallow the lump in my throat that surfaces from hearing my dad speak with such emotion. It's not that he's closed off, but he's not exactly an open book either...not like my mom. "I'd do it again."

"I know you would, son. And so does your mother. Which is why she ran out of here like her pants were on fire."

It's quiet for a bit as we both focus on eating the rest of our meal. I shoot glances toward the kitchen, knowing from experience she'll be in there until there's no trace of her tears, and then she'll waltz in, probably carrying a pie, like nothing happened.

My dad clears his throat after a few minutes of silence. "Have you thought about maybe staying? The shop is as much yours as it is ours. And we're getting up there in age. Wouldn't mind retiring while I still have some years left to enjoy it."

I roll my eyes. "Dad, you're fifty-eight. I don't think the Grim Reaper is knocking on your door just yet."

"Doesn't change that I'm getting itchy. Just something to think about."

And the thing is, I *have* thought about it. More than I'd care to admit. Especially now that things with Paige have been progressing positively, despite her temporary freak-out over the R-word. We've continued on our non-dates weekly, doing shit most people would probably think was unromantic, but it's on those nights, seeing her all sweaty and competitive, that I want to fuck her the most. Though, really, there's never a day when I *don't* want to fuck her.

But there's one thing that keeps tripping me up when I play that future out in my mind—a future where I'm back here, doing exactly what I wanted to get away from. I moved away, went to school in Colorado and got a degree in accounting so I never had to deal with this kind of life. Keep away from the ups and downs and uncertainty that comes from owning your own business. From the sleepless nights and bottomed-out savings accounts and scraping by week to week for half the year. From the lack of security of not working a sure and steady job.

That's to say nothing of the loyalty I feel toward Ken and his accounting firm. During the four years I was in college in Colorado, he and his wife took me in whenever I couldn't afford to come home—holidays, long weekends, even just whenever I needed a place to do laundry and didn't have the quarters to go to the Laundromat. And now? He gave me three months off, no questions asked, knowing how important it was to me to be able to help my parents.

But also knowing without a doubt I'd come back. I can't leave him in the lurch. More than that, I don't know that I want to.

I can't deny how much I've enjoyed these past several weeks working at the shop, using my mind as well as my body. Feeling *accomplished* at the end of the day. But I know, too, that high is circumstantial, because we only had up to go. My parents hit rock bottom before I got here, so *any* improvement was improvement. I'm here on the upward swing, but it won't stay that way. It'll fluctuate, the earnings and subsequently my *life* fluctuating right along with it.

And it kills me to deny my parents, because if I don't step up to run the business, it's going to be sold to a third party. My sister isn't uprooting her life to run it, besides the fact that it was always a chore for her. Even still, I won't lie to him. He deserves at least that much. "I have thought about it, Dad, and I can't. You know that. We've talked about it before."

He nods and glances down at his plate, picking at his food. "Doesn't hurt to ask again."

"You're right. Doesn't hurt."

He's hiding his disappointment well, but I can see it. I've just learned really well how to block it out.

AN HOUR AND two slices of pie later, I don't feel any better about turning down my dad. My mom didn't say anything when she finally came back into the dining room, pretending like nothing happened just as I knew she would. What I also know is as soon as I left, my dad told her exactly what he asked. And exactly what my response was.

Exhaling a deep breath, I unlock my apartment door and

walk inside, tossing my keys on the counter and scrubbing a hand through my hair.

"Hey, honey, you're home!"

The sound of Jase's booming voice scares the shit out of me, and I jump. "Jesus Christ! You fucker."

His answering laugh is the only thing that greets me, which just pisses me off more. He picked a bad time to show up. Walking into the main room, I narrow my eyes at him sprawled out on my couch, grin on his face and beer bottle resting on his knee as the TV blares in the background.

"Did you steal my beer?"

He shrugs. "Of course."

I blow out a sigh. "What the fuck are you doing here?"

"It's so good to see you, too." He lifts his bottle in my direction before tipping it back to take a drink. "And what the fuck am I doing here? I'm bored. It's girls' night at my place, and I've been forced out by way of estrogen. They're probably going to set off fucking glitter bombs and shit. Figured I could drag your ass with me to harass Cade instead of suffering through that. Thought we could play the whole, 'This food was horrible. I'd like to talk to the chef' game. You know how much that pisses him off. But *first*," he says, pulling something from behind him and dangling it between his fingers, "I have a more important question for you. Whose panties are these?"

I stalk over to him and snatch the tiny scrap of purple lace from him and stuff them in my pocket. I know without a doubt they're Paige's. I just saw her ass in them last night when she swung by after a Pilates class for a quick hello. A quick hello that led to her riding me on the granny panty couch.

Jason's smile grows. "From the scowl on your face, can I assume those belong to none other than our sweet Paige?"

I try to ignore his use of the word *our*. Try and fail. "She's not *your* anything." I clench my teeth and close my eyes, pressing my thumb and forefinger to them, because *goddammit*. That infraction is definitely not going to be ignored by Jase. For one blissful minute following my outburst, there's nothing but silence. Sweet, sweet silence. And then his laugh rolls out of him, the force of it causing him to fall back on the couch, clutching his stomach as he guffaws.

Crossing my arms over my chest, I glare harder at him. "I don't know what's so fucking funny."

"You don't—" He starts laughing again, shaking his head as he stares at me. "Holy shit, this is the best thing I've seen all goddamn week, and that includes sitting across from Cade in a pink hat at one of Haley's tea parties."

I definitely need to have some alcohol in my system if I'm going to continue to be subjected to his presence, so I grab a beer from the fridge. "I have no idea what the hell you're talking about."

"This," he says, gesturing to me with his bottle. "*You.* The purveyor of relationships. Mister Rigid and Regimented is falling hard for the one-night stand. Jesusfuck, this is comedy gold."

And the thing is…he's not wrong. I don't know if I'm in love with Paige yet, but there's no doubting I'm falling. And it's futile to ignore it any longer. She's the first person I think of when I wake up, the last person I think of before I go to sleep, and the only person I think about all goddamn day. And the really fucked up part is, I'm not even thinking about all the outstanding sex we have. I'm thinking about random things. How I love when she tucks her feet under my thigh when we're watching those ridiculous horror movies, and how she doesn't get scared or cower while we watch, but instead heckles the actors and points out everything totally implausible. How she makes everything into a competition between us—even eating pizza—and takes it as seriously as she would a national championship game. How she makes extra coffee in the mornings for me, because she knows I don't have a pot at my place.

I'm so fucked.

I flick the bottle cap at his forehead. "I'm glad my misery amuses you."

"Oh, misery? Is that what we're calling it when hot girls leave their panties in our couches?"

Collapsing next to him, I take a deep pull from my beer. "No, misery is what I call it when I find a girl I think could actually be *it*, and I'm leaving in two weeks. Misery is wanting to stay here, but knowing I can't. Misery is also knowing, with absolute certainty, that the girl who might actually be *it* will be fucking some other dude a month after I'm gone."

He stares at me for a moment, then drains his beer. "Well, shit, when you put it like that, it does sound pretty damn miserable." He stands and heads into the kitchen, tossing his bottle in the garbage before coming back with two glasses and a bottle of Jack. "Fuck going to see Cade. This calls for liquor and lots of it. He can bring his ass here when he's done." Jase pours way more than three fingers in each glass, then lifts his to me. "To women rotting our fucking brains and us being stupid enough to let them."

paige

Tessa, Winter, and I are crammed on Tessa's couch, Haley long since passed out and hauled off to her bedroom. She tried to hang with the big girls as long as she could, but by nine, her eyelids were drooping more and more. Now it's just the three of us, a pile of chips in front of us, and enough tequila to cause some trouble.

"All right, Paige. Spill," Tessa says, bouncing in her seat as she stares at me over the rim of her glass.

"Spill what?" Lord, I knew this was coming. And, really, it's my own damn fault. I haven't said much—or anything really—to Tessa about how things have been going with Adam. In fact, she doesn't even know it's become a thing. A bonafide Relationship—capital R—even if it's an unspoken law that Adam and I never refer to it as that. How I've managed to avoid talking to her about it is beyond me. Except I think it has a lot less to do with what I was doing to distract her from getting me to talk about it and more to do with the fact that Tessa *allowed* me to distract her.

"Nope, you don't get to play that." Tessa shakes her head. "I've let you avoid it for *weeks*. Time's up. Besides, you're the only safe one I get to hear sex stories from. Winter obviously can't tell me what my brother's doing." She shudders and Winter laughs. "Don't deprive me."

"Yeah, Paige, don't leave the poor girl hanging," Winter chimes in, wry smile on her face. "And, I mean, I wouldn't mind hearing some stories, either…"

I take a sip of my strawberry margarita, buying myself some time. Then I stuff some chips in my mouth, looking thoughtful as I chew. When I reach for another handful, Tessa slaps my hand away and throws a chip at my head, the pointy end stabbing me right in the forehead. "Ouch! What the hell?"

"Stop procrastinating! I don't know when Jason will be home, and I want to hear the story already."

"All right! Jesus. You don't have to get violent." Blowing out a deep breath, I sink back into the couch. "So, Adam and I are fucking. It's good. Next topic, please."

They both bark out laughs, shaking their heads. Winter glances at me, her margarita poised in front of her lips. "I'm fairly new to this whole 'girl time' thing, and even I know that's not gonna cut it."

"What do you want me to tell you guys? You wanna know the last position he fucked me in? Or how many times he's gone down on me? How many orgasms I've had because of him and his magical cock or how big said magical cock is?" I close my eyes, my memories like a dirty flipbook in my mind. "Because the answers are: cowgirl, too many to count, and he's ruined me for all others, vibrators included."

"Oh my damn. He's better than B.O.B.?" Tessa asks seriously.

Laughing, I say, "Girl…there's no competition. Not even a little."

"Whoa." She takes another sip of her drink, emptying her glass. "Thank God for tequila. Otherwise, I'm not sure I could handle hearing this about the first non-related boy I ever saw naked."

My spine snaps straight. "Hold on…what'd you say?" I can't keep the hard edge out of my voice, and I'm only slightly embarrassed that my jealousy is rearing its head in front of the one person who knows me better than anyone else. I've never been a jealous person. I've never needed to be, I guess, with how my relationships—or lack thereof—usually go. But even with Bryan, I didn't feel like this—like I want to claw out the eyes of any and all girls who've been with Adam before. Apparently that goes for girls who've seen him naked before, too.

"Oh, chill out, Xena Warrior Princess. I was seven. Pretty sure he's changed quite a bit since then."

I settle back into the pillow, letting my ramrod straight back relax into the cushions. "Well, okay, then. You could've *led* with that tidbit of information. How would you like it if I said I've seen Jase naked?" That wipes the smile from her face, and I laugh at the scowl she's wearing instead. I'm smug as I say, "Yeah, that's what I thought."

"Okay, I think we can all agree none of us want any other girls to see our guys naked," Winter says.

I start to nod in agreement, then stop myself. My guy? Adam's not my guy. Not even a little bit. He's just a guy I hang out with sometimes. Just a guy I talk to every day, and I sleep with nearly every night. Just a guy I'm fucking for an extended period of time.

Just a guy I'm in a Relationship with for the first time in five years…

Before I can well and truly freak out, Winter tilts her head. "How much time does he have left before he goes back to Colorado? From what Cade's told me, Adam's parents' shop is back on track. He might even be able to leave early."

I don't miss the heavy silence that falls around us, or the worried look Tessa shoots my way, but I can't focus on it. I can't focus on anything except the gaping wound that somehow opened up in my chest at Winter's words. Adam and I haven't talked about the end of the summer. It's been this abstract thing, just sort of hovering in the back of my mind as an expiration date. My safety net. But now, hearing that I might not have as long as I'd originally thought with him? It churns my stomach, makes my palms clammy, sends my mind spinning. Makes me wish I didn't have that stupid safety net.

Makes me wish I didn't need it.

TWENTY-SEVEN

paige

A couple hours later, I pull into a parking spot at my apartment building and climb out of my car. While I wanted nothing more than to get absolutely smashed in the face of the epiphany I had at Tessa's, I knew I had to drive home at some point tonight, so I cut myself off. Funny how thoughts of *what the hell am I doing?* can sober you up really damn quick.

The front door to the building opens just before I get there, and Cade and Jason walk out, both looking a little rough.

"Hey, guys. Bar brawl tonight?"

They glance at each other, then back at me, neither cracking a smile. "Yeah, something like that," Cade says, rubbing the back of his neck.

"Ooookay..." I shift my eyes between them, taking in everything with a scrutinizing eye. "You both okay to drive? I can drop you guys off if you need me to..."

Cade waves me off, grabbing his keys from his pocket and

tossing them into the air before he catches them. "Nah, we're all right. The third person in our party, though? Not so much."

"Adam? He got drunk?" I fail to keep the surprise out of my voice.

Jase looks at the building and shakes his head before turning back to me. "I think drunk is a bit too tame for what he is right now."

"And fair warning," Cade says, "he's parked on the floor outside your apartment door. Dragged his ass out there and refused to go back into his place until he saw you, despite how many times we assured him it was a bad fucking idea. I can haul him in there, though, if you need me to."

I'm so shocked at the fact that *Adam*—follow the rules, responsible Adam—is shitfaced and sitting outside my apartment door that I don't take Cade up on his offer, despite my epic freak out from earlier. Despite the fact that I could really use some time to myself. "Nah, that's okay. I'll slap him a couple times and give him some coffee. He'll be all right."

"Don't slap him too hard, Paige. He had a rough night." Jason isn't serious very often, but there's an edge to his voice now as he steps off the stoop, Cade following.

"Why? Did something happen at the shop?" I turn around as they walk past me and toward the street where both their cars are parked.

Cade tips his head toward the building. "You'll have to ask him. See ya."

I offer a wave, then head inside, unsure of what I'm going to find when I get to the bottom of the steps.

Whatever I thought I'd see doesn't live up to what I'm actually met with. Adam is slumped over in front of my door, his black-framed glasses sitting crookedly on his face, his hair a mess. He's resting his head on the doorjamb, and his eyes are glazed as he brings a mostly empty bottle of Jack to his lips.

"Okay, drunkie, you've probably had enough tonight, don't

you think?" I ask as I squat in front of him, taking the bottle from his hand.

"Hey, baby," he slurs, then makes a face. "That one *sucked.* Gimme a minute. I can do better."

I breathe out a laugh, ignoring the flip of my stomach, and tug his arm. "That's okay. How about we get you up so we don't give Mrs. Connelly a show, huh?"

"That old bat loves me. She told me she was gonna steal me away from you. I told her you wouldn't even put up a fight for me, so she could steal me whenever."

His words are like a wrecking ball through my chest. While I've never thought of Adam as particularly withdrawn, it's clear he's sharing a lot more than he ever would if he were sober. And the thought that he thinks I wouldn't fight for him hurts. The fact that I know I probably wouldn't? It's too much.

What I need is some breathing room. To get away from Adam and be by myself so I can think. Figure out what this maelstrom of feelings spinning around inside me are. Unfortunately, I have over six feet of hard-bodied male slumped against my door, so it looks like my needs are going to be put on hold for a while.

"Come on. Let's go." I reach up and unlock my door from where I'm squatting in front of it, then push it open, causing Adam to catch himself from falling back.

He looks up at me, then back into my apartment, then back at me once again. He tilts his head to the side. "You're gonna let me stay with you tonight?"

The confusion in his voice at the question should confuse me. Except it doesn't. I know exactly why he's asking that…because he doesn't stay the night anymore unless we have sex. That's been an unspoken rule since our middle of the night talk a few weeks ago. It wasn't something I asked for…wasn't even something I thought I wanted or needed until he gave it to me without me even voicing it.

That shouldn't break my heart as much as it does.

I avoid his underlying question. "Are you going to puke in my bed?"

"Don't think so. Can't be sure, though."

"Well, I can't be sure I won't shove you off the bed so you puke over the side instead of on me, should it come to that. If you can handle that, come on."

I stand, then offer him a hand and try to help pull him up, but attempting to yank up a two-hundred pound pile of solid muscle—solid, *drunk* muscle—is about as easy as it sounds.

"Can't believe you're gonna let me stay, even if we don't fuck. I mean, I'll try. I'm always hard for you, but I can't guarantee I won't pass out mid-thrust. You could get on top, though, if you wanna. I love it when you ride me and your tits sway in my face."

I laugh, shaking my head as I pat his chest, one shoulder tucked under his arm as we walk in. "You are such a sweet talker, but I wouldn't want to take the chance of you puking on me. How about we skip it tonight?"

"This is the first night since the last time."

"What is?" But I know before he even says a word. It's exactly what I just thought about, and the fact that it's obviously been weighing on Adam, too, but he's done it for me? Just another knife in my already bleeding stomach.

"That we're not fucking when I stay over. Since we had that talk. The R-talk. You know, that word we don't say. The one you're still avoiding, even if you pretend you're not."

My stomach churns, dropping at what he says, but he's right. While I've kept up everything with Adam—our non-date dates and our evenings in and our mind-blowing sex—I've put him in a very distinct section in my head, and it only got more defined after that talk. He's in a box that clearly states our relationship is sex-based.

But more than that, what we have is labeled with bright red Sharpie, permanently marked: TEMPORARY.

AS SUSPECTED, ADAM passed out as soon as he hit the mattress. He's sprawled out on his stomach on his side of the bed, arm hanging over me…still finding a way to touch me even though he's dead to the world. And here I lie. Eyes wide, blinking up at the ceiling, stomach churning at everything that whipped through my overactive mind tonight.

I can't even pretend I didn't know it was coming. It's been building. I know that. I can avoid it all I want, but at the end of the day, the shit always catches up with me.

What's throwing me for a loop are all my conflicting feelings about it. I thought there'd be relief when Adam's time came to a close. Instead I feel…sad. Helpless. Like sand is slipping through my fingers, and I have no way of catching it. I've been waiting for this abstract day, a time that seemed too far away and yet too close at the same time. I've been stashing it away as my get out of jail free card, and it turns out…I don't mind being in jail so much?

I don't know what the fuck is going on with me. I have no idea where my head is, or how to work out this jumbled mess of shit taking up residence there. And since I'm not going to get time by myself to just think, what with Adam's deep breaths rumbling in my ear, his arm a heavy weight over my stomach, what I need is straight talk from someone who's seen the shit end of relationships. I need a no BS answer from the one person I can trust to give it to me, especially now.

Fifteen minutes later, I'm knocking on Dillon's door, clad in a vintage My Little Pony T-shirt, ripped sweatpants, and a pair of flip-flops. I glance at the time on my phone—4:05 a.m.—and cringe. At least it's Saturday—or very early Sunday, anyway—so he doesn't have to work. And he's always been a night owl. Plus, there's a blue glow coming from behind the shades in the living room, so I know he's still awake. Sure enough, thirty seconds later, he opens the door, his eyebrows shooting up on his forehead when he sees me.

"Punky?" He glances behind me, then looks around, like he's

expecting I brought trouble with me right to his doorstep. "Everything okay?"

"Yeah." I nod, brushing stray hairs away from my face. "Yeah. Everything's totally fine. Super great."

He narrows his eyes at me, one hand resting on the doorknob. "There's that 'super great' thing again." Pushing the door open wider, he gestures me inside. "When you're 'super great', you don't show up on the doorstep of your big brother at ass o'clock in the morning."

"Yeah, sorry about that. I didn't wake you, did I?"

"Nah, I was watching some TV." He doesn't say it's because he has a hard time sleeping...has had a hard time sleeping since his tours, and even more trouble since everything that happened with Steph. "You want a beer or something?"

"No, I definitely don't need more alcohol tonight."

"Ah, so this is alcohol induced," he says as he sits on the couch, feet propped up on the coffee table.

I toss my keys on the table and take a seat next to him, tucking my leg under me as I face him. "Yeah, you could say that. Funny thing is, only half of it was *my* consumption of the alcohol."

He shakes his head. "You lost me."

I take a deep breath, running my thumbnails over the pads of my fingers. "There's this guy..."

Dillon groans, head thrown back against the couch, as he scrubs a hand over his face. "Can't you talk to Mom about this? Wouldn't that be more appropriate, anyway?"

"It's not about sex, idiot."

That only makes him groan louder. "Jesus Christ, why does everyone in this family insist on reminding me you're having sex?"

"Dill...I'm twenty-three. What were *you* doing at twenty-three?"

He's quiet for a minute, then he inclines his head toward me. "Fair point."

I reach down and pick at the tattered hem of my sweat pants, not able to look at him. "So here's the thing…I've done something stupid."

"Gonna have to be a bit more specific, Punky."

Glaring, I backhand him in the stomach. "Don't be an ass. I'm trying to have a moment with you."

"All right. I'm sorry. What's going on? What'd you do that's stupid?"

Shaking my head, I wave a dismissive hand, brushing off his question. He doesn't need to know that I set this thing up with Adam with the full intent of only taking what I wanted—sex—and leaving all the rest—emotions—by the wayside. Or that my plan hasn't exactly worked. Or worse, that it's actually backfired. "The details aren't important. What I need from you is honesty. I need you to tell me that love is a fairy tale. That relationships are a waste of time. That what Mom and Dad have is the exception, not the rule. They're the one in a million we hear stories about, but they're the kind of stories that never actually happen to the rest of us. I need to hear it's nothing but heartache and agony and bitterness when it all inevitably comes crashing down."

He stares at me, his face unreadable. "Jesus, he really did a number on you, didn't he?"

My brow furrows. "What? Who?"

"Bryan."

I huff out a humorless laugh. "Yeah, I guess he did. But that's my point, Dill, it's not just him."

"Well, it's more than just Mom and Dad who have a good relationship. What about Tessa? She's happy with Jason."

Grudgingly, I admit he's right. "Yeah, okay, and Cade and Winter, too, but that's three couples out of *alllll* the others. I've watched too many people get their hearts stomped on. I've seen enough heartache happen around me that it affected me, too. Or have you forgotten Steph?" I immediately feel like a jerk when he snaps his mouth shut and clenches his jaw. "I'm sorry. That was a shitty thing to say. I'm an asshole."

"No argument from me." He leans forward, resting his elbows on his knees, and looks over at me. "Look, you want honesty, right?"

Straightening up on the couch, I nod. "Yes. Do your worst."

"Okay…honestly, I can say you shouldn't be afraid of this stuff now, Punky."

I'm so shocked by his answer, I can only blink at him for a few moments. Then I sputter. "What? No. No, that's not—what about everything that happened? What about last year and all the hours we clocked on Skype? I *know* it still hurts. I can see it in your eyes. You lived it, just like me. I know what kind of pain that causes."

He presses his palms together, looking down at them as he gives a short nod. "I did. And you're right. It hurts like a bitch… still. But the thing is, I'm thirty-three. I've had a decade of living, of wading through the shit, that you haven't even experienced. You shouldn't give up before you even have the chance to start."

"So you're saying, what, exactly?"

"I'm saying…you need to wade through the shit, Paige. Yeah, my marriage was crap, but there were relationships before her that weren't all bad. Relationships I learned things from—things about myself, and things about how to be involved with someone, and things about how *not* to be with someone. It's a mixed bag, but that's how it is with anything you do. Not everything's perfect."

"You telling me you're gonna get married again?"

"Fuck no. What I'm saying is you can't let the mistakes of others stop you from figuring out your own. You're a work in progress. Don't be so jaded that you ignore the parts of you that still need to grow."

Shaking my head, I blow out a breath. "Well, fuck. That's not what you're supposed to say. You're supposed to remind me of everything that's bad about relationships."

"Actually, I think you do that fine on your own. I think you need me to remind you of everything that's good about them."

"He's leaving, Dill. Moving back to Colorado in two weeks. There's no way this can have a happy ending."

"Then enjoy it while it's here, and then let it go. Just don't get all tied up in him, and you'll be all right."

It's great advice. Too bad it's too late.

TWENTY-EIGHT

adam

I wake to an empty bed and cool sheets, a marching band stomping around in my head and a dead rodent in my mouth. Groaning, I roll over on my back and blink at the ceiling in the early morning light coming through the sheer curtains in Paige's room.

How the hell did I end up in Paige's room?

As I close my eyes, bits and pieces of last night start coming to me. Talking to my dad about not taking over at the shop. Jase showing up at my place unannounced. The Jack he took out so he could commiserate properly. Then Cade coming over, and me spilling my guts to both of them—that I was falling for Paige.

And at some point during the night, coming to the realization that I'm not *falling* in love with her.

I'm already there.

Which is a cruel joke if I've ever heard one. I've been searching my whole life for a girl who could be mine. Permanently. And the one I finally find? Doesn't want to be anyone's.

But the thing is, I want more. I've always wanted more, and I thought I could pretend otherwise. I thought I could be okay with getting only half of her. Turns out I'm not. I want the whole thing. The good and the bad, the messy and ugly along with all the shiny, near-perfect parts. I want all of her to be mine.

And I want her to come with me.

That realization hit me somewhere around my third glass of Jack, but the certainty behind it is still there now, in the light of day. After spending all this time looking for someone like her, someone who fits me so perfectly...someone who challenges me and makes me laugh and turns me the hell on...I know it's not going to come again for a long, long time. If ever.

And I'm not willing to throw that away without trying. I'm done avoiding and I'm done tiptoeing around the subject because she needs me to. We're not putting it off anymore. I'm scheduled to leave in a little less than two weeks, so there's no better time than now to have the talk.

But first, I have to deal with this massive hangover and then find out why she's not in bed with me. Grabbing my glasses, I stumble my way to the bathroom, rummaging for some Ibuprofen to help with this headache, then swallow them with a few handfuls of water from the faucet. By the time I make it into the living room, I still haven't heard any noise from anywhere in the apartment. Paige isn't curled up on the couch. She isn't in the kitchen. Her entire place is empty, and just as I start to get a little worried about where the hell she could be, a key sounds in the lock, and in tiptoes Paige, clad in her pajamas.

She doesn't see me as she kicks off her flip-flops and quietly sets down her keys on the counter, before she turns to walk toward her bedroom.

"Did I actually manage to scare you out of your own apartment last night?"

She screams, jumping and spinning to face me. I can't help

but laugh, and that, mixed with her scream, does nothing for my raging headache.

"Holy shit, Adam. What are you doing up? It's not even six."

I rest my ass against the back of the couch, bracing my hands on either side of my hips. "I could ask you the same thing."

"I…" Clearing her throat, she avoids eye contact, glancing off to the side. "I, um, needed to talk to Dillon."

Raising my eyebrows, I ask, "You needed to talk to your brother in the middle of the night?"

She nods, running the pads of her pointer fingers over the tips of her thumbnails, but otherwise doesn't say anything. She doesn't have to, though. Her nervous gesture speaks volumes.

"Ahh…" I nod and glance down at my bare feet before looking back to her. "About me, huh? Guess I should take that as a compliment. What horribly awkward things did I say to you in the name of Jack? Because I have to be honest… I don't remember a lot after my fifth glass."

"You called me baby."

"That's horrible."

She laughs and her posture relaxes, and I feel my shoulders lose a bit of tension. "That's what you said last night."

"What else did I say? Because something sent you to your brother, and I'm guessing it's not me calling you baby, despite your aversion to it."

A small smile graces her lips, and she shrugs. "Not much else. Just something about how you never stay the night unless we have sex."

I clear my throat, scrutinizing her. "Well, that's true."

"It is."

"Anything more?"

"Um…you said Mrs. Connelly was going to steal you away from me and how I wouldn't even put up a fight. That I wouldn't fight for you."

I swallow, tightening my grip on the back of her couch and brace myself for the answer to the question I need to ask. "And what about that? Is that true?"

"I…I don't know. Does it even matter? Our time is almost up."

"It matters to me."

"Adam…" She exhales and looks down, her words tinged with a sadness I haven't heard from her before. "We only have a couple weeks left."

I'm silent as I study her, trying to read the quiet cues she's giving. I know I'm not misreading the resignation I heard in her voice when she mentioned me leaving. That gives me the encouragement I need. "That's not all it has to be. It can be more, if we want it to be."

She snaps her head up to look at me, her eyes flitting back and forth between mine, and she takes a step toward me. "What do you mean? Are you…I mean, do you think you might move back here?"

I let the hopeful tone in her voice reassure me and take a deep breath, ready to lay my heart on the line and trusting she won't stomp on it. "Actually, I was kind of hoping it could be the other way around."

Her brow furrows, and she shakes her head. "I don't understand… What other way around?"

"I was hoping you might want to move. To Colorado. With me."

TWENTY-NINE

paige

Jesus. This can't be happening. No, seriously, this *cannot be happening.* How much growth is one girl expected to do on any given day? Because this? Adam asking me to uproot my life? To move with him? After I *just* decided I could throw caution to the wind and go all in for the two whopping weeks he has left here?

What in the actual fuck.

I sputter, soundless words falling from my lips as a million scenarios fly through my mind, the dozens of reasons I can't go whipping behind my eyes. "But...I have to finish my master's. And then there's the full-time analyst position I've been working toward."

"Your master's is done, though, right? You just have to finish your internship and defend your thesis? And there are analyst positions there. Denver has a police department, you know." He's teasing, the lilt in his voice and the smirk on his face telling me so, but none of that soothes me. Because all I can focus on is how he's rewriting all my plans.

And all I can think about is the fact that I've been here before. When I was seventeen and too stupid to know any better. When I let a guy take an eraser to everything I worked toward, to my life plans, and scribble his in over top of them. Then I stood by when he decided he had enough. I watched him crumple up the paper with my new life scrawled in his script and throw it away when he didn't have a use for me anymore, taking all my plans—the ones I made with him, and the ones he erased that I'd made for myself—with him, making me scramble to put myself back together in the end.

The redesigned me Adam wants to rewrite now, too.

I wipe my sweaty palms on my pants, then cross my arms against my chest. My entire body is covered in a light sheen of sweat borne of uncertainty, but my jaw is quivering, my whole body a live wire, my stomach a twisted ball of nerves. As calmly as I can, I say, "I can't just leave, Adam. My family's here. And my friends. And, yeah, Denver has a police department, but I'd have to start all over there. I've worked hard for this. I've busted my ass, and I'm pretty damn sure they're going to offer me the position. I can't leave that…"

He's quiet for a moment, then he glances up at me from under his ridiculously long eyelashes, behind the frames of his black-rimmed glasses. "Not even for me?"

That snaps my spine straight, and my anger rears its head. "Don't do that. That's an asshole move. It's not fair, and you know it. Don't put that on me. What about you? Why can't you stay here? Your parents' shop is here, and you're doing a fantastic job of running it. Why can't you do that? After seeing you working there, I can't imagine you being happy sitting in an office all day on the computer."

He shakes his head, looking down. "I can't. I moved to Colorado to get away from all that. No, sitting in an office all day isn't the most exciting job in the world, but it's *stable*. I don't want the uncertainty that comes with running the shop. Coming back here would be like throwing away the last seven years of my life and everything I've worked toward."

"And it wouldn't be like that for me? I'm working toward stuff, too. Why is your reason more important than mine?"

"It's not about whose issues are more important, Paige. Sometimes you have to compromise in relationships."

"And yet I'd be the one compromising everything and you wouldn't be compromising anything." Just like before. Once again, I'd be the one bending to someone else's will. Once again, I'd be abandoning my plans for the happiness of someone else.

He laughs, but the sound is hollow. "I think we both know who's been compromising the past three months, and it hasn't been you. Maybe it's your turn."

"Maybe it's—" I cut off, shaking my head and taking a deep breath, not wanting to fight with him over something he's never mentioned, even offhandedly. We've never, not once, discussed the possibility of me moving there. Hell, we've never discussed what would happen in *October*, after he was set to leave. "This isn't fair. That night when I freaked out—you said nothing had to change between us. And now you're trying to change it into something you knew I never wanted."

"*We* changed." He flicks his finger between us, his voice hard. "Whether you're too goddamn stubborn to admit it or not, we changed. And you were in this with me, one hundred percent, whether you pretend you weren't or not. I'm just asking you to be with me one hundred percent in Colorado."

Shaking my head, I press my fingers to my eyes, inhaling a shaky breath. "I don't know where this is coming from or why all of the sudden—"

He steps into my space, pulls my hands away from my face, and looks at me, his thumbs caressing my palms. "I love you. I'm in love with you, Paige. That's where it's coming from. That's why I want you to come with me. I want us to be together. I want you to be mine, for real and for good. None of these safety nets you've put in place. No expiration date. Just me, you, and Colorado." He entwines his fingers with my shaking ones. "The question is, do you want that, too? Do you feel this thing between us?"

Memories of my time with Adam come to me, flooding my mind with happiness. With laughter and fun and intensity and passion. It's been the best summer of my life; there's no denying that. But is that enough?

Suddenly the picture book behind my closed eyes changes, and in place of the past few months with Adam, I'm remembering things from years ago, things I've tried hard to forget, tried for years to block out. Making plans around Bryan's. Rewriting my college picks to be the places he got accepted. Missing the deadline on my number one school because of it. Paying my deposit for FSU—the school we were going off to together—two days before finding him fucking that other girl in my car.

Remembering that shuts me down cold. I won't go through that again. Won't change my life for a guy. Not when I can't be sure he'll stick around.

I tug my hands away from his and cross my arms. "I can't believe you'd ask me to do that, to uproot my life because you want me to, after you know everything Bryan did to me."

His jaw tics as he stares at me, and this is the maddest I've ever seen Adam. He doesn't get upset. Doesn't get riled or worked up. He's even-tempered and calm, but right now there's a storm brewing behind his sky blue eyes. "And I can't believe you're still comparing me to some asshole from your past who I am in no way like, and I've proven that time and time again." He runs a frustrated hand through his hair and shakes his head. "But you're not ever going to get that, are you? I'm always going to be compared to the guy who broke your heart. Whether we're five or a thousand miles apart, we never had a chance."

I don't say anything. Find I can't, because maybe he's right. Maybe this was doomed from the start.

The room falls into a heavy silence, and I don't dare look up at him, instead focusing on the carpet under our feet. I wish I hadn't dropped his hand. Suddenly I want to feel it in mine, because I know this will be the last time. Any minute now he's going to pull away and walk out that door, and that'll be it. He'll be gone from my life, and it'll be just another reminder of exactly why I don't traverse this pothole-ridden road that love and commitment are on.

I hold my breath when he reaches up, brushing the hair back from my face as he closes the distance between us. He tilts my head back, and I close my eyes before I can see him, before I can look into those bottomless eyes, and then his lips are on mine. His kiss is soft and tentative, just the barest whisper of his mouth on mine, and it's not enough. I don't have time to memorize the feel or the taste of his lips or what his body is like against mine before he steps back.

"Goodbye, Paige."

I sense him moving away from me, but I don't dare open my eyes. I'm too afraid of what I'll see. Too afraid I'll crumble and go after him, agree to his ridiculous plans because...what? Because we had a great time for two months? Like that's enough on which to build a lasting relationship. Like that's reason enough to uproot my life, to totally fuck over my career, and start over.

The quiet snick of the door shutting behind him is like a foghorn in the otherwise quiet room, and I exhale a deep breath, my shoulders curling forward as the weight against my chest presses harder.

He's gone, walked away from me when I wouldn't change everything in my life, rewrite it to fit his. I shouldn't have listened to the advice Dillon gave me. I should've listened to my gut. Since the beginning of this thing with Adam, it's been whispering for me to leave, to get the hell away. And this just proves why all my avoidance was necessary.

All love brings is heartache and pain, and no matter what lesson I got out of this *relationship*, it isn't worth the tears trailing down my cheeks, or the stabbing pain in my heart, or the agony twisting my insides.

It isn't worth shit, and I'd do good to remember that.

THIRTY

adam

It's my last day here before I go back home. *Home.* The word puts a sour taste in my mouth, the idea that my home be somewhere other than here all wrong. Funny how I've been in Colorado for seven years and it has never felt like home like this place does. Even my shitty apartment across from Paige felt more like home than my place in Denver ever has.

Paige.

Just the thought of her name brings an empty feeling to my gut, an ache to my chest. The morning I walked away, I had to force myself not to turn around. Not to go back and tell her it was the hangover talking. That I'd be happy to take whatever she could give me.

But I forced myself to stand my ground, because the thing is, I know I won't be satisfied with the tiny bit she was willing to give, and there's no more denying the way I feel toward her. Not now. Not after I'd tasted those words on my tongue, looked in her eyes when

I told her I loved her, and watched the sheer terror reflected back at me in hers. She's running away from everything I've ever run toward.

But more than that, she's *terrified* of it.

And it makes me an idiot for thinking it could ever work between us. How did I delude myself enough to think I could be happy with the scraps she tossed my way? That I'd be happy being in an extended one-night stand?

Except I know it was more than that. *We* were more than that. Paige can deny it all she wants, but I know. We were in a relationship, even if we never defined it until that middle of the night panic attack. Even if we didn't use the label, never said the word, it doesn't change what it was well before that night, either.

I've dealt with breakups. I might not be as versed as Cade or Jase when it comes to having dozens of girls in my bed, but I'm a step ahead of them when it comes to the messy parts—the parts they never wanted to deal with. The tears and the harsh words and the heartache that comes from giving up on something that's been a part of you for so long.

My shortest relationship before Paige was just over a year, and that breakup didn't hurt nearly as bad as the split from my high school girlfriend of two and a half years. I don't know if it was the fact that Nikki had been my first in everything...if it was because we broke up not because of some fight or disagreement or loss of interest but instead because of circumstances—she was going to school in Texas and I was going to Colorado, and we decided it'd be best to cut our losses. If it was the fact that she was my longest relationship, and thus I had the most invested in it.

It doesn't feel that way now, though. Logically, Paige should be the easiest to get over if I'm going by time invested. Two months is nothing in the grand scheme of things. It's the blink of an eye, a blip on the radar.

But if that's the case, why do I have this hollow feeling in my chest? This *ache* that's radiating out, spreading everywhere until it's all I can feel, even after more than a week since I've seen her face or heard her voice. Since I've had her pressed up against me, listened to her heckle me about some sport we went head to head on. Since I've gotten a ridiculous text about how they make the fake blood for horror movies.

I've never had to deal with unreciprocated love, and I can honestly say a kick in the nuts with a steel-toed boot would hurt less.

"You're all packed?" Cade's voice interrupts my thoughts, and I shift on the chair on the back patio, grateful for the distraction.

"Yeah, got everything loaded last night, so I could leave whenever today." I have the few things I brought from home shoved in my car, my suitcase full of clothes stuffed in the trunk.

Cade, Jase, and I moved everything out of my apartment and back into my parents' basement yesterday. I don't know if it was a blessing or a curse that I didn't see Paige once. Not in person, anyway. I've dreamt about her, though. Every night, and there's no getting around it. Everything's back to just like it was after that night in December—the night that changed everything.

Except now it's a thousand times worse, because I know who she is. Paige isn't just a pretty girl anymore, someone with a gorgeous face and a killer body who knows her way around a bedroom. She's sarcastic and funny and adventurous and smart and not mine.

Now when I dream of her, I know exactly what I'm missing.

Cade stretches his legs out in front of him and takes a sip of coffee from the mug my mom handed him. She's been flitting around for the past two days, hovering with that sad look on her face, shooting me worried glances. My parents have always met all my girlfriends. Even the ones who lived in Colorado. It seems weird that they don't even know about Paige when she's taken up such a huge part of my life for the summer. But even without knowing her, even without knowing I was seeing someone, I think they realize something's up. My mom especially. She has this weird sixth sense about stuff like that.

"You gonna try and drive straight through?" Cade asks, glancing over at me.

"Nah." I shake my head. "I think I'll stop somewhere in Iowa. The last couple days have been long, and I don't wanna fall asleep at the wheel."

Jase shifts in his seat, but he doesn't say anything. They both know it's more than a couple days that have been long. Neither of them has asked anything about Paige, but they don't need to. You don't have two decades of friendship under your belt without knowing certain things, and they've been with me enough through other break-ups that they know what one looks like.

"I sure am gonna miss these apple pies your mom's been fueling me with," Jase says as he pats his stomach. "Though it's probably a good thing. I was starting to get a pudge."

I breathe out a laugh and shake my head. "You know she'd bake you one whenever you want. In fact, I'm pretty sure she'd *love* it."

"Yeah, but I'm just a substitute for the real deal." He pauses as he takes a sip of his coffee. "A much funnier, much better looking substitute, but a substitute all the same."

Cade laughs but the joke falls flat for me, because Jason's words ring a little truer than I'd like. I've never felt guilty before when leaving. I don't know what's different about this time. No, I haven't been home for a summer in a few years—not since I graduated—but this isn't the first one I've spent back here. It's also not the first one I've spent working at the shop. It shouldn't feel any different.

But it *is* different. In all the times I've worked at the shop, that's all it's been. Just me, running the register, helping customers, being a fill-in for any other worker. This time, though, I *did* something. I revived the business, breathed life into it, and it almost feels like I'm leaving a piece of myself behind.

"You guys remember that time we snuck out of here to go to that party at Mallory's house in high school?" Cade asks. Jase laughs as I groan, remembering that night like it was yesterday. "That much funnier, better looking substitute got us out of a shitload of trouble. I still don't think your mom called our parents," he says to me. Then he turns to Jase. "How'd you manage that, anyway?"

"A professional flirt never shares his secrets."

"Hey, asshole, you just admitted to flirting with my mom," I say, though there's no heat behind it. Jase's been flirting with her for as long as I can remember. "Breaks bro-code, dude."

"He's right." Cade tips his head in my direction.

"Yeah, well, I didn't see either of you complain when we were sixteen and didn't get our asses handed to us by our parents. I can't help that moms love me. And some *love* me." He breathes a deep sigh, closing his eyes. "Remember Mrs. Wheeler?"

"Oh Jesus," Cade and I groan the same time. Then I say, "Do we really have to hear this story again?"

"Did either of you ever get with a hot cougar when you were eighteen? No? I didn't think so, so shut the hell up and live vicariously through me like good goddamn best friends would." He reaches up, rubbing his jaw and looking thoughtful. "I should really send her some flowers or something in thanks. She taught me how to eat pussy. And *that* has come in handier than anything else I learned my entire high school career."

"*Dude.*" Cade shoots a sharp glare at Jason, and I can only snicker behind my mug.

"What?" He shrugs. "You never complained about my stories before. And now that it's your sis—" Jase holds out his coffee mug when Cade pushes off his chair to stand. "Don't take another step, man. I have hot coffee, and I'm not afraid to use it."

"I have fists and I'm not afraid to use them, either. Keep your fucking mouth shut." Cade shoves a finger in Jase's direction as he sits back down, grumbling under his breath about best friends and baby sisters and the horror of it all.

All I can do is laugh. I've loved being around them while I've been home. With college and jobs and life, it's been too long since we've had more than a couple days at a time to hang out. I'm going to miss it. I'm going to miss *everything* about this place.

Cade breaks the silence a few minutes later. "All joking aside, it's been nice having you home. It'd be great to have you here all the time."

"Yeah, especially since I can't even breathe a word about Tess around this asshole before he gets his panties in a twist," Jase says, hooking his thumb toward Cade.

"Don't pretend like you don't call me and talk about that shit all the time." I stretch my legs out, folding my hands together over my stomach. "It has been nice, but I can't stay. You guys know that. Don't start in on me, too. My mom hasn't let up. Every day, I get another pleading look or a bribe pie."

"All right, we'll drop it." Jason clears his throat, and I don't miss the glance he shoots at Cade. "So, uh, have you talked to Paige lately?"

It was too much to think I could get away with not talking about it with them. I should just be happy they've given me a reprieve from everything since The Night of Epic Drunkenness. I grab my coffee off the patio table and take a sip, really wishing it were something a little stronger, even with the memory of that alcohol-fest fresh in my mind. Might make saying this out loud a little easier.

I shake my head. "Nope. Not for a while."

"So that's it?" Cade asks.

I shrug. "Not much more there could be."

"You're not even going to try to keep something going long distance?" Jase looks over at me, but I avoid his gaze, staring out at the backyard.

"There's no point."

"Did she say that?" Cade cuts in. "That she didn't want to try?"

"Not in so many words."

"What words did she use, jackass?" Jase asks. "Jesus, you're worse than Tess when she's pissed. Give us something to work with."

I take another drink of my coffee. Blow out a deep breath. Cross my arms against my chest. All in all, that takes about seventeen seconds. Not nearly enough time to prepare myself to say the words out loud, but I do. "I told her I loved her. Asked her to move with me. She said no. Not sure what else there is to say."

The silence that follows is so heavy, it might as well be a ton of bricks pressing down on me. Finally, Cade clears his throat, and Jase starts in on that one time we dyed the pool purple in high school and managed to never get caught. Before long, they both have me laughing again, despite the hollow feeling in my gut at the thought of leaving.

That laughter, almost more than anything, is what I'll miss when I'm gone.

THIRTY-ONE

paige

I love my family, but I'm starting to get a little sick of them. I've managed to rotate between both my brothers' places and my parents' house over the last week and a half, limiting the time I spent at my apartment. Not because of any reason other than I missed them. It definitely didn't have to do with a certain tall, dark, and handsome hottie who reached into my chest, pulled my heart out, and put it through a meat grinder.

I think they can all tell something's up, but other than Dillon, none of them knows anything. When asked, I blame it on the stress at the station, worrying about getting the job offer, and defending my thesis. That it helps me relax to be around them. So far, they've all bought it, but I don't know for how long that's going to last.

And I'm not sure when I'll be able to walk through the doors to my apartment building and not have a sinking feeling in my stomach, a dread in my chest. Not be bombarded with memories of the past few months.

"Punky! Your phone's been blasting like a motherfucker. Answer it already. Jesus," Tanner shouts from the kitchen, mixing up another batch of margaritas to go with our chips and queso and our marathon sit-in of *24*.

Dragging myself up from the couch, I go into the kitchen and grab my phone off the counter while Tanner turns on the blender. I have four missed calls, all from Tessa, and a text that simply says, *call me*. Walking away from the whirring noise and down the hall, I dial her number and wait for her to answer.

"Hey," she says, relief in her voice.

"Hi, what's up? Everything okay?"

She's quiet for a minute. "I was going to ask you the same thing."

Furrowing my brow, I glance around. "Yeah, I'm fine. Why would you ask?"

She clears her throat and avoids the question. "Where are you?"

"Tanner's. We're marathoning *24* and having margaritas."

"Have you, um, have you been home lately?"

She doesn't need to know I crashed at Dillon's place the past two nights because I was too chickenshit to go to my apartment. Too afraid I'd run into Adam again and the pain in my chest would increase tenfold. It was all I could do to tell her about it the day after Adam decided to throw me for a fucking loop. I made it seem like it wasn't a big deal, shrugged, then pretended I needed a new pair of red wedges, so I dragged her to the mall and partook in some retail therapy. Since? I haven't said a word about that jerk with the meat grinder, and neither has she. I'm not going to start now.

Evading a bit, I say, "Not for a while, why?"

"I just wanted to make sure you were okay." There's movement on her end of the line, then she blows out a breath. "You know...with Adam leaving."

It's just a handful of words. Certainly not enough to make it feel like the ground disappeared from under me. Like I'm in a free fall to a black and bottomless hole. It shouldn't feel like all the oxygen in the room's been sucked out, and I'm gasping for air. It was only a couple months. A handful of days. How was he able to affect me so much?

I clear my throat and try to keep my voice even. "I, uh, I thought he was leaving next week?"

Tessa's voice is tentative, her *I'm sorry* and *I didn't know how else to tell you* and *How can I help?* clear in every word. "He got things squared away at the shop, so he decided to go early."

"So he's...he's gone? He left?"

"Yeah. Jason and Cade helped him move out of the apartment yesterday. He left this morning."

"Oh."

That's good, though, right? He's gone now. I can go back to my apartment. I don't have to couch hop between every one of my family members. I don't have to worry about pulling into the parking lot at the same time as him. Don't have to worry about running into him as I get my mail, or as I'm on my way out. Don't have to worry about him tagging along to whatever activity I'm getting up to.

I should say all of that, tell her I'm okay. That this is good. It's totally fine. Better this way, really. Instead, all I manage is another, "Oh."

"What season are you on?"

"Huh?"

"*24*," she says. "What season are you watching?"

"Oh, um, we're just starting Season 2."

"Really? That's perfect. I never saw the second season. Maybe I can come over? I'll bring ice cream. Does Tanner still love rocky road?"

I want to cry. I want to sag against the wall and slouch down to the floor, tuck my knees to my chest and sob. Sob until I expel all these feelings, the ones weighing me down inside, the ones making it difficult to talk or think or dream or breathe. I don't know if it's better or worse that Adam left earlier than planned. It shouldn't change anything; I haven't seen him since that morning in my apartment, so this doesn't affect me. Not really. Except now, it feels like he's a million miles away. Out of my reach. Like even the possibility of more has been snatched away, taken out of my grasp, and there's no going back from that.

There's no hope for us now. It's done. Over. For good.

Pressing my forehead against the wall, I close my eyes. "Yeah, it's his favorite." My voice is scratchy, the product of me denying the tears that want to come, but Tessa doesn't comment on it.

"Rocky road it is. And double fudge brownie for us. Since I'll be at the store anyway, I was maybe thinking I'd grab some of those lemon bars from the bakery. And I saw this thing on Pinterest for peanut butter s'mores dip. God, it looked *amazing*. I think I'll grab stuff to make that, too. Can't have too many munchies for a TV marathon."

"You're going to make me gain twenty pounds."

"I love you, too. I'll see you soon."

I press the end button on my phone and stare at the black glass screen, tears blurring my vision. I'm not sure how long I stand there before Tanner calls from the living room, "Who was that? Tess? She comin' over? See if she can bring some of that salsa Cade makes. That shit is fucking delicious."

Huffing out a laugh, I shake my head, blinking the tears out of my eyes and allowing them to trail down my face. Those are it. The last tears I'll shed for Adam. The last ones I'll allow myself.

I chose this path. Made this decision to let him walk away without me, and I'm sticking with it. I've got my family and friends here. A job I can't wait to start. I'll be all right. I'm living the life I love.

Even if it is a life without Adam.

THIRTY-TWO

adam

Even after a couple weeks of being back in Colorado, time I've spent at the office, doing the job I've been anxious to get back to, I'm still waiting for that sense of accomplishment to come when I leave at the end of the day. Will it hit me today, when I walk in through my door? When I take off my crisp white shirt and pressed black pants and don't have to shower off dirt or sweat, will I think about what a great job I did today? How I achieved something, helped to make something stronger by my day's work? Or will it be the same as it's been every other night for weeks?

While I'm supposed to be engrossed in a client's project, all I can think about is the shop. How it's doing. If Mom and Dad have remembered to change out the signs advertising the new classes coming up for the fall. If they've hired the new guides yet. And if they have, are the people they got qualified enough to handle everything?

As I push through my door and toss my keys on the counter, I try to remember what it was like before I left. How I felt at the end of each day, because it had to have been there before, right? That sense of accomplishment at the end of the day. At some point before I went back home and before I worked at the shop and before I brought it back to life, I felt it... At some point while working here, I felt it, didn't I?

I unbutton the crisp white shirt I've come to hate as I head toward the shower, even though I don't need one. Doesn't matter. It gives me something to do, and it takes my mind of things. Things like...what if I didn't feel that accomplishment? What if I've *never* felt it, but I didn't know any better? And I spent the time at my parents' shop thinking it'd be here when I got back, only to find it was never here in the first place.

I spent the summer in Michigan waiting to get back to this place, with its stability and reliability and predictability, counting down the weeks until I'd be back on solid ground, not fumbling through miles and miles of uncertainty and doubt. And all I've been able to think about since I've been back is everything I left behind. *Paige.* Everything I turned my back on because it wasn't the safe route or the easy route. *Paige.*

And that makes me wonder how much of my life has been planned out with those thoughts in mind? I went to UNC not because it was my top choice, but because I was able to get a nice scholarship there, easing financial strain. I eventually shoved baseball aside, even though I loved it, even though I was damn good at it, because I never saw it as a plausible future for me. I got my degree in accounting not because I love working with numbers, but because I'm good at it, and I knew I could make a solid living doing it.

Has any part of my adult life been something I've chosen because I *wanted* to? Because I loved it too much to turn my back on it, to choose a different, easier path?

Every memory I have is tainted with thoughts of what I've done under the guise of this misconception that I needed to live this way. The girls I dated...have I really liked the quiet, docile types, or did I just gravitate toward them because it was easy? Because they didn't challenge me? Not like a certain opinionated, outgoing blonde does.

A certain opinionated, outgoing blonde who turned her back on me. Who made her choice.

Looks like I made mine, too.

paige

I thought it would help, knowing Adam's gone, but it doesn't. Walking through the door of my apartment building has been just as hard as it was that last week before he left. Harder, because even though I didn't want to see him, there was a part of me that sort of hoped I would. Now, though, that possibility is squashed.

Even with things keeping me busy at the station with Detective Dodd having me track down leads, I think about him too much. Especially when I'm home with nothing else to occupy my time. And it's not like I can do any of the things I used to love. Whenever I try watching a favorite movie, I have the sudden urge to text Adam a stupid line from the dialogue. One time I barely caught myself before pressing Send, and *God*, wouldn't that have been a bitch to explain? *Oh, hey, Adam, just can't stop thinking about you is all, even though I let you walk away...*

What's worse, I can't even go out and do any of the activities I used to love, because I've done them all with him, thanks to those stupid fucking non-date dates. I see his face at yoga, when I go rock climbing or rappelling. Paintball, laser tag, biking along the lake... even running in my neighborhood. Wherever I go, whatever I do, he's there, his eyes penetrating, his lips unmoving, as he stares at me. Untouchable.

He even ruined B.O.B. for me, the bastard, and I haven't been able to get myself off since he left. Not that I even have the urge anymore, but sometimes I wake up in the middle of the night, my body on fire, the sheets wrapped around my ankles and my panties wet, totally unsatisfied because I can't even dream of him without pulling myself away.

And isn't that just a bitch? I won't go after him in real life, and I punish myself for it by not even allowing it in my dreams.

I don't realize I'm frozen in front of Adam's door, just staring blankly at it, until a throat clears from the staircase.

"'Scuse me, dear, do you know where I'd drop this key off? My son forgot to return it. I thought there'd be an office somewhere, but I can't find one, and I've been all around the property. Do you live here?"

I glance over my shoulder, and when I spot the woman standing there, we both freeze. All the air vanishes from my lungs—just, *poof,* gone. I try to remember how to talk. How to smile. How to *something,* but I can't. Mrs. Reid recovers before I do, a huge smile sweeping over her face as she continues down the steps until she's on the landing next to me. "I remember you. Rappelling gloves, right?" She glances at the door I was just staring at, the door that was Adam's, and when she looks back at me, she has this knowing glint in her eyes. I didn't say a goddamn word, but it's like she knows everything without me having to. "This makes more sense now…"

I finally find my voice. "What does?"

"My son scrambling to move in here when he had a perfectly usable room at our house." She smiles then, clasping her hands in front of her. "Can I assume your apartment is one of these four?" She gestures to the four doors leading to apartments. "And that you didn't meet for the first time when you came into the shop?"

Not seeing the point in lying, I nod. "Yeah, I'm this one." I gesture behind me toward my door. "And no, we didn't. Adam and I have actually known each other for years, just in passing, though, until this summer. I'm Paige, Tessa's best friend."

"Well, I'll be…" she says as she pats my arm. "Of course, of course. I go to her to get my hair cut, you know. I just love that girl. And her daughter, oh. What a doll. Makes me so happy she and Jason got together. Jason's like a second son to us, you see, especially now after everything with his parents, well…" She tuts and shakes her head. "I'm sure you know. I'm surprised Tessa didn't mention this to me, about you and Adam. Though you know most of the time it's the clients yapping the ears off the poor stylists, just blabbing about anything they can think of." She laughs and pauses, her smile welcoming, her eyes open and bright, telling me it's my turn to talk now after her monologue.

Except I don't have any idea what to say.

Your son told me he loved me, and I ran scared. Like I always do.

I think I might love him, too, but it's too late.

I thought I was happy with my life here, but he's ruined that, too. He's ruined everything.

"Um, it was nice meeting you, Mrs. Reid, but I have a yoga class I need to get to, so I better go…" I jerk my thumb toward my door and pull my keys out.

She looks at me—really looks, the same way Adam does, and it makes me want to cower, to duck away, to *hide*, but I know it'd be no use. She can probably see through me, too—and then she nods. "Oh sure, sure. Nice to meet you, too, Paige. You go on ahead. Sorry to have kept you."

"It's no problem." I try to smile, but it feels more like a grimace, and by the way her brow furrows, her lips tipped down at the corners, I'm sure I'm not too far off. I glance down at her wringing hands and see the key, remembering why she was here in the first place. "Oh, and you can drop the key off upstairs. Apartment 8 is the manager."

"Thank you, dear." She nods, then heads up the stairs and calls over her shoulder, "Hope to see you again soon."

I choke out some sort of reply, but I have no idea if it comes out as anything remotely recognizable because I can't get into my apartment fast enough. Letting my purse and messenger bag fall at my feet, I collapse against the closed door and try to focus on anything but what just happened. About her parting words. I think about my internship, which is done next week, and Captain Peters is letting us know on Friday who got the full-time analyst position. I have a million things I should be concerned about, should be concentrating on, but whenever I close my eyes, it's his I see.

Is that ever going to change?

THIRTY-THREE

adam

Before I left Michigan, I switched the shop to new accounting software, one that lets me to log in from anywhere and keep track of the numbers. I didn't want to allow the shop to slide into a deep hole like the last time…wanted to be able to stop it earlier, if I needed to.

The first week I was home, I saw a decline in sales at the shop. I figured that was to be expected. My mom and dad were still getting their footing with all the changes we made. But then week two was much the same, only worse. Week three? A steady decline. Now, a month after I've been back in Denver, there's no more avoiding it. No more denying it. All the progress I made while I was there is getting erased in the face of declining sales.

Knowing I can't avoid it any longer, I press the speed dial on my phone for my parents and wait for one of them to answer.

"Hi, sweetie! This is a nice surprise," my mom says.

"Hey, Mom. How's it going?"

"Oh, it's going great. We're keeping busy here, but we sure

miss you. Jason's been stopping by more, though. He brought Haley the other day—I tell you what, she's just the sweetest little thing, isn't she? Makes me miss my grandbaby. Can hardly wait for the new baby to be born. Sure would love to spend a couple weeks down there, to help Aubrey." She tuts. "Having a toddler, plus a newborn, Lord, that girl is gonna run herself ragged. She's gonna be a wreck. Just a wreck. Wish there was more we could do. Maybe I'll be able to sneak down for a bit and your dad can run the shop for a while."

This is how every conversation with my mom is. I could set the phone down and walk into another room for ten minutes, not saying a word, and she wouldn't have the faintest idea I'd done it.

Needing to cut in, I say, "That's a good idea. I'm sure she'd appreciate it."

"And I'll get to soak up some of those baby cuddles. Oh, it can't get here fast enough! Now, since it's not Sunday and you're calling anyway, something must be on your mind. What is it, honey? You feeling better now?"

"Better? I've been feeling fine."

"I just meant after you left here…"

I close my eyes, knowing it was too much to hope that she didn't notice anything while I was there. "Yeah, Mom, I'm fine."

She heaves a deep breath. "I was trying to wait patiently for you to tell me this on your own, but it's clear that's not going to happen, so I guess I'll just have to come out with it."

"Out with what?"

"Who the girl is."

I pause, my entire body frozen. "What girl?"

"It's a little late to play dumb, Adam. You forgot to drop off the key to your apartment. I tried calling you, but when I couldn't get through, I tried Jason. He gave me the address, so I thought I'd just run it over." I curse under my breath and close my eyes, because I know what's coming before she even says anything. "Funny thing…I ran into that girl who came into the shop a while back. The stunning blonde getting rappelling gloves. You remember her?"

"I remember," I mumble.

"Mhmm, I just bet you do. I guess I should be happy about it. Makes me feel better that you moved into that apartment to be closer to her. I thought you were doing it to get away from *me!*" She laughs, and my dad's training is hard at work. I keep my mouth shut. "So that's why you were moping around here those last couple days. I couldn't figure it out, but I should've known it was over a girl. You always have been my little lovebird, haven't you? Since you were little. So how are things going with that? I didn't want to ask her—thought that might be overstepping. But she looked—well, I hate to say this. Don't want it to seem like I'm gossiping, you know—but, well, she looked a little run down. Sad. Maybe you need to call her more. Do those video talks and whatnot."

The fact that Paige doesn't look like herself shouldn't fill me with relief. It makes me a Grade A Asshole that it does, but I can't help it. Because maybe it means she wasn't as unfeeling about this whole thing as she led me to believe.

Clearing my throat, I say, "Um, yeah. We dated while I was there, but that was it. We're not still seeing each other."

"No? Hmmm…"

I can practically hear the wheels turning in her mind, and before she can dive into something that I most definitely don't want to get into with my mother, I break in. "Actually, Mom, the reason I was calling is about the shop. Is Dad around? Can we talk on speakerphone?"

"Oh, sure, sweetheart. One sec, let me grab him." She puts the phone away from her mouth and calls for my dad, then they're both there, on speakerphone and waiting for what I have to say.

"How's it been going since I've been gone?"

There's a pause. "Good, good, son. We're playing catch up a bit, but we expected as much. You were doing such a great job of running everything while you were here."

"Dad. Come on, don't BS me. I've got the numbers right in front of me. The first week or two could've been you getting your footing, but a month? What's going on?"

He heaves a deep breath, and I hear my mom whisper, "Just tell him, Calvin."

"Tell me what?"

I don't have to be there to know my mom is looking at my dad with that pointed stare, one eyebrow raised, arms crossed with her finger tapping on the opposite elbow. Dad clears his throat and then turns my whole world upside down. "We're looking into selling the shop, Adam. It's time. Our hearts just aren't in it anymore. We want to travel and see the grandbabies. We want to be able to come out and visit you—you know we've never once been out there? Can't even see what you've worked so hard for. We've loved the shop, but we're tired of being tied to it. We're ready, and we want to do it before it slips much farther and we can't sell it for what it's worth."

"How—" My voice breaks, and I clear my throat at the overwhelming emotion clogging it. "How far are you in this?"

"We've got the name of a Realtor. We haven't called yet, but it's coming."

"Does Aubrey know?"

"No, no…we'll tell her soon, but she never loved it like you did," my dad says.

"We don't want you to think we don't appreciate everything you did when you came out here, honey." Mom's voice is watery. "We do. So much. But we just can't keep it up anymore. And we don't want to let it slide until the damage is irreparable, and we can't sell it for what we need to. We hope you understand."

"Of course." I swallow, rubbing a hand over my chest, because it hurts. Physically hurts—at the thought of someone else coming into my shop and doing things wrong, screwing up everything I've worked for. And not just what I've spent the past three months working for, but well before that. My whole life. It's my family's legacy, and I don't know if I can let it go. I don't know if I want to.

Somehow, the three months of living in Michigan, working at the shop and *doing* something, was enough to make me hate everything I used to love. But more than that, it was enough to shake the foundation of everything I used to crave. And in the past couple weeks, I've been asking myself daily how I could have ever been satisfied with it. With the monotony of the day-to-day life. No variety, just the same thing day in and day out.

I've hated every fucking second of it, and maybe it's time I stopped lying to myself about it. Before it's too late to get what I want.

paige

This is the day I've been waiting for. The day I've worked my ass off for for the past five years. I sacrificed for this. I readjusted my plans, took on more, just to prove to myself Bryan didn't break me. *Couldn't* break me. I wasn't going to let his deceit change my outlook anymore. I was going to fight for what I wanted, and I was going to get it.

And I did.

In a bar around the corner from headquarters, Tanner's laugh is loud, several of his buddies and fellow cops crowded around us on stools. After Captain Peters offered me the permanent position, boasting about my tenacity and drive, Tanner wanted to take me out for a beer to celebrate.

I should be fucking thrilled right now, especially since I had the chance to throw my promotion in the face of that asshole Jared as if to say, *see? Told you I'd get the job.* I should be slinging back beers with the rest of the guys—the guys who are now my colleagues. I should want to shout at the fucking moon, *I did this!* Despite the challenges thrown my way, despite wrenches being thrown in my plans and things not working out how I originally thought they would, I got here.

Somehow, though, I thought it'd feel different. Maybe it's the build up. I've been striving for this for a long damn time, so when it finally came, maybe it was inevitable that it fell a little flat. That it feels a little hollow.

Except I know why it feels flat…why I feel hollow…and it has nothing to do with the job, and everything to do with He Who Shall Not Be Named.

A while later, after I've managed to say about fourteen words the entire time, I walk out to my car, Tanner following. It's dark, the streetlights on and the chilly fall air comforting in a way I love. Tanner opens my door for me, but blocks it before I can get in.

"Sorry, I forgot you like hugs now," I say and wrap my arms around him, squeezing, before pulling away. When he doesn't move out of the way, I raise my eyebrows. "I have to pay a toll now to get into my car?"

"Just wanted to see what's up with you. You've been weird lately, and you didn't tell one crass joke in there the whole time. Wondering where my baby sister is."

"She's right here. I'm just stressed," I lie, averting my eyes and leaning in to toss my purse on the passenger's seat. "Once everything is wrapped up next week and I can focus on the job, it'll be better. I promise I'll be back in all my crass glory."

Tanner stares at me, his Cop Gaze in full effect, but I don't flinch away, and eventually he relents with a nod. Pulling the door open farther, he lets me get in, then leans into the open space. "Sorry we can't marathon season six this weekend. But I'll see you at Mom and Dad's on Sunday, right?"

"Yep, dinner at six. I'll see you then."

"Bye, Punky. Text me when you get home." He shuts my door for me and stands guard until I've pulled away. I should be out having the time of my life tonight, celebrating until all hours of the morning. Instead, I'm going home alone.

Back to my apartment that holds nothing but ghosts.

I'D HAVE TO be blind to miss the worried glances my brothers are shooting to each other across the table. Plus, Tanner hasn't hassled me once, or teased me about how I look or smell, so he's definitely going easy on me. It doesn't take a genius to figure out he must've talked to Dillon after Friday night at the bar, and Dillon no doubt filled him in on our little talk from last month. The Code of Silence doesn't mean shit when it comes to these two. Like a couple of gossiping old ladies.

"How's your dinner, honey?" Mom asks. "I wanted to make your favorite to celebrate. We're so proud of you." She smiles at me and glances at my dad, who nods.

"Told ya you'd get that job, Punky," he says.

I force myself to take a bite of lasagna and smile around my fork. "Thanks. And it's awesome, Mom. Super great." I cringe, knowing my brothers are going to call me out on that, but when silence greets me, I relax into my seat and continue picking at my food. Food that used to be my favorite, but now is tainted with Adam. Just when I think I'm getting past this bullshit, the bastard pops up when I least expect it. I remember him telling me his mom made sure he could do three things before he moved out—his laundry, clean a bathroom, and make one dinner. The dinner he perfected being lasagna. He promised he'd make it for me. Turns out he's a liar.

But the fact that he never made it for me is kind of my own fault.

Okay, no *kind of* about it.

I pushed him away, but what other choice did he give me? He didn't give me the option of continuing what we had long distance. It was move there with him, or it was over. And after everything that happened, everything from my past, how could he think for a minute I'd be okay with that?

I justify my actions on days when I'm missing him the most. Play out an alternate ending, one where we're still on talking terms. Sometimes, it's because we stayed friends, and while it would hurt to hear him talk about other girls, at least I'd get to talk to him. Because somehow in the short months he was here, he wormed his way into my life, fixing himself front and center, right next to Tessa as one of my best friends.

Other times—and these are the ones I never admit to, allow myself to fantasize about it, then act like it never happened—I pretend we're still together. That he stayed here or that we made it work long distance until I could get a bit more time under my belt as an analyst, make it easier to transfer. That's usually when I snap myself out of it, because knowing that I think about transferring proves the one thing I've been trying hard to ignore. The thing I've been fighting against since last December.

I'm in love with him.

When the plates have been cleared and Tanner and Dillon are on dish duty—their week—I sneak outside to shoot some hoops by myself. This was one thing Adam and I never did together, and I'm grateful for the reprieve, shooting three-pointers while Buddy watches from his perch on the garage floor.

After a while, the back door opens and out come my brothers, their looks of worry replaced with smug expressions. "Who's up for some old school H.O.R.S.E.?" Tanner asks. "I'm feeling the need to kick a little ass."

"You couldn't kick ass if it was bent over in front of you," Dillon says, snatching the ball from me.

This is what I need. The easy back and forth I have with my brothers. Getting lost in a physical sport, letting my body lead for once instead of my head—or worse, my heart.

The reprieve doesn't last for long, because by the time the game is done, when we've all heckled each other within an inch of our lives, I can't help the thought that I wish Adam had met Dillon and

Tanner. Despite being the dude sleeping with their baby sister, Adam would've gotten along great with my brothers.

Before I know it, I'm being surrounded by sweaty man muscle, sandwiched between my brothers in a bear hug, and tears prickle at the corners of my eyes. They used to do this when I was younger, to make me feel better. When my first goldfish died. When we found out we were moving after a whopping three months in Georgia. When Dillon went to boot camp in Missouri.

I manage to keep the tears at bay. At least until Tanner says, "You'll be all right." And then Dillon follows it up with, "Just wading through some shit, Punky. It'll all work out in the end."

I bury my face in the sweaty chest of one of my brothers—it doesn't matter which one, because they're both here to provide the same purpose. And the thing is, I know Dillon's right. It will work out, eventually. Eventually I'll get to a point where I don't think about Adam every day, don't dream about him every night. Where I don't see his ghost in everything I do, everywhere I go.

Eventually.

THIRTY-FOUR

adam

"Am I out of my mind for doing this?" I ask for the millionth time. "Driving twelve hundred miles for the third time in six months?"

"Yeah, you are," Jase's voice booms over my Bluetooth. "Isn't it great?"

"Not helping, asshole."

"Look, man, what do you want me to say? You need another pep talk? Because I gave you one when you called me three weeks ago and suggested it in the first place. I've given you one every day since then. And I *know* Cade's been giving you them, too. Shit, dude, how much dick licking do you need before you get off? Goddamn."

"What the fuck?"

"Sorry, I'm a little preoccupied. Horny as fuck and Tessa's not home."

"Well, Jesus, go look at some porn or something. Don't talk about licking my dick."

"I wasn't talking about licking your—fuck, never mind. When

are you gonna be here?"

"GPS says a little over two hours."

"Cool, Cade and I'll be at your parents' place around then. Haley's been asking to go over this week, anyway."

"My mom is going to adopt her as a grandchild if you're not careful."

He laughs. "She already has, and I have no objections. Neither does Tess."

With Tessa's parents long gone, Haley's dad out of the picture from day one, and Jason on the outs with his parents, that means Haley doesn't have any grandparents to dote over her. Not by choice, but by circumstance. And I was willing to leave my parents—who've always been supportive and damn cool when it came down to it—just because of security.

I didn't know what the hell I was doing. What kind of life would I have had in Colorado? A quiet life with a quiet job and a quiet wife. Boring. Dull.

No more.

Giving my two weeks to Ken felt more exhilarating than my first climb. Getting to the top of the rock and looking out at how far I'd climbed had nothing on taking control of my life and doing what I wanted instead of what I thought I needed.

Calling my parents and telling them to stop everything, that I wanted the store to stay in the family, and I wanted to come home and run it was a kind of high I've never experienced. For the first time in my life, it felt *right*. Not just correct, like it was the proper route, but *sure*, straight to my bones.

"Speaking of your parents, how long are you planning to stay at home this time?"

I laugh, shaking my head. "Well, Aubrey's about to pop, and Mom wants to go down for a couple weeks to help out, so it'll give me some time to find something."

"Plus she'll probably stock the freezer with meals for when

she's gone…"

"Yes, you can come over."

"I knew you were my best friend for a reason," he says. "Oh, hey, Tess is home. I gotta go."

"Hey, wait a sec. Can I talk to her quick?"

"Uh, sure. Hang on."

There's muted voices over the line, and what I'm pretty sure is the sound of them making out for a good thirty seconds, then Tessa says, "Hi, Adam. What's up?"

I clear my throat, unsure how I should pose this question, but still needing to know. "Hey, um, listen…I know this probably breaks girl code or whatever, but I was wondering…Paige talk about me at all?"

"Adam…"

"Yeah, you're right. Stupid idea to even go there. Hey, will I see you tonight?"

She's quiet for a minute. "Yeah, I'll be there. Can't wait to have you home."

"Me, too. See you soon."

I don't wait for a reply before I end the call. And then have the urge to bang my head against the steering wheel. I'm going back to Michigan for all the right reasons—wanting to be a part of my family's business, wanting to do something I love rather than just getting by. Even knowing all that, I can't help the what ifs from going through my mind.

What if I didn't tell Paige I loved her like that?

What if I didn't tell her it was all or nothing?

What if I'd made this decision to come back five weeks ago?

But even with all the what ifs, I fear we would've come out the same way. Because no matter how you cut it, Paige just wasn't ready.

I wonder if she'll ever be.

THIRTY-FIVE

paige

I practically skip out of the station, those leads we were hunting down finally coming to fruition and getting a break in the case we desperately needed. Nothing can ruin my mood, not even *that asshole* and the leer he shoots me as I walk through the parking lot. Oh, yeah, he totally knows Tanner is fucking with him because of me, but I don't even care. Some guys are just born assholes. I flutter my fingers at him in a wave and smile, then dial Tessa's number as I hop into my car.

She answers after a couple rings, "Hey, girlie. What's shakin'?"

"Not much. Just totally had a lead pan out and give us the break we need!"

"I...have no idea what that means, but you sound super excited, so I'm going to go out on a limb and say it's something awesome."

"You are so astute."

"I really, really am."

"So what do you say? How's about helping me celebrate? I feel like sushi. You want in on this party, or what?"

"I'd love to, but I...can't."

"What? Why? This isn't best friend protocol."

"I know, I'm sorry. But I sort of have this other...thing."

"What thing? Why are you being weird? You better not be going to a party without me or you're on BFF hiatus again."

"No, there's no party. We were just—" She doesn't get to finish before Jase is in the background, hollering for her to hurry her ass up so they can get to Adam's.

And my whole fucking world stops.

"Tessa Marie Maxwell. What the hell is he talking about? You guys headed for a last minute trip to Denver I didn't know about?"

She blows out a breath. "Look—"

"Are you fucking kidding me? You're starting with 'look'?"

"What else should I start with, Paige?"

"How about the truth? How about how long Adam's been in town for, and how long he's staying, and why you didn't tell me he was visiting."

"Because he's not visiting."

"And then you can tell me why—what? What do you mean he's not visiting?"

"Exactly what I said. He's here to stay. And that's why I didn't tell you. I didn't know how. Wasn't sure how you'd take it. You've finally gotten your spunk back—"

"Are you seriously talking about spunk right now?"

"—and I didn't want you to lose that. Not again."

"I deserved to know, Tess."

She blows out a breath. "You're right. And I'm sorry I kept it from you for this long..."

I swallow, gripping the steering wheel. "How long's he been back?"

There's a lengthy pause on the other end of the line. "About a week."

"And how long have you known?"

"Um…longer than that."

A million thoughts run through my head, but they all come back to the fact that I'm…crushed. Hurt in a new way I didn't think was possible, because even though Adam and I ended things, I still thought we were friends. That when he came back to town, we'd manage to be civil around one another. And now I find out that not only is he back, but he's here for good, and he didn't even bother to shoot me an impersonal text telling me so? It crushes.

And there's no more denying it.

He was more than just a hook up for me. Over the course of the summer, he managed to work his way in and became the closest friend I have besides Tess.

"Text me his address," I finally say.

"Right now?" she asks. "I'm not sure that's such a good idea. You're mad and I don't think—"

"Text me his fucking address, Tess!" Then I take a deep breath and flick myself in the forehead. "I'm sorry. That was bitchy and I flicked myself for you. Will you please text me his address? And give us a bit before you bring in the troops. Thank you." I hang up before she can say anything and wait for the ping of my phone.

I'm done running away from the feeling that's been overwhelming me since Adam Reid drove me home on that cold night in December.

I'm ready to take a leap and wade through some shit if I have to.

ADAM'S PARENTS' HOUSE is in a nice neighborhood, not far from Cade's place, the one he and Tessa grew up in. It's an older ranch style and after meeting his mom, I assume it probably has really nice landscaping. She seems like the type to keep up on gardening and such. Probably has some of those poofy fall flowers, even. I don't stop to look, though. Don't stop to see anything, actually, before I'm pounding on the front door loud enough to draw the attention of the neighbors. All I can focus on is the fact I'm going to see Adam again.

When no one answers, I pound again, harder this time, and glance toward the driveway. Adam's car is there, all right, so I know the little bastard is here, and if he thinks I'm walking away without having this little meeting, he doesn't know me as well as I thought. And sure enough, at my next pounding, he opens the door and there he stands, looking completely fuckable in that goddamn red Henley again from that night at the pub and those worn jeans and his fuckhot glasses, and I am definitely not thinking about that right now. Definitely not.

"*Why didn't you tell me you were back?*" I'm too far gone now to even try to get my voice in some semblance of normal volume, so I don't bother cringing when my question comes out in a screech.

Adam raises his eyebrows and crosses his arms over his chest—good Lord, I've missed those muscles—as he leans against the door frame. "Hi, Paige. How are you?"

"Oh, don't give me that bullshit." I wave a hand in front of his face. "Answer the question."

"Well," he says, drawing out the word, "according to you, we were never in a relationship, so why would it matter if I told you?"

The urge to kick him in the shin is so heavy I have to grit my teeth to keep my feet firmly planted on the ground. Instead I shove him in the chest, hard. "We were *friends*, dammit. Friends tell each other that shit. Friends don't let friends think their best friend is halfway across the country when he's actually seven blocks away, even if we did break up. Friends don't change something monumental about their life circumstances and not even tell the other. Friends don't—"

"I'm your best friend, huh?"

"I…what?"

"You said—"

"I know what I said," I snap, more mad at myself than I am at him for exposing that weakness so early. But I'm in it now; might as well go balls to the wall. "Yeah, you're my best friend. So what. Why don't you get smug about it? Then you can get smug about the fact that you made me love all this shit about you. Like those stupid ass nicknames you gave me. And the way you heckle horror movies just like I do. And how you enjoy doing all the things I do. And do you know when we compete in shit you don't even let me win? And I find it really fucking hot? Why is that, Adam? *Why?*"

He clears his throat, his lips pursed, and it looks a hell of a lot like he's fighting a smile. "I'm just going to go out on a limb here and say it's because you love *me*, not just all those other things."

I glare and shove him in the chest again. "Yes, you idiot, I love you, but that doesn't change the fact that I'm really pissed at you for not telling me you were coming home."

"Just so I'm clear, are you going to yell every time you tell me you love me, or just this time? Because I gotta tell you, it's kind of turning me on."

"*What?* I'm trying to have a heart to heart with you and you're talking about getting turned on by my yelling? What the hell?"

He chuckles under his breath and reaches out to tug my belt loop, pulling me flush against him, and I can feel exactly how turned on he is. "Yeah, see, that's what I mean. Why does it make me hard when you get all worked up at me and start yelling?"

"Because you're crazy?"

"Crazy in love, snoogiewoogums."

I roll my eyes, but inside I'm melting. "Okay, Romeo, that was a little far even for you."

"It's only because I'm so far gone over you, sprinkledoodle."

"Oh Jesus, how many more have you got in you?"

"For you? I can go all night…want me to prove it?"

I huff out a breath and stomp my foot. "Can you be serious for five seconds please?"

"Okay, I'm sorry." But he doesn't look contrite at all. He looks smug as hell, but I don't even care because he's here. He's *here.*

I keep my eyes on my fingers brushing over the cotton of his shirt. "So you're really back?"

He runs his hands up my back until they're cupping my face and tilts it back, forcing me to look into his eyes. "Yes. I am. It wasn't just you who learned about the things you love this summer." His thumb makes soft passes along my neck, and between that and his words, I'm afraid I'm going to dissolve into a puddle of girl-goo. "I realized everything I picked for my life I chose for the wrong reasons. Running the shop isn't going to be easy, and if you're sticking it out with me, that means a lot of years are going to suck." He doesn't pose it as a question, but I hear it all the same.

But the prospect of that doesn't terrify me. Doesn't even scare me a little, because this is Adam. I've already lived without him, and I'm not willing to do it again.

"I'm sticking it out with you."

The smile starts slow but soon sweeps across his face, and he leans toward me, his lips close to mine. "I was hoping you'd say that."

"So what do we do now?"

"I have a few ideas..." he says, getting closer with each word.

"Yeah? Do any of them include clothes?"

"Can't say as they do, no."

"How about you start with a kiss and we'll go from there?"

"With pleasure, sugarlump."

He leans down to capture my lips with his, his breath mingling with mine, and it's everything I remembered and more than I ever thought it could be. Because being kissed by Adam is one thing. Being kissed by the man I love knowing he loves me back?

That's worth any amount of shit I have to wade through. Especially if I know he's at the other side waiting for me.

EPILOGUE

adam

I'm being a horrible co-best man. Absolute shit. All the guests stand to watch the bride walk down the aisle, and I should be looking there, too, watching her walk toward one of my best friends. My eyes shouldn't be focused on the blonde across from me, standing up while two of our closest friends promise each other forever. But they are.

They haven't strayed from her, if I'm honest. Catching glimpses of her here and there, posing for pictures, not able to do anything but caress her with my eyes. She's statuesque in her bridesmaid dress, her hair piled on her head, her bare shoulders taunting me, and this day is going to kill me.

She stayed with the girls last night, Cade, Jason, and I all relegated to the hotel to avoid the groom seeing the bride, so I didn't get to see her before it was too late to get her alone. We were surrounded by dozens of people, too many to be able to cop a feel. To be able to slip my hand under her dress and see if her text telling me she left her panties at home was the truth or not.

Instead, I had to offer her my arm like a gentleman and walk her down the white-cloth covered aisle outside, white folding chairs set up on either side to hold the few dozen guests.

And now I'm stuck here, watching her watch the bride, a huge, beaming smile on her face, and I can't believe she's mine.

She's *mine*.

For good and for real, she's with me in it, one hundred percent.

Vows are spoken, rings and kisses exchanged, and then we're all walking back the way we came, and finally her arm is in mine again.

"You didn't even look at them," she whispers, the reprimand clear in her tone. "You're lucky you didn't have to carry the ring or they'd have been fucked."

"That's probably why they didn't give me the job. I had something more important to look at, love muffin."

She rolls her eyes, but her fingers tighten on my arm. "You're starting early. We've got a long way to go until we can sneak off to the hotel room."

"Who said anything about needing a hotel room?" I lean down and whisper in her ear. "Meet me in the downstairs bathroom in fifteen."

She doesn't say anything, her lip caught between her teeth, attention focused straight ahead. And then she gives the subtlest nod, and I want to fist pump, but I restrain myself.

The next fourteen minutes are the longest of my life. I manage to sneak off after twelve, going to the bathroom and locking myself inside, praying Paige will be able to get away, as well.

When sixteen minutes comes and goes, and then seventeen and eighteen as well, I start to think she couldn't sneak off, but then the doorknob rattles, and I whip open the door to see her standing there.

"Didn't think you were coming."

"I have five minutes, tops. Told the girls I lost an earring in my car. Think you can get it done in that time, big boy?"

"You know I can get you there in three," I say, already unzipping my pants and rolling a condom down my shaft. "Climb up, hot pants."

She breathes out a laugh, but she does as I tell her, gripping her bouquet as she wraps her arms around my neck. I slip my hands under her dress, groaning when I palm the bare skin of her ass. "Jesus, you've been walking around all day with your pussy bare out there?"

"Uh huh. Knew you'd want to do this. Thought I'd save us a step."

"Always prepared." I grip her in my hands, hauling her up against me.

She laughs as she wraps her legs around me, and then groans when I slide through her wetness.

"You been thinking about this, Paige? Been thinking about me fucking you? Because you're wet as hell."

"Stop with the chit-chat. You've got three minutes."

"You'll get off, don't worry." With that, I place myself at her entrance and slowly sink into her until we're pressed together as close as we can get.

She exhales against my lips, her eyes open and focused on me. No more secrets. No hidden emotions. Nothing between us now. This new relationship between us is almost a year old. A year of ups and downs. Of fights and misunderstandings and more make-up sex than I can count. But through it all, we've stuck it out.

I reach between us and thumb her clit as her forehead presses against mine, my name a whispered plea against her lips, and I never want to be anywhere else. Wrapped up in the arms of a girl I never knew I wanted but now could never see my life without.

As she comes around me, pulling me along with her while she whispers her love for me, I realize I spent my life looking for her in the wrong places. I spent my life looking for something only she can give me.

Forever.

ABOUT THE AUTHOR

Brighton Walsh spent nearly a decade as a professional photographer before deciding to take her storytelling in a different direction and reconnect with her first love: writing. When she's not pounding away at the keyboard, she's probably either reading or shopping—maybe even both at once. She lives in the Midwest with her husband and two children, and, yes, she considers forty degrees to be hoodie weather. Her home is the setting for frequent dance parties, Lego battles, and more laughter than she thought possible. Visit her online at brightonwalsh.com.

CPSIA information can be obtained at www.ICGtesting.com
Printed in the USA
LVOW07s0140160316

479198LV00001B/17/P

9 780997 125818